M

AND OTHER STORIES

JAMES HANLEY, novelist, short-story writer and playwright, was born in Dublin in 1901 and brought up in Liverpool. He ran away to sea at thirteen, joining the Black Watch Battalion of the Canadian Expeditionary Force to see action in the First World War. He spent nine years working at sea, and it is these experiences that provided the settings for many of his early novels. His second novel, *Boy* (1931), was prosecuted for obscene libel, and this gave him a notoriety that may have led to the unjustified neglect of his powerful and startling work. He published forty-eight books, including *Drift, Men in Darkness, Ebb and Flood, Captain Bottell, The Furys, Stoker Bush, The Secret Journey, Broken Water, Grey Children* and *Hollow Sea*. He died in 1985.

James Hanley

THE LAST VOYAGE

AND OTHER STORIES

With an introduction
by Alan Ross

THE HARVILL PRESS
LONDON

This edition first published in Great Britain in 1997 by
The Harvill Press
84 Thornhill Road
London N1 1RD

1 3 5 7 9 8 6 4 2

"The Last Voyage" first published in 1930
" The German Prisoner" first published in 1930
"Greaser Anderson" first published in 1931
"A Passion before Death" first published in 1930
"Narrative" first published in 1931

A CIP catalogue record for this book is available from the British Library

ISBN 1 86046 316 9

Designed and typeset in Walbaum at
Libanus Press, Marlborough, Wiltshire

Printed and bound in Great Britain by Butler & Tanner Ltd
at Selwood Printing, Burgess Hill

CONTENTS

INTRODUCTION

James Hanley's book of sketches, *Don Quixote Drowned* (1953), consists of an anatomy of the Welsh village where he lived for twenty years. "Llangyllwch is an island surrounded by mountains," it begins; and with the word "island", and its association with the sea, Hanley is immediately considering his cottage as a ship, the mountain as a vast wave.

> I often look at it through my window, and it does at times seem to me to hold within it the very momentum of a living wave. Nor have I ever ceased to imagine that beyond it there may lie an unknown sea. Sometimes I have expected it to come crashing down, sending spray flying. But in the clear morning light it looks just a hard, grey, granite mass, sparsely covered with vegetation, solid and unyielding, yet, too, it seems to shoulder a wave in some far-off ocean. In the fading light of the evening it can carry an unearthly glitter, one might almost say a skin, yet the moment I glance at it there is a ship rearing to the first long bow wave.

A little further on he writes:

> If I should one day breast this hill, I might yet see a wide, far-stretching sea, the new horizon. The trees that I pass as I climb will surely be the masts of many sleeping ships. I may yet hear the reverberations from their bells.

Hanley is in the classic situation of most of his own characters. The grey heaving sea, the green limpid waters, are constantly moving past him, carrying their echoes of ice, their indulgence of sun. Isolated, contained in his cottage, he is like "the sailor", that anonymous, removed hero-victim of his novels, in his ship or lifeboat. He understands the language of the elements, he reads the sky for prophecies. Yet within his confined space, limited in action, he is not only secure, he is capable of everything, for he can dream. Hanley's sailors, barely distinguishable from one another – for they are all men born to a particular kind of life, with its own brand of anguish and suffering – are, while spare of words and clumsy in expression, at the same time locked in dream. That is the true seaman's condition: he is alive in the past and future; the present is something to be endured.

Hanley in his cottage, where he is visited by a variety of characters (Jones Pompous, Price Post, Vaughan Conductor and Lloyd Dynamo and Salvation among others), gradually widened his field of vision, but, locked in his own sea-dream, shaping his prose until its rhythms were the rhythms of the sea itself, he never tried to lighten the burden of those who were still bound to the sea. He had the professional sailor's love and hatred for his element, and he never made it more palatable than it was. The result is always sombre, intense, uncomfortable; sometimes – for Hanley is a writer who goes all out for singleness of effect – it can be monotonous. Yet it is never false; the author never forces a climax, he has little use for anecdote, he makes no concessions to romance or even readability. His sailor is a man forced to the sea by circumstances, and it is in his realization that these circumstances do not basically alter, that for the seaman life is dangerous when it is not monotonous, that Hanley's psychological mastery lies. He never plays to the gallery; his sailors are not lively talkers, they are not involved in any great drama except their ultimate fate. There is poverty at home, the struggle to get a job on a ship, the boredom and hard living of the actual trip, and usually a torpedo at the end of it. That is the sequence of events in his novels, and there is no avoiding it. If a ship comes back unscathed, there is another journey to be endured with the same possibilities. Hanley does not help out his characters (or his readers) by giving them exciting reminiscences to dream over, flashbacks to kinder pasts. His men are seen on duty, in situations where they exist in conditions altogether more basic. They have carried their feelings about with them so long that they are obsessed by them – by the fear of putting them to the test, by the fear of disappointment. They are ordinary, sane men driven by delirium, whose interior life, nursed during weeks, months, even years at sea, becomes so intense at the end that reality can never approach it. Hanley is an uncompromising realist and never more so than when his realism is extended into what appears to be fantasy – a fantasy extracted from reality, something moving under the ice. Clausen, in the short novel *Quartermaster Clausen* (1934), carries the image of a woman about with him for twelve years, yet when the moment of seeing her arrives and she is on the quay waiting for him, he refuses to recognize her because, aged by twelve years, she is not identical to the image he has of her. Confronted by difference, he simply remains on board.

Certain themes recur with great frequency in Hanley's novels, not because he seems to be obsessed with them as ideas so much as that, in his constant reconstituting of life within severe limitations, they force themselves on him. These themes, or rather states of being, are all conditional to men who have no choice of action, either because their circumstances are such that they must take what they can get, or else because they are men whose lives have been suspended – men undergoing long voyages as in *Hollow Sea* (1938), men on a raft as in *Sailor's Song* (1943), or a lifeboat as in *The Ocean* (1938). They may be waiting for a ship as in *Narrative* (1931) – seven out of 300 struggling men are taken on; they are the lucky ones, and within twelve hours the ship has gone down – or they may be waiting for an air-raid to end, like the sailor in *No Directions* (1943). They, like Hanley in his island-cottage, are stationary; it is the water flowing by them that moves, it is the ship that throbs under them, taking them away from what they know to what nobody knows. It is time that passes while they wait for rescue, or for the bombs to stop dropping, or for death to come. These characters are like the figures sculptured by Henry Moore – still, enduring people, under sentence of history, confined by the rhythms of sleep and exhaustion, but dreaming action under the bone. Like the sea at whose mercy they are, they are static and moving at the same time. Some of them have names; more often they are simply "the sailor", the anonymous man sandwiched between the remorseless pressure of poverty and war.

Few of Hanley's sailors choose the sea; they may be chosen by the sea, the compulsive siren-song of escape drumming in their ears, but usually they are forced to it. Their predicament is the more moving because it is involuntary: their basic situation, allowing them little physical action, puts them at the mercy of their untutored imaginations. They are stripped of all extraneous aids to behaviour, all distractions and diversions. They are naked in character, and it is character alone that will see them through. Relentlessly the author takes the ordeal of his characters (and in the stories that are not about the sea it is usually ordeal by social humiliation) to its limits. At the end of their resources, their weaknesses or vices or human strength or compassion are in relief, they reveal themselves as what they are. Deliberately, like a man tightening a tourniquet, Hanley increases the pressure on his characters' ability to endure. He subjects them to shock first of all: they are torpedoed, machine-gunned, wounded and exposed in open boats. They are delirious through lack of water, or surrounded by dead men. They are made victims of depravity, brutality or contempt. Loneliness and despair, disappointment, and failure aggravated by drink have confused their minds so that half the time they are uncertain of what their element is, sea or air or land, past or present. They are men off balance, on tilting decks, obsessed by ice and fire, greenness and water, holding vaguely on to the last split second before the torpedo, the bomb or their own foolishness turns the world turtle. They mutter names of women, they try to focus on a known face or room, but whatever they reach out towards has been torn away from them and there are only interchanging fragments, glass into ice, dream into nightmare, beauty into ugliness.

> After the deluge of sound ceased, after the wind passed, the sailor fell, was sick. They were in a desert of air.
> "Goddam! Get me out of this," the sailor shouted. "Stand up," the little man said; he began to pull. Crunching sounds came up.
> "It's ice," the sailor said. "Get me out of this." Falling again, hands became feelers, pawed about. "I know ice," he said, "always something moving under ice. I know."
> "Glass, you crazy bastard," the little man said, the cheap raincoat dripped water, his tin helmet

kept falling over his forehead. "Stand up!" Half-
bent, arms encircling the sailor, pulled hard.

"Damn and blast you," he shouted, "why, you're
drunk."

This opening passage from *No Directions*, a novel set in a
lodging-house during the night of an air-raid, shows how
economically and powerfully Hanley gets his effects, how he
establishes the ambiguities behind confusion of mind and lost
equilibrium by the simple statement, held back to suggest
shock and horror, that the sailor is only drunk. Yet his drunk-
enness is in fact an escape from horror, the sailor is at the
centre of a world that is spinning under his feet, and the glass
broken about him is the ice of his real voyage, "white, then
bluish, towering, great walls, sheets, layers, a world of it, blue,
shining, cold, silent, where no man was".

This "horror" is the routine background of Hanley's world;
it is a delusion sometimes, but it conveys the reality of a lived,
nightmare past that each of his merchant seamen has behind
him. "The sailor" who appears in the first sentence of *The
Ocean*, for example, does not really need to be described. The
novel opens: "When the light broke the sailor got up and looked
about him. Clear sky, silent heaving masses of water. No other
boats. Horizon's line a blur." The word "sailor" means Arthur
Fearon, in *Boy* (1931), forced to leave school at thirteen beaten
by his father, reduced to stowing away; it means Morgan,
leaving wife and three children to sign on as a fireman in the
A02, jumping to the wilderness of water from an open boat the
same night; it means the crew selling food to the soldiers on
the troopship A10 in *Hollow Sea*, the troopship out to an
unknown destination that was to kill both exploiters and
exploited; it means Peter Fury, in *The Furys* (1935), home after

eight years, seeing his parents on the quay, suddenly ashamed of them, of his too loving excited mother, his father in his black cap and black silk scarf. It means also the raving sailor in *Sailor's Song*, any old sailor and every sailor:

> That one who curbs frenzies in a sea
> That great hauler on the ropes.
> That one who plies a fire, and that one who
>   watches a star.
> That one who tells a tide.
> That one stood sentinel in the wilderness.
> Have mercy on them, O Lord.

as the words float to the raft-bound survivor dreaming his whole sea-past in the great prose poem of that book.

Generally speaking, Hanley's sea novels and stories can be viewed as one novel; they are component parts of a single experience, swept by a powerful searchlight that moves about in time as well as in space. The men, however different, are aspects of the same man and they are complementary to each other. Only the searchlight picks them up at moments that are decisive in a different way for each. Hanley, however, is concerned with their common human situation, their shared qualities as a race of men involved with the sea. The sea is what forms them, it gives them stature, a heroic quality even, though heroism is not something the author outwardly makes much of.

Hanley's successive experiments with prose rhythms have gone further in capturing the sea's likeness, as a sailor sees it, than any previous writer's. The sea, it might be said, is the central experience of his novels because it dictates the actions of their characters. *The Ocean, Hollow Sea* and *Sailor's Song* especially contain visual effects no other writer has achieved. They are effects created by spareness of imagery, by a sculptural sense of language, above all by an ear for the contrary sounds of the sea. The result is tautly poetic, because the writer has aimed, sometimes obliquely, sometimes directly, at transcription more than description. He has, in this sense, remained an experimental novelist, a novelist who does not plan, who has no cut-and-dried story, but whose work is the journey back into his own consciousness. He is guided by instinct, by the desire to make words get as close as possible to their subject. The sea, as well as forming his characters, forms his own style. The shape of his books is usually a voyage, and he moves along it knowing that there are only a limited number of destinations.

His impressive gifts of concentration, his dramatic skill, his poetic energy, work best in stories, as here, and in the short novel, when his compassion and anguish, pared down to the bone, create an often sublime intensity. For this reason his greatest achievements are almost certainly *Boy*, *Sailor's Song*, *The Ocean*, *No Directions* and *The Closed Harbour* (1952). Captain Marius, pottering hopelessly from one shipping company to another in *The Closed Harbour*, going out of his mind because the suspicion raised against him on account of an obscure incident in the past prevents him from getting another ship, indicates as well as anyone the narrow dividing line between actuality and fantasy in Hanley's world. Fate, as seamen believe it to be, is gravely ironic; men have doors shut on them for mysterious reasons, and moon about uncomprehending because that is the way the world is. Some, the employers, have the power to say yes or no; others, the seamen, have to accept what is offered to them. They are not expected to understand what is going on, they are at the mercy of others' whims, they are a prey to rumour. The men – and it is with the unprivileged that Hanley deals – see it that way and as a result they exist in a kind of maze, searching futiley for clues.

Hanley does not have much in common with Conrad, whose sea-captains were mostly men of a certain standing, able to trade for their own benefit in romantic parts of the world. Hanley's men have little free will, no gifts of expression or anecdote, only a stale repetitive jargon. They are mostly to be found covered in grease below decks, not on the bridge or smoking a cigar in the captain's cabin. The comparison, if one can be made, should be not with Conrad but with the mysterious B. Traven – with *The Death Ship* (1925) and *The Treasure of Sierra Madre* (1934) – or with Malcolm Lowry's *Ultramarine* (1933). In this foetid, animal world of cursing firemen and trimmers, scheming stewards and vicious bo'suns, every man has to fight for himself. He may expect nothing but squalor and betrayal, and he may be right. He may also find a common humanity which perhaps he never believed to exist. Hanley's stories and novels put the case for both views equally. They may not always do so entertainingly but entertainment is not necessarily what he has aimed at. Of the greatness of his power, however, of the force of his pity, there can be no doubt. Of all writers about the sea he is the most consistently memorable.

ALAN ROSS

THE LAST VOYAGE

THE EIGHT TO TWELVE WATCH had just come up. The fo'c'sle was full. The four to eight crowd were awake now. Some were already getting out of bed.

"Where is she now?" asked a man named Brady.

"She's home, mate. Look through the bloody port-hole. Why, she's past the Rock-Light."

And more of the four to eight watch began climbing out of bed. They commenced packing their bags. The air was full of smoke from cigarettes and black shag. A greaser came in.

"Reilly here?" he asked gruffly.

A chorus of voices shouted: "Reilly! Reilly! Come on, you bloody old sod."

A figure emerged from a bottom bunk in the darkest corner of the fo'c'sle.

"Who wants me?" he growled.

"Second wants you right away. Put a bloody move on."

The man put on his dungaree jacket, a sweat-rag round his neck, and went out of the fo'c'sle.

"His goose is cooked, anyhow," said a voice.

"Nearly time too," said another.

"These old sods think they rule the roost," said another.

"He's just too old for Rag-Annie," said yet another.

3

And suddenly a voice, louder than the others exclaimed: "What the hell's wrong with him, anyhow? If some of you bastards knew your work as well as he does you'd be all right. Who says his goose is cooked?"

"The doctor."

"The second."

"Everybody knows it."

"That fall down the ladder fixed him all right."

"The old fool'll get gaol. D'you know he's sailin' under false colours?"

"False colours?"

"Yes. False colours. The b——'s sixty-six, and he's altered his birth-date. They've got him down on the papers as fifty-six."

"Has he been found out?"

"I don't know."

"Some lousy sucker must have cribbed."

"Give us a rest, for Christ's sake," shouted a Black Pan man. "You'd think it was sailin' day to hear you talkin'. Don't you know it's dockin' day? We'll all be home for dinner."

"And a pint of the best, eh?"

The packing of the bags continued, whilst the flow of conversation seemed unceasing.

"This ship is the hottest and lousiest I ever sailed in," growled a trimmer. "A real furnace, by hell."

"Oh, listen to that," said a voice. "You want to sail on the *Teutonic* if you like the heat."

4

Suddenly the man Reilly appeared in the fo'c'sle. He walked back to his bunk past the crowd of men, who were now so occupied with bag-packing that they hardly noticed his return. Suddenly a voice exclaimed:

"Well, Christ! Here he is back again."

"Who?"

"Old Reilly."

All the faces turned then. All the eyes were focused upon the man Reilly.

"Did you get your ticket, mate?" asked one.

"Did he kiss you behind the boiler?" asked another.

"Are you sacked then?" asked another.

Everybody laughed.

"He went down to kiss the second's —," growled one.

The man Reilly was tall and thin. His eyes, once blue, were black. Heavy rings formed beneath them. His skin was pasty looking, his hair was grey. He was very thin indeed. When he took off his singlet, they shouted:

"His fifth rib's like a lady's."

"His arms would make good furnace slices."

"He's like a bloody rake."

"The soft old b—. Why doesn't he go in the blasted workhouse."

Suddenly Reilly said: "Go to hell."

Then he commenced to roll up his dirty clothes.

"Here, you! Shut your bloody mouth and leave Reilly alone," exclaimed a man named John Duffy. "If half you suckers knew your job as well as he does, you'd get on a lot better."

"He's an insolent old sod, anyhow," said a deep voice in the corner.

"I've been twenty years in this ship," said Reilly.

"Aye. And by Christ, the ship knows it too. I'll bet you must have been growlin' for that twenty years.

"Who's growlin'?" shouted Reilly. "You young fellers think you can do as you like," he went on. "Half of you don't know your damn job, but you can come up to us old b— and get the information though. Who the hell told you I was sacked? Don't you believe it. You'll have me here next trip whether you like it or not."

"Oh Christ!"

"By God! I'll look for another packet, anyhow."

"So will I."

"Why in the name of Jesus don't they let you take the ship home with you? Anyhow we don't all kiss the second's —."

"That's enough," shouted Duffy.

A silence fell amongst the group in the fo'c'sle. Reilly, having packed his bag, went out on deck. He sat down on number 1 hatch. The ship already had the tugs, and was being pulled through the lock. He walked across to the rails and leaned over. He glared into the dark muddy waters of the river. He thought:

"Good God! All my life's been like that. Muddy."

Duffy came out and joined him. He spoke to him.

"Hellow, Johnny," he said. "How did you get on with Finch?"

Finch was the second engineer, a huge man with black hair and blue eyes, and a chin with determination written all over it. It was known that he was the only second engineer who had ever tamed a Glasgow gang from the Govan road.

"This next trip," said Reilly, "is my last. It's no use. I tried to kid them all along. But it wouldn't come off. I just come up from the second's room now."

"What did he say?"

"'Reilly,' he said, 'I'm afraid you've got to make one more trip, and one only. You'll have to retire.'

"'Retire, Mr Finch,' I said.

"'Yes. You're too old. I'll admit I like you, for I think you're a good worker, a steady man. You know your job. What I have always liked about you is your honesty and your punctuality. I have never known you fail a job yet. That's why I've hung on to you all this time. You're a man who can always be trusted to be on the job. I'm sorry, but you know, Reilly, I'm not God Almighty. The Superintendent Engineer had you fixed last trip. but I asked him a favour and he did me one.'

"'D'you mean that, Mr Finch?' I asked him.

"'Yes, I do. Look here, Reilly. What have you been doing with that book of yours? You're down as being ten years younger than you are.'

"'Can't I do my job?' I asked him.

"'Of course you can, Reilly, but that's not the point. You're turned the age now. Once you become sixty-five the company expect you to retire.'

"'On ten shillings a week,' I said to him.

"'That's not my business, Reilly,' he said: 'I repeat that I'm sorry, very sorry, but I'm not very much higher than you, and if I disobeyed the Super, I wouldn't be here five minutes.'

"'By Christ!' I said.

"'Look here, Reilly,' he said, 'it's your last trip this time. I can't stand here talking to you all day. I'm sorry, very sorry. It might have been worse. You ran a chance of getting gaol, altering the age in your book. Here. Take this.'"

"He gave me a pound note," said Reilly to Duffy.

"He did?" Duffy wiped his mouth with his sweat-rag. "He's not a bad sort himself, isn't the second. Not bad at all."

"Not much consolation to me though," said Reilly, "after thirty-nine years at sea. By Jesus! I tell you straight I don't know how to face home this time. It's awful. I've been expecting it, of course, but not all of a sudden like this. But d'you know what I think caused it?"

"What?" asked Duffy, and he spat a quid of tobacco juice into the river.

"Falling down the engine-room ladder three trips ago."

"But that was an accident," remarked Duffy.

"Accident. Yes," said Reilly. "But don't you see, if I'd been a younger man I'd have been all right in a few days. But I'm not young, though I can do my work with the best of them. I was laid up in the ship's hospital all the run home."

"Ah, well. Never mind," said Duffy.

"S'help me," exclaimed Reilly, "but those young fellers fairly have an easy time. Nothing to do only part their hair in the middle, and go off to French Annie's or some other place. By God! They should have sailed in the old ships. D'you remember the *Lucania*?"

"Yes."

"And the *Etruria*"

"Yes."

"D'you remember that trip in the big ship when she set out to capture the Liverpool to York speed record?"

"Aye."

"D'you remember Kenny?"

"I do," said Duffy. "The bloody sod! All he thought about was his medal and money gift from the bosses, but us poor b—! Every time we stuck out faces up to the fiddley grating to get a breath of air, there he was standing with a spanner, knocking you down again:

"'Get down there. Get down there.'"

"Half boozed too." said Reilly. "I'll swear he was."

"He was that," remarked Duffy. "All in all, nobody gives a damn for us. Work, work, work, and then—"

"You're a sack of rubbish," said Reilly. "And by Christ I know it. I know it. All my life. All my life. I've worked, worked, worked, and now—"

9

"Will you have a pint at Higgenson's when we get ashore," asked Duffy.

"No. I won't. Thanks all the same," said Reilly, and he suddenly turned and walked away towards the alleyway amidships.

"It's hard lines," said Duffy to himself, as he returned to the fo'c'sle. All the men were now dressed in their go-ashore clothes. Duffy began to dress.

"Where's the old boy?" they asked in chorus.

"I don't know," replied Duffy, and he put on his coat and cap. Overhead they could hear the first officer shouting orders through the megaphone; the roar of the winches as they took the ropes; the shouts of the boatswain as he gave orders to the port watch on the fo'c'sle-head. The men went out on to the deck.

"She's in at last. Thank God."

She was made fast now. The shore-gang were running the long gangway down the shed A crowd of people stood in the shed, waiting. Customs officers, relatives of the crew, the dockers waiting to strip the hatches off and get the cargo out. All kinds of people. The gangway was up. The crew began to file down with their bags upon their backs.

"There he is!" shouted a woman. "Hello, Andy!"

"Here's Teddy!" shouted a boy excitedly.

And as each member of the crew stepped on to dry land once more, some relative or other embraced him. The men commenced handing in their bags to a boy who gave each man a receipt for it. He placed each one in his cart. Now all the crew were ashore. The shore-gang went on board. An old woman stood at the bottom of the gangway. She questioned an engineer coming down the gangway.

"Has Mr Reilly come off yet, sir?" she asked.

"All the crew are ashore," he replied gruffly.

But they were not. For Reilly was in the fo'c'sle. He was sitting at the table, his head in his hands. His eyes were full of tears.

* * *

"What a time you've been Johnny," exclaimed Mrs Reilly, when eventually her husband made his appearance. "The others came down long ago."

"I had something to do," said Reilly, and there was a huskiness in his voice. Near the end of the shed he suddenly stopped and put his bag down. "Have all those fellers cleared?" he asked. "I wanted to send this bag home with Daly."

"I'll carry it, Johnny," said his wife.

"How the hell can you carry it?" he said angrily. "I'll carry it myself. Only for this here rheumatism. I've never been the same since that there fall down the stokehole."

He picked up the bag and put it on his shoulder. They walked on. At the dock gates they had to stop again, whilst the policeman examined his pass.

"I haven't got it," exclaimed Reilly, all of a flutter now for he suddenly remembered that he had left it on the table in the fo'c'sle.

"You're a caution," said his wife. "Indeed you are."

"If you haven't a pass, mister, I'll have to search your bag. Are you off the *Oranian*?"

"Yes. I am. You ought to know me, anyhow. I've been on her for years."

"I don't know you," said the policeman gruffly: "let's have a look at it." He picked the bag up and took it into the hut.

"Good heavens," said Mrs Reilly. "How long will he be in there? I'm perished with the cold."

"Serve you right," said her husband angrily. "Haven't I told you time after time not to come down here, meetin' me? It's not a place for a woman at all."

"There were other women here as well as me," said Mrs Reilly.

"The other women are not you," said Reilly, more angry than ever. "Anyhow, here's the bloody bag."

The policeman said: "Everything's all right. Goodnight."

Mrs and Mr Reilly walked away without replying. They passed through the dock gates. The road was deserted. Suddenly the woman exclaimed: "Did you take those Blaud's pills while you were away, Johnny? I've been wondering. How d'you feel now?

"Rotten," he replied.

They walked on in silence.

"Shall I get you a glass of beer for your supper?" asked his wife.

"No."

Again silence.

"Mary's husband got washed overboard," said Mrs Reilly quite casually. "Of course, I wrote to you about it."

"Jesus Christ! Andy? Andy gone?"

"Yes. Poor feller. He was coming down the rigging after making the ratlines fast."

"My God!"

They reached the end of the road. Turned up Juniper Street. Reilly spoke. "How's Harry? Did he get any compensation?"

Mrs Reilly looked at her husband.

"He got twenty pounds. Lovely, isn't it? And him with his jaw gone."

"Poor Andy, poor Andy," Reilly kept saying to himself. "Poor Andy." And then suddenly he said aloud: "Holy Christ! What a life! What a lousy bloody life!"

"It's God's Holy will," said his wife. "You shouldn't swear like that, Johnny."

"I dare say I shouldn't," he said, and he stopped to spit savagely into the road. They reached the house. The three children, twelve, fifteen, and sixteen, all embraced him.

To the boy, Anthony, who was sixteen, he said: "Well, are you workin' yet, Anthony?"

"No, dad. Not yet."

The father sighed. He turned to Clara, twelve years of

age, and took her upon his knee. "How's Clara?" he asked her.

She smiled up at him, and he smothered her in a passionate embrace.

When the children had gone to bed, Mrs Reilly made the supper. They both sat down.

"Eileen has to go into hospital on Wednesday," said Mrs Reilly

"What for?"

"Remember her gettin' her arm caught in the tobacco cutting machine?"

"Yes. But I thought it healed up?"

Mrs Reilly leaned across and whispered into his ear' Don't say anything, John."

"I'm sorry I came home. By God, I am. Coming and going. Coming and going. Always the same, trouble, trouble, trouble."

He put down his knife and fork. He could not eat any more, he said, in reply to his wife's question. He drew a chair to the fire and sat down. Mrs Reilly began clearing the table. She talked as she gathered up the dishes.

"Trouble. God love us, you don't know what trouble is, man. How could you know? Sure you're all right aren't you? Away from it all. You have your work to do. And when you've done it you can go to bed and sleep comfortable. You have your papers and your pipe. You have your food and your bed. Trouble. God bless me, Johnny, but you don't know what the word means. The rent's gone up, and then

Anthony not working, and Eileen's costing me money all the while. And she'll end up by being a drag on me. How can the poor girl work? I get on all right for a while and then something happens. You see nothing. Nothing at all."

Reilly jumped up and almost flew at his wife. She dropped her hands to her side. She looked full into his face.

"See nothing! Jesus Christ Almighty! You don't know what I see. You don't know what I have to do. What worry I have. You don't know what I think, how I feel. No. No. God's truth, you don't. Me! ME! An old man. And I have to hop, skip, and jump just like the young men, and if I don't, I'm kicked out. And where would you be then? And all the children. In the bloody workhouse. I have to put up with insults, humiliations, everything. I have to kiss the engineer's behind to keep my job. By heavens, you're talking through your hat, woman!"

"Am I? How do you know I'm talking through my hat? Was I talking through my hat that time you fell twenty-five feet down the iron ladder into the engine-room? Was I? Was I? Was I talking through my hat when I made you come away from the doctor who examined you? Was I daft? You with a piece of your skull sticking in you brain, and no jaw, and all your teeth knocked out, and three ribs broken. And you actually wanted to take a lousy twenty-three pounds from the shipping company's compensation doctor. The dirty blackguards! You tried to kiss *his* behind. That I do know."

"Look here, woman. I'll cut your throat if you torment me much longer. You don't know what I have on my mind. God! you don't. Kiss his backside? I had to. Supposing I had done as you say. Asked for a hundred pounds compensation. I know it would have been all right if we had got it, but we didn't get it, did we? And I knew we couldn't. So I took what they offered – twenty-three pounds, and my job back."

"Did that pay the doctor's bill and rent and food, for all the eleven weeks you were ill in bed on me? Did it? No. You had a right to ask for the hundred pounds. It's too late now."

"I had no right."

"You had. Good God! You know you had."

"Damn and blast you, I tell you I had no right. I could never have got it. Didn't the union try? Didn't everybody try? It was no use. I got off lucky. I got my job back anyhow, didn't I?"

"Your job," said Mrs Reilly, sarcastically.

"My job! My job! My job!" he screamed down the woman's ear. "My job."

"The people next door are in bed," she said.

"I don't care a damn where they are."

"I do," said his wife.

"Christ, you'd aggravate a saint out of heaven. I feel like chokin' you."

"Go ahead then. You hard-faced pig. That's what you are."

"Oh, go to hell," said Reilly. He walked out of the

kitchen. Went upstairs. He undressed and got into bed. He lay for a while. Suddenly he got up again. He went into the children's room. They were sleeping. He went up to each one. He kissed them upon the forehead and upon the lips. He kissed Clara, murmuring: "Oh, dear little Clara. Dear little Clara. I wonder what you'll do. I wonder how you'll manage." Then he kissed Eileen.

"Poor Eileen. Poor darling Losing your little arm. Your poor little arm. And nothing – NOTHING can save it."

He kissed Anthony and murmured: "Poor lad. God help you. I don't know how you'll face life. No, I do not know. Poor boy."

Then he tip-toed out of the room and returned to his bed. All was silent in that house now. Below, Mrs Reilly was sitting in the chair just vacated by her husband. She was weeping into her apron. Above – he lay.

* * *

He thought. "First night home. Good Lord. Always trouble. Always something. And me – me defending my job, and I haven't got one after this trip. Finished now. All ended now."

Mrs Reilly came up to bed. Neither spoke. She got into bed. Lay silent. No stir in that room. All dark outside. Roars of winches and shouting of men they could hear through the window. Mrs Reilly slept. The husband could not sleep. He got out of bed again, and went into the children's room. Anthony was in one bed. Clara and Eileen in the other. He lay down on the edge of the boy's bed.

"Nothing. Nothing now," he said. "Things I've done. All these years. Nothing now. How useless I am. Poor children. If only I had been all right. Oh, I wonder where you'll all be this time next year. I wonder." He closed his eyes but could not sleep. Was nothing now, he felt. Nuisance. And young men coming along all the time. Young men from same street. Street that was narrow, and at the back, high walls so that sun could not come in. "No sun in one's life," he thought.

Mrs Reilly woke. Felt for her husband. Not there.

"O Lord!" she exclaimed. "Where is he? Surely he hasn't gone."

She called. And her voice was thin and cracked and outraged the silence of that room. "Johnny, are you there?" she called.

He heard. He would not reply. Was crying quietly, and one long arm like piece of dried stick was across Anthony's neck. She called again.

"Oh my God! Where are you, Johnny?"

He did not answer. Were now strange feelings in him. Heart was not there. Was an engine in its place. Ship's engine. Huge pistons rose and fell. He was beneath these pistons. His body was being hammered by them. All his inside was gone now and was only wind there. Wind seemed to blow round and round all through his frame. Gusts of wind. Were smothering him. Many figures were

tramping in him. Voices. All shouting. All talking together.
He could hear them. They were walking through him.
Third engineer was one.

"You soft old bastard. Didn't I tell you to watch the
gauge?"

"Don't you get mine!"

"Yes. But it's not enough, Johnny," she pleaded. "You
know Anthony is a strong lad. He would be all right as
a trimmer."

"I don't want any of my children to go to sea," he said.

"You're very particular in your old age," she said, with
sarcasm.

"In my old age! Particular! Christ! Shut it."

"Anyhow he wants to go," she said. "Is tired being at
home. No work for him. Poor lad. Other lads working and
money for cigarettes and pictures. None for him."

"We're a lucky bloody family," said Reilly angrily.

"Won't you try?" she asked. "Will help us all this getting
him away as a trimmer. Will make a man of him. He wants
to go."

"Make a man of him," said Reilly, and he laughed.

"Yes. Will make a man of him," she said, and was angry,
for colour had come into her cheeks that looked like taut
drum-skins. "How bloody funny you are."

"Me funny. Don't kid yourself, woman. I have to see the
doctor in the morning. Nothing funny in that. For the love
of Jesus shut up about Anthony and everybody else. Why
don't you go to sleep?"

He was angry too, for eyes were burning with strange fire. He turned over on his side. Mrs Reilly mumbled to herself. They both lay on their sides with their backs to each other. He thought:

Bring Anthony with him? No. How funny. What made her suggest that? Especially this next trip. No. He would not.

"Are you awake, Johnny?" she asked him.

"I am," he replied.

"Are you all right? I'm worried about you. Won't you have that glass of bitter that's downstairs?"

"No."

Of a sudden were strange sounds in that house. And silence was like a fast revolving wheel that has just stopped.

"What's that?" asked her husband.

"It's Eileen. Poor child. In the night her arm pains awful."

"Go to her."

His wife got up and went in to Eileen. The girl was sitting up in bed. All dark there for though moon shone, light could not get in through high wall that faced window. It had a crack in it.

"What's the matter, child?"

"Oh, mother!" she said. "Oh, mother!" Mrs Reilly held her child to her. And in her heart a great fear arose. Could feel now tiny heart of child pulsating against her own, whose tick was slow, like little hammer taps, or like dying tick of clock that is worn out.

"Oh my arm!" sighed Eileen.

"There, there," said the mother. "Don't cry, darlin'. God's good."

Was nothing but heavy breathing of mother and little sobs of Eileen in that darkness.

Mrs Reilly shuddered. Eileen clung to her. In the other bed Anthony snored. His curly hair was a dark mass on the pillow.

Mr Reilly turned and lay on his back. He was muttering to himself.

"There's owld Reilly home again."

"He looks bad, doesn't he?"

"Sure that owld devil's as hard as leather."

Reilly passed a pub where men were standing outside. Were old seamen out of work and they were talking.

"Hello, Johnny! How are you keepin' old timer?"

"Not bad," Reilly said.

"See you coming back," he added, and they smiled.

One man was small and had a face like a bird. He smacked his lips for Reilly coming back meant two rounds of drinks at Hangmans.

"He's a tough old devil, all right," said this man.

Reilly had turned the corner. He had nearly been knocked down by a car. He had jumped smartly out of the way. A man who was young and very tall laughed. He said to the girl who was with him: "Can't beat that, can you? An old sod like that trying to appear like a schoolboy."

Reilly walked on. He was near the docks now. He walked down the shed. Were many men in this shed who knew him. They halloed him. Waved hands.

"Hello there?"

"Hello?"

"How goes it, Jack?"

"How do?"

Reilly smiled and shouted: "Fine." "Middlin'." "Not so bad." "In the pink." He was walking up the gangway now. A large number of men were standing about in the alleyway, waiting to pass the doctor.

"Hello there?"

"How do?"

"Christ, he's back again!"

"Bloody old sucker."

"How do, Reilly, old lad?"

All the men shouting and joking with him. He stood by the wall. He had his book in his hand.

"Whose — will you kiss this time?"

"How's your arm?"

"Did you have a bite this time home?"

All men taunting him. Were young men. Could not protest. Must hang on to his job.

"Leave the old fellow alone."

"He's all right."

"A wet dream is more correct."

Reilly's heart was almost bursting. Could do nothing. Was tragic for him. "I feel like a piece of dirt," he said to himself. He was nearly in tears through anger, humiliation, threats, taunts.

"Doctor."

All the men commenced to move down the alleyway. Reilly was last. He shivered. Was afraid. He drove his nails into the palms of his hands but hands were hard and horny through much gripping of steel slice. He bit his lip until some blood came.

"Jesus, help me!" he said in his heart. "Don't shiver. Don't be afraid. Be like the others. Remember now. All at home waiting for you. Waiting. Waiting for money. Little children expecting something. Wife expecting to go to the pictures. Keep cool." The thoughts careered round and round his brain. He felt he was in a kind of whirlpool. "Keep calm."

The file moved along and it came Reilly's turn. He was in the doctor's room now. The doctor was young, and whilst Reilly dropped his trousers down, he cast look of appeal at doctor, whose cheeks were rosy, and his teeth beautifully white. Very clean he was. "Like those men from University with white soft hands," thought Reilly as he looked him in the face. Terribly clean. And strong too. The doctor spoke to him.

Reilly looked up at him with the eyes of a dying dog. "Tell the truth now," he said to himself. "Anyhow it's your last trip."

"How old are you?"

"Sixty-four, sir," replied Reilly. "I've been in this ship since she was built."

"That doesn't mean that you can stay in her for ever," said the doctor. Was cruel. Was like a stab in the heart. Was bitter, Reilly thought.

"Step over," he said to Reilly.

The man stepped across and stood before the doctor. He was a head above Reilly. He examined his chest.

Then he looked lower down. He stroked his hair with his hand. He placed his hand on Reilly, and he felt how soft it was. Like silk. Beautiful hands. And his own were like steel. "How long have you had this rupture, Reilly?"

"About six years, sir. I think I got it in the *Lucania*."

"You didn't happen to get it anywhere else," said the doctor.

"Again he is sarcastic," thought Reilly.

"Oh," exclaimed the doctor. "Who's been passing you with these varicose veins?"

There was a bitter taste in Rei!!y's mouth. Like gall.

"On and off, sir," he said: "Dr Hunter always passed me. I can do my work well. Second engineer will tell you that, sir."

The doctor smiled. "I don't want to know anything about that," he said. "I am quite capable of handling you, thank you."

"Christ!" muttered Reilly: "how bitter he can be. Bitter as hell."

"Bend down," said the doctor.

Reilly bent down. Doctor looked hard at him. Felt him. All over. Legs, thighs, heels.

"All right," said the doctor. "But I won't pass you again after this. Next."

The blood stirred in Reilly's heart. He was angry. He did not, he could not, make any reply to the doctor. He seemed to fly from that room.

"Did you get tickled?"

"Did you cough?"

"Did you do it?"

Again were voices in his ears as he walked down the alleyway. Again were many men waiting to pass through to the pay table. Suddenly a voice of a master-at-arms shouted: "Pass through as your names are called."

Pay table was in grand saloon where rich carpets are deep and feet sink into them. Was beautiful and rich. Very quiet. Warm. Beautiful pictures on walls. Great marble pillars stretching up to ceiling. Was a place where first-class passengers dined on trips to America, but crew were not allowed to go there, for crew must stay for'ard in fo'c'sle. Crew must eat off wooden table through which iron poles were pushed up to deckhead, to hold table and prevent food from upsetting when weather was rough. Was well for'ard, the men's fo'c'sle. Where, when ship was up against heavy head swell, fo'c'sle seemed to pitch and toss, and often when she pitched badly food would be flung from table into men's bunks. And was dark too, for port-holes were down near water-line, and must have dead-lights screwed over them, for fear waters poured in, drowning men in their bunks. Men filed past the pay table.

"Reilly."

His name now. And he stood whilst another man said: "Five pounds, eighteen and threepence." Was handed the notes, and they were new and crackled in his horny hand.

"Your book." And another man handed him his book.

"John Reilly, ship's fireman." He passed through another room, where he signed on. He handed his book to the officer. He passed out to the other side, and walked along saloon deck, which crew were not allowed to stand on during voyage, descended the companion ladder, walked along well-deck, and then down gangway. Again many men in the dock shed. "Union," one said, and that was seventeen shillings.

"Help the blind!" said a voice, and that was one shilling.

"Here y'are," and it was a bill for carrying the bag to and fro from ship to house for four trips, and that was eleven shillings.

Near gates were Salvation Army women with boxes, and these rattled, for were full of poor men's pennies, that kept hostels open for poor men. Was also a man holding a large box for collection. A card read: "For widow of Bernard Dollin. Scalded to death on the *Europesa*. No compensation. Please help." More shillings. Reilly hung desperately on to his money now. He put two shillings in the box for Dollin's widow. On dock road was a woman selling flags that were made of yellow rag. Was for homes for tired horses at Broadgreen.

"Jesus Christ! For tired horses!" exclaimed Reilly, and

laughed aloud. He turned up Juniper Street. At Hangmans he stopped and went in with men who had been waiting for him.

"Have a drink on me, mates," he said.

The bar-lady served seven pints of bitter. "Good health, Johnny. Best of luck next trip."

All wished him good health and good luck. He said "same to you," and drank his pint quickly, like a thirsty horse drinking at a trough.

"Same again," he said to the bar-lady. "I must go now, lads," he said. "See you again. Good luck."

"Good luck, Johnny," all said in chorus, and he went out.

He came up the street and again were women talking on steps as he passed. Also children like pigeons in gutters.

"Good day, Mr Reilly."

"Good day," he said.

"Hello, Johnny, how are you?"

"Not so bad," he said.

People were nice in one's face, and some people had cursed him when he had gone up the street. Was at his home now. Mother had clean table-cloth on the table and children were waiting for him.

"Hello, dad," said Clara, and then Anthony said, "Hellow, dad," and Eileen too. "Hello, dad," she said. He kissed them all. He sat down in the chair by the fire. Looked in the flames for a long time. Children looked up into eyes of father who had come to them out of great ocean and dark night and was wonder in their eyes. Mother came in from back-kitchen and said: "Dinner is ready, Johnny."

He said he was ready too and sat down. Children were seated now. Wild freshness of youth on their faces was a feast for his eyes, and his dinner was going cold through watching them. He looked at them longingly and blood stirred in him when he remembered humiliations of last trip.

"Lovely children. God help them," he said in his heart.

The children were finished dinner so they got up and went out.

"Here," he said, and gave each of them sixpence, and they smiled. he kissed them all. "How happy they are," he thought. They went out then.

Mrs Reilly said: "Did you sign, Johnny?" and he said: "Yes."

He pushed back his plate and put his hand in his pocket. Gave her four pounds.

"Is that all?" she asked, and was a sadness in her voice.

"That's all," he said. "Had to give seventeen shillings to union, and coppers here and there. Was going to buy a pair of drawers this trip, but can't afford it."

"Good God!" she said. "That's terrible, Johnny."

"Good Jesus!" he said. "Can't do any more, can I? You get my allotment money. You can't have it both ways, woman. If you hadn't drawn thirty shillings a week from my wages I could have given you about eight pounds."

"God! I don't know," she said, and sighed deeply.

"Can't do any more," he said. "Will you go to the pictures to-night?" He stood up and put his hands on her shoulders.

"I don't know," she said.

"Heavens above," he said. "Always something wrong. What would you do if I hadn't signed?" He became suddenly silent. No use to talk like that. Forget all that. Try and be happy.

"Come on, old girl," he said, "get cleaned up. We'll go to the theatre or somewhere."

"All right," she said. "You go and have a lie down."

Reilly went upstairs to bed. He was not long with his head on the pillow before he snored. Below Mrs Reilly cleaned up. When she was finished she washed herself. Changed. Was all ready now and sitting by the fire. Kettle was boiling on the hob. At five Johnny came down. Was feeling a little better after his sleep. He said: "Good. I see you're ready. Where'll we go, old girl?"

"Anywhere you like," she replied.

"Righto," he said, and went to get a wash in the back-kitchen.

When the children came in she said to them: "Your father and me are going out to the pictures. Now please be good and look after the place." And to Eileen she said: "Look after them, Eileen. To-morrow me and you will go somewhere."

Were gone now and children all alone in house.

Mrs Reilly and her husband got on a tram and it took them to the picture-house. Was dark in there but band played nice music and Mrs Reilly said she liked it. He said nothing at all. When picture came it was a story of a man and two women. Mrs Reilly said last time she was at the pictures story was about two men and one woman. Johnny laughed. "Story was very nice," he said. Always the people in the pictures were nice looking, and always plenty of stuff on the tables and no trouble for them to get whisky. She said women wore lovely dresses. Interval then and lights went up. Band played music again.

"Come on," he said, and they got up and went outside. They went to a pub, and he said: "What'll you have, old woman?"

She said: "A bottle of stout."

"All right," he said.

He drank a lemon dash himself. Was all smoke and spit and sawdust in the pub. Many men and women were drinking there. He said: "It's cosy here."

"Have another?" said Reilly, and she said: "No. Not now."

"I'm having another dash," he said. When it came he drank it quickly. Back to pictures. All was dark again. In the next seat to them they could hear the giggling of a girl.

"Gettin' her bloody leg felt," he said and lighted his pipe.

"Ought to be ashamed of herself," she said, and was

looking at a picture of a comic man throwing pies when she said this. He laughed, and she thought he was laughing at the picture and she said: "He's a corker, isn't he?"

He said: "I should think so," and was thinking of the man who was with the girl who his wife said should be ashamed of herself.

"I'm tired," he said. "Shall we go?"

"Near the end now," she said. "Wait, Johnny."

Comic man had just been chased by a policeman. He knew it was near the end of the picture. Did not want to stand when "God Save the King" was played by band.

He said: "Come on," and pulled her arm. They went out. They hurried home in the tram through dark roads where pale light of gas lamps made all people's faces look yellow as if everybody had yellow jaundice.

"I feel so tired," he said.

"Will you have a glass of bitter?" she asked him as they were walking up the street.

"No," he said. "I'm going to bed now. Too tired for anything." When they got in he went upstairs. As he was closing the kitchen door, he said: "Don't be long now."

Mrs Reilly made herself a drink of tea before she went up herself. She ate some bread that the children had left. "Poor Johnny," she said. "Gets tired quickly these days. Is not the man he used to be: God help him."

She put out the light and went upstairs. Undressed and got into bed. Candle was burning on table at his side of the bed and light fell on her husband's face. His eyes were closed.

"He is asleep," she said. Looked at his face. Was very thin, she thought. "Good God!" she whispered. "I hope he doesn't catch consumption." She kissed him on the forehead where many furrows were. She fell asleep watching him.

* * *

Morning for going away had come and he was up early. Mrs Reilly and the children were up. Bag was packed and was standing in the corner by the door. Was beautiful and clean for his wife had scrubbed it well. Was hard work for it was made of canvas. All were at the table having their breakfast. Egg each and some bacon. It was the same each sailing day. An egg each and a slice of bacon for the children. Mr Reilly was shaving in the back. Was sadness in his eyes and he did not like looking at himself in the glass whilst he was shaving. He tried to look downward just where razor was scraping. He finished and washed himself. Came into the kitchen. Were two eggs and a piece of bacon for him. He could not eat all that, he said. Wasn't hungry, he told his wife. But she said, "Try, because you haven't ate much this trip," and children were looking from father to mother and to his plate, and each was thinking: "He will give me the egg that's over." Mr Reilly started to have his breakfast. His wife said: "Won't you eat any more?" and he said: "No." Children looked only at the mother now, but were disappointed for she said: "I'll have the odd egg myself."

Children had gone out into yard. Was quiet now and clock could be heard ticking. Was five past seven by it.

"Must go now," he said and voice was soft.

"Now, Johnny," she said, and got up from the table.

Whilst she crossed to the back door to call in the children to say good-bye to their father, she wiped pieces of egg from her mouth, for her husband always kissed her on the lips on sailing day. Children came in. He embraced each one, saying: "Good-bye. God bless you." Now his wife. She clung to him.

Nearly in tears he was, for was much in his mind, and "the heart is a terrible prison," he said to himself.

"Good-bye, Johnny," she said. She hung tightly to him. "God bless you. Take care of yourself now. Don't forget to take the Blaud's pills. Good-bye. God bless you."

"Good-bye," he said, and bag was on his back and he was through the door. She closed it and went up to the window, where children were trying to look out into dark street and with their noses pressed flat against the window pane.

"Poor Johnny," she said in her heart. "Didn't eat much this trip, was looking very bad, poor fellow. Ah, well!"

"Draw the blind down again," she said to Eileen, for it was still dark and gas was lighted yet. Dark until eight o'clock. The children came away from the window.

Mother's eyes were misty and they were looking at her. Reilly walked down the street in the direction of the dock where his ship lay. Was dark, and all silent. Streets were terribly quiet. Everything seemed gloomy and sad. Raining too. Turned the corner now. Argus Street, Welland Street, Darby Street. Good-bye. Good-bye. Juniper Street, Derby Road. Good-bye. Good-bye. Was near the docks now. Some men were coming out of the gate. They knew him for he was just walking under the lamp when they came out.

"Good-bye, Johnny. Good luck." they said.

"Good-bye. Good-bye," and his voice was a murmur low in their ears. Ship was there. Like a huge beast, sleeping. Was a light from an electric cluster hanging over number 2 hatch. Was like huge beast's eye. Some steam was coming out of the pipe near the funnel. Was like hot breath coming out of huge beast's nostrils. Was slowly waking. And from funnel itself was much smoke coming. It came out in clouds, then in the air became scarf-shaped. All was very silent except for low moaning. Steady whirr, whirr within ship. It came from for'ard where beef-engine was running. Was never stopped for place where food is kept for passengers must be always cool. The morning was very cold. At the gangway the watchman shivered. As Reilly ascended the gangway, the watchman took his nose between his fingers and blew hard into dock.

"Mornin'," he said dryly as Reilly passed him. Reilly made no reply. Was on his ship now. Going for'ard. In some hours to come he would be right down inside this beast. Down inside huge belly. Sweating. Half-past seven. Suddenly many noises filled the air. Ship was full of action. Ship was like great hippopotamus where all ticks were feeding on body. Decks were alive with men. Derricks were moving like long arms, and men seemed like pygmies on the great decks. Crew were now coming on board. All were hurrying towards fo'c'sles and gloryholes, for first there was best served. Last trip Reilly had to take a bottom bunk in firemen's room, where rats as big as bricks stood up defiant against the men when they tried to get them in the corner and kill them with big holy-stones. Reilly had a top bunk now. Was first man in. Another man came in. His name was Campbell.

"Hello, cocky. You took my bloody bunk," he said.

Reilly did not reply. Thoughts in him were calm. He said in his heart: "Your last trip. Keep calm. Remain silent. Stand things for sake of wife and children. When you go home you can get the old age pension."

"Well, Holy Jesus!" said Farrell, coming in. "The dozy swine's back again."

Reilly remained silent. Calmly he unpacked his bag. Was something hard in it. Like a little box. "Good God!" he murmured. "Fancy that. Poor Eileen. Bought me a box of soap. God bless the darling child." He fondled the box as if it were made of solid gold. Were many noises now for fo'c'sle was full. Again voices in his ears. He wished they were full of cotton-wool.

"Old Reilly's back."

"Oh Christ! Is he?"

"Can't you see him?"

"Hello there. You old sucker."

Was a message flashing through Reilly's brain. "Keep calm." Nine o'clock now. Second engineer came down the crew's alleyway. He crushed past a small trimmer. Said to him: "Tell Farrell to pick his watch." Trimmer went into fo'c'sle. Spoke to Farrell. Farrell shouted: "Outside, men." All the men went out on deck. Some were already wearing their dungarees. Some wore their best clothes. Many were drunk. Farrell looked at the men. His right forefinger was pointing. As if he were pointing a gun at them all. They watched him.

"Ryan. Duffy. Connelly. Hughes. Hurst. Thompson. Reilly. Simpson."

Eight men stepped forward.

"Eight to twelve watch," he said. "Stand by till twelve o'clock. Have your dinner. Then turn in." He walked off amidships.

On the deck also were boatswain and his mate. They picked their port and starboard watches. Look-out men. Day men. Lamp trimmer. Storekeeper. Came a little man, bald, with a sandy moustache. He called eight firemen and they were for Black Pan watch. Then a man named Scully; he picked the "gentleman's" watch.

Hatches were being put on. The chief engineer was coming along the deck. He was shouting and his face was as red as a turkey-cock. "God damn you. Can't you hear five blasts on the whistle! Get these men up on the boat-deck."

Was a terrible fuss now, for no watches should have been picked before boat muster. Boat drill first because that was most important. Was very important because men must be good sailors in case of ship striking iceberg, and helpless passengers to be saved. Was not right to pick watches before this had been done as it gave men a chance to pick mates and make other arrangements. Confusion. All the men diving into bags for jerseys and sailors' caps that made some look like monkeys. Was necessary company said even if they looked like monkeys to have ordered ones.

"Like the bloody navy," said Duffy, whose hat would not fit him and he had just paid five and sixpence for it at the slop chest. "Robbers," he growled. "Dirty robbers."

The crew ran along all decks and on flush deck some tripped over hatch combings and falls from the drum ends. Cargo men cursed them. Crew swore too. Reilly was one. Fell right over hatch cover.

"You dopey old bastard. Where were you last night?" growled a ganger. He did not hear the remainder of the sentence. He did not run up companion ladder to the saloon deck, rather he hopped up like a bird. "I feel like a poor bloody sparrow," he said in his mind.

All excitement.

"Lower away."

"Slack your falls."

"Hey! What the hell are you doin'!"

"Easy there."

"Heave away."

"God blast you! How can you lower away with your rollocks like that?"

"Get clear of chocks."

The boats were ascending and descending. Then a whistle blew. The men dispersed. Reilly went along the deck with Duffy.

"How are you, old timer?" asked Duffy.

Reilly said: "Not so bad." They passed up the alleyway. Reilly undressed and turned in. All the men looked at him.

"Oh hell. He's started again."

"Who? Oh, him. How are you, my pigeon?"

"Leave the old sucker alone."

"He's all right."

"Tickle his ribs."

"To hell with him!"

Duffy's face went red for was fifty himself and remembered sailing with Reilly years ago when he was young and strong and a good worker. Would not let him be put on, he said.

"You're as bad as him."

"Who said that?"

"I said it." Farrell was speaking. Was a glint in his eye.

"Come out on deck," said Duffy.

Reilly was shivering in his bunk. Was cold. For ship's blankets were thin and iron laths of bed pierced through straw palliasse. Was in singlet but no drawers. Good Christ!" he said to himself. "All this over me. All this fuss. All will hate me now." Some men playing cards at the table were growling.

"Throw the old bastard over the side. Bunk and all.

"There's always something wrong when he's here.

"Awful," said Reilly in his heart, "and I wanted to keep calm. Say nothing."

"Come on. Come on the bloody deck!"

"Put a sock in it."

"Pipe down."

Silence then for a moment.

"What time is it?"

"Nearly four o'clock."

The cook, who was half drunk, came up the alleyway from galley and said did any of those b—'s want dinner. Was not going to wait there all day for them. Was going to kip.

Seven bells. Four to eight watch were dressing. All had clean sweat-rags round their necks. Some smoked ciga-rettes, others black shag. They passed out of the fo'c'sle in silence. Down alleyway and along well-deck. Through starboard alleyway and along well-deck number 2. Was a great stink now. Very warm. They could hear the thunder of the pistons pounding. Walked slowly. Some dragged their legs after them.

"Bloody steam up all day. Just to keep you working Lousy bastards." From the alleyway could see the entrance to the engine-room. The steel ladders glistened. All disappeared through the steel door between two high walls of steel, that were black. One wall was scaly with salt. In the fo'c'sle Reilly fell asleep. He dreamed. Was with the children in a park. Were playing with a rubber ball. All were jolly. Laughing. He bought them ice-cream sandwiches. He stroked their heads. They disappeared. He called after them. Could not find them. "Hey! Hey!" he called aloud. "Hey! Where are you all?"

"Where the hell are you? Shut your confounded trap. People here have to do their four hours below as well as you."

Blood rushed to his head. He had been dreaming all right. Raised his head a little. Very quiet in the fo'c'sle now. Eight to twelve watch fast asleep. Suddenly he felt cold. Felt in the bed. Was nothing. Felt on top of blanket and his hand was wet. Greasy. Someone had thrown slops on top of him whilst he was sleeping. Was angry.

Show a leg there! Show a leg there! Seven bells! Seven bells!"

Reilly sat up quickly.

"How soon the time passes," he said.

Somebody laughed. "Were you dreaming about her?"

Some were now climbing out of their bunks. Were sullen and silent. They had been drinking heavily and their heads were large and painful. All were ready now.

Five to eight.

"Righto."

Eight to twelve watch left the fo'c'sle and towards amidships. Reilly stopped to tie his boot with a piece of string.

"Come on, dozy," shouted Farrell, and to himself: "I'll sweat that sucker this trip."

Descended ladder now one at a time. Reilly was shaking. Each time he was on a ladder his whole body shook. Remembered that trip falling twenty-five feet on his head. They reached the engine-room. Passed through into stokehole. Was all heat and smell of water on ashes for men they were relieving had been emptying their bladders. Was much sweat on these men.

"Number 3, you," said Farrell, and Reilly went to number 3.

A man said to him: "What time did she pull out?"

"Half-past four."

"Oh! Must be in the channel now."

"Yes."

"Farrell! Are you there?"

Farrell turned round. Reilly was standing there with singlet off and bare to waist. Ribs shone in red glare of furnace.

"What the hell do you want now?" asked Farrell.

Reilly was afraid. Was a sickness at the pit of his stomach. His blood was stirring. It was anxious for rest.

"Number 3. Who is he?" asked Reilly.

"What's that got to do with you?"

"A lot," said Reilly. "Isn't he the man I relieve this trip?"

"Well?"

"He wasn't here when I came down."

"What about it?"

"He should be here. The lousy sod. Look at that."

"Look at what?" said Farrell, and he smiled.

"You bastard," said Reilly, but only in his heart.

"The mess he left," said Reilly. "The mess he left. What a worker. A pile of bloody ashes here and half the furnace raked out."

"D'you know who you're relievin'?" asked Farrell.

He bent low towards Reilly, who shivered now.

"Who?"

"My wife's brother," said Farrell. "You get on your job, old cock. By Jesus! I'll watch you."

Was a man stoking up hard at number 4 furnace. Also a little trimmer running to him from between boilers. Had come from bunkers with heavy steel barrow full of coal. Ship lurched and trimmer was pitched forward on to his face.

"You awkward bloody worm," said Duffy.

"Come on. Christ! Look at him. Standing there," said Farrell. "D'you want me to use your slice for you? Hell. Sit down. I'll hold your hand for you."

"O Jesus!" said the old man to himself. "Be calm."

Farrell walked away. Reilly looked towards number 4 furnace. Was a cloud of steam. Duffy had done it on ashes. He could not see him. He looked at his own furnace. Suddenly bent down. Looked right into it. A trimmer had shouted: "Righto." Had tipped his barrow for Reilly. Heat was terrible. Reilly took his shovel. Dug into coal and heaved a shovelful into the furnace. Flames roared. Flame licked out at him, scorching his face and thin chest. Reilly said: "The mean bastard! Knew it would happen. Told trimmer to heave me a load of slack. God strike him dead!"

He shovelled again. Must get her going. Must watch gauge. Gauge going down. Must watch bloody boiler. Might burst. He heaved in again. Flames licked out at him like many little tongues. Suddenly he flung down his shovel. Folded his arms and stared into the roaring furnace. "How tired I am. How sick and tired of it all. After forty years. O Jesus! How can I go to them? To see her face when I say: "I'm sacked. Too old." How can I? Poor children. Nothing for them. Nothing for them." Was silent. Tears were running down his cheeks and drying on his chest. Saw in flames all his past life. Every thought. Every word. Every deed. All endeavours, trials, braveries of the flesh and spirit. Was now – nothing. All ended. Nothing more now. Nothing more now. "What is it all for?" he said in his heart. "Who cares? Nobody. Who feels? Nobody." Saw all his life illuminated in those flames. "Not much for us. Sweat, sweat. Pay off. Sign on. Sweat, sweat. Pay off. Finish. Ah, well!" Were voices in those flames now. Were speaking to him. He understood their language which was in sounds of hot air. And suddenly he said, half aloud: "All to her. All to the sea." He gripped his shovel. Then suddenly dropped it. He picked up the steel slice. And suddenly dropped that too. All to her. All his life, hopes, energies. Everything. The flames licked out at him.

"ALL," he shouted, and leaped.

"Hey! Jesus Christ" HELP! HELP! Reilly's jumped in the furnace."

THE GERMAN PRISONER

JUST AS DUSK WAS DRAWING in, the battalion pulled into Boves. It had marched thirty kilometres that day. The men were tired, black with sweat, and ravenous with hunger. They were shepherded into one of those French houses, which now seemed more stable than house, alas. After some confusion and delay they were served out with hot tea, stew of a kind, and bread. The food was attacked with a savagery almost unbelievable. The heavier parts of kit had been thrown off, men sprawled everywhere. They filled the rooms with their sweat; their almost pesty breath.

"The Battalion will move off in three hours time," announced a sergeant, the volcanic tones of whose voice seemed to shake the house itself. He also made the following announcement.

"Those who have not yet made out wills, had better see the orderly sergeant at once."

Then all became silent as before. In the darkest corner of one of the rooms on the ground floor, lay two men. They were facing each other, and even in this recumbent position their physical contrasts were striking. The taller and more hefty of the two, one Peter O'Garra, said:

"I hope this 'do' won't be as big a balls up as the last lot."

47

He spat upon the floor, following up the action by drawing the flat of his hand across his mouth.

"I don't think so," said his companion, a man from Manchester, named Elston.

"You never know," said O'Garra; "these funkin' bastards at the back; you never know what game they're up to."

"We'll see," replied the Manchester man.

Peter O'Garra was forty-four years of age. He came from Tara Street, known as the filthiest street in all Dublin. He had lodged there with a Mrs Doolan, an old hag who looked more like a monstrous spider than a woman. O'Garra was very well known in Tara Street. In those fifteen years he had been known as, "a strange man – a misanthrope – a Belfast Bastard (his birth-place) – a lousy bugger – a rake – a closet – a quiet fellow – a tub of guts – a pimp – a shit-house – a toad – a sucker – a blasted sod – a Holy Roller – a Tara lemon – a Judas – a jumped up liar – a book-worm – a traitor to Ireland – a pervert – an Irish Jew – an Irish Christ – a clod."

It was rumoured that he had never worked, and had at one time been crossed in love. It was known that he used to stand beneath the clock in Middle Abbey Street, stalking the women, all of whom are supposed to have fled in terror. O'Garra could never understand this, until he discovered it was his ugly mouth that used to frighten the women. It was his most outstanding characteristic. It made him something more than a man. A threat. The children in Tara Street used to run after him, calling him "Owld click", because he made a peculiar clicking sound with his false teeth. But all Tara Street was surprised when he went for a soldier. Not only the men, women, and children, but even the houses and roofs and chimney pots, the very paving stones, joined in song. They became humanized. And the song they sang was that Peter O'Garra's blood was heavy with surrender.

"His blood is heavy with surrender," they sang.

As soon as the blood is heavy with surrender *Act*. O'Garra had acted. And Tara Street saw him no more. Perhaps what it had already seen of him was enough. Already there were a number of lines upon his fore-head; the years had traced their journey-work through his hair; his eyes resembled the dried up beds of African lakes. But it was his mouth above all that one noticed. If one wished to know O'Garra, one looked at his mouth. Once Elston had asked him what he thought of the war. He had said:

"Well it's just a degree of blood bitterness, and bitter blood is good blood. Personally, it is a change for me from the rather drab life of Tara Street, with its lousiness, its smells, its human animals herded together, its stinkin' mattresses."

Elston had yawned and remarked:

"My views are different. There is nothing I long for so much as to get back to the smoke and fog and grease of Manchester. I like the filth and rottenness because it is warm. Yes, I long to get back to my little corner, my little world."

In Dublin, a fellow like Elston, a kind of human rat, would get short shrift. To O'Garra he was "the Hungry Englishman" par excellence. And he had little time for Englishmen, especially the suck-holing type. Still he remembered that he was his bed-mate, his one companion in this huge mass of desperate life. When first he had set eyes on Elston, he had despised him, there was something in this man entirely repugnant to him. He had once written on a piece of paper, the following lines:

"There's an Englishman named Elston
By the living Christ I swear
Necessity has never hewn
One like him anywhere."

"Have you any idea at all?" asked O'Garra – "as to where we're goin'?"

The Manchester man smiled. His small ferrety eyes seemed to blink.

"Gorman thinks we're marchin' up to the jumpin-off point, to-night. I suppose they'll want us to take back all the bloody ground the fifth lost, last year. God blast them."

"Division you mean?" queries O'Garra.

"Yes," replied Elston.

"I suppose we'll be met by a guide. Time they were movin' anyhow. See the time," and he showed Elston his watch. "Remember the last time, don't you? Confusion, delay, roads blocked up. Guide drunk and lost himself. Result. Caught in single file at daylight. One of his uckin' observation balloons at work. Next thing a salvo of five-nines and seven men lost."

"Hope it won't be like that this time," said Elston in a quiet voice.

A voice blasted out – FALL IN. And the men filed down the stairs and into the yard. O'Garra and Elston filed out too, and took their places in line with the others. Darkness, gloom, and silence. This darkness was so intense that one could almost feel it. It is just that kind of darkness which falls with the most dramatic suddenness. The men could barely see one another. By feeling with their hands they became aware that they were in line. All was in order. Gorman came out, though he was not discernible. But one recognised the voice. Names were called and answered LEFT TURN. QUICK MARCH.

The files moved. In that blackness they resembled the rather dim outlines of huge snakes, as they turned out of the yard and on to the white road. In the road they halted once more. Nobody spoke. The officers came up. Another order, and the men began to nose their way towards the line. One could not say they walked erect, but just that they nosed their way forward. In five minutes order had given way to confusion. This was inevitable. Roads were blocked. All space around seemed to be festered, suffocated by this physical material; by guns, limbers, ambulances, mules, horses, more guns, more wagons and limbers. And men. Suddenly O'Garra slipped into a hole.

"Jesus Christ! Already," growled Elston.

He dragged O'Garra out, following up the action by falling in himself. One saw nothing. Nothing. There was something infinite about the action of feeling. One was just conscious that the night was deluged by phantom-like movements. That was all. Far ahead the sky was lighted up by a series of periodic flashes. Then a vast concourse of sound, then silence. The roads were impassable. The men were separated, relying on an occasional whisper, an occasional feel of a hand or bayonet, to establish contact with one another. Crawling beneath wagons and guns, now held up by mud. A traffic block.

"Elston man," said O'Garra; "how in hell are they goin' to get all this lot up before day-light. It's impossible. They'll never clear the road."

"Think of yourself," replied Elston. "We have to go a mile and a half yet. And let's hope the guide is there. You know it's not the trenches I hate. No. It's this damned business of getting into them, and out of them again too. Every time I think of those sons of bitches at the base, I get mad."

There was no reply to this remark. The men wormed their way ahead. In that terrible moment when all reason seemed to have surrendered to chaos, men became as it were, welded together. Occasionally one saw a humped back, the outline of a profile, the shadow of legs. A huge eyeless monster that forged its way ahead towards some inevitable destiny. Nothing more. At last the road seemed a little easier. Elston spoke.

"I was over this same ground, last July. I believe we turn here. The trench-system proper commences somewhere about here. To the right I think. Funny though. I once saw an aerial photograph of these same trenches. Took it off a Jerry who crashed. Looked like a huge crucifix in shape."

"You mean a cross," said O'Garra.

"Yes."

"H'm. Cross. The bloody country is littered with them. I once saw one of those crosses, with the figure of Jesus plastered in shite. Down on the Montauban Road."

"Had somebody deliberately plastered it?" asked Elston.

"No. A five-nine landed behind it, and the figure pitched into one of those latrines," replied O'Garra.

"Did you ever make a point of studying the different features of these figures?" asked Elston.

"Saw half-a-dozen. Didn't bother after that. Reminded me of the Irish Christ. All blood and tears."

Again silence. Suddenly a voice whispered – PULL UP.

The order was passed down the line. PULL UP.

More confusion, bubble of voices, whisperings, curses, threats.

"What's the matter?"

"Lost the way."

O'Garra shivered. Pulled out his watch and noted the time. He said to the man from Manchester:

"Won't be long before it's light. Must have been over four hours pawing about these blasted roads."

Elston gave a kind of growl. O'Garra growled too. One had to do something. After all it was better than standing still, helpless. He, O'Garra, once said that the war had quickened his critical spirit:

"After all the end of man is rather ignominious. No. I don't blame even the simplest of men for endeavouring to go down to the grave in a blaze of glory."

Again an order. In almost a whisper.

"Get contact and move on."

Once more the men moved along in single file. The road seemed clearer here, and the officer knew that but a thousand yards ahead a guide would be waiting to take them up to the old trenches of "16".

That officer, whose name was "Snow-Ball", was at present worrying over his men. He must certainly get them under cover before it got light. It might be too late in half-an-hour or so, and then progress was so slow. There were, of course, two reasons for this state of mind. Firstly, he might lose a few men; secondly, it might disclose (more important still), the movements of troops, going up for what, to the Germans, would be an attack on the grand scale. Far back, at the very tail end of this file of men, the Irishman was explaining to his English friend that:

"It looked as though the guide had failed to turn up,

54

after all. I had a curious feeling something would happen," he muttered.

"Cheer up," said Elston.

"It's turned half-past-six, you fool. Cheer up. That bugger in front wants to cheer up. Doesn't know what to do, I'll bet. Same old thing every time. Flummoxed. I think they get a bug on the brain sometimes."

"Yes. It's getting light now alright," remarked Elston, and there was a frightfulness about the tone in which he uttered these words.

"We can't arse about here much longer. Wonder those fellows up in front don't have something to say to him."

Down the line came an order. FILE MOVE ON.

The men moved on. And now, what had merely been a germ, became a disease, an epidemic. The torment was no longer private, but general. To all these men it became apparent that something had happened. When something went wrong the more sensitive spirits became agitated. One saw it in their eyes. Like a man conscious of Death, who begins to sense the earthiness of the grave about him. Elston remarked that it was about time they reached the trench.

"I know the ground well, at least I think I ought to. To the direct North of this trench-network, you'll find a trench once begun but left unfinished. We used it for shelter on one occasion during heavy shelling. We were changing positions one night. It's not much in an emergency, but better than nothing. Only about three feet deep. No covey holes either. Jerry has it spotted too."

Suddenly there was a low whine. Someone ahead shouted LOOK-OUT, and the line was thrown into confusion once more. The shell exploded about twenty yards ahead of Elston and O'Garra. There was a scream.

"Christ!" exclaimed Elston. "He's feelin'. Now we're for it."

"I should think so," growled O'Garra. "Its gettin' light already. When is that bastard in front goin' to do something?"

"He can't do anything if the guide is lost, or failed to turn up."

Already it was light. The men now began to murmur threats against the officer in front. Far ahead somebody had espied a balloon. Somebody shouted from the middle of the file:

"Has that soft runt gone mad? He'll get one bloody quick himself. I suppose he'll ask us to form fours and march in ceremonial style."

It was quite light now. One could see the wilderness all around. Here and there a gnarled tree-stump. Far back one visioned the packed roads and became tearful of consequences. O'Garra thumped Elston.

"Let's go to him. The fool's crazy. Stark staring mad."

"LOOK OUT."

There came another shell, exploding right in their midst so it seemed. Out of the smoke and stench there came sounds of moaning.

"That's only the beginning," said Elston. "Someone caught it alright."

It got seven men. An order was passed down from one to the other.

RUN FOR IT.

Both Elston and O'Garra made for a rise in the ground. Elston said:

"In here. Quick."

Both men sprawled into this unfinished trench.

"This way fellows," shouted Elston.

Soon the remaining men had skeltered across the broken ground, and had jumped into the trench.

"We're here for the bloody day," remarked a lance-corporal.

Elston and O'Garra agreed.

The Irishman still saw in his mind's eye, the mangled body of Gorman. Elston had helped him get the papers from his pocket. He had vomited too, for Gorman's brains were splattered on his forehead.

"Think I'll go to kip for a while," said O'Garra. Elston agreed too. The other men were endeavouring to make themselves comfortable, when the sergeant, named Grundy, said he was going to post certain men. On hearing this, all and sundry broke into loud cursings and obscene oaths.

"If that son of a bitch – well by Christ – I – I –"

"I feel rotten tired," sighed Elston.

As soon as darkness set in they were going to move out

again, and continue their march until they reached the jumping-off point. An officer was expected up before they moved out. But Grundy knew that no officer would arrive. He was quite prepared to take the responsibility of getting the men up to the jumping-off point mapped out for them.

Finally Grundy had men posted every four hours until night-fall. He knew how lucky they had been to escape so lightly. And what a blasted rotten trench they were in. No protection from flying craft. Exposed to everything.

"If that officer gets here safely," thought the Sergeant, "it'll be a miracle."

At ten fifteen the men broke cover, and continued on in single file across the broken ground, pitted here and there by yawning shell-holes filled with stagnant and stinking water. A voice was heard then.

"TAPE LINE HERE."

And each man felt that at last he was near his final destination. O'Garra himself has espied this tape-line, well concealed in the grass. Only the bundles of twigs indicated to the men that that long line of white tape was their infallible guide.

"We follow this I suppose until told to pull up."

"Correct," said the Manchester man. "It won't be long now."

They gripped each other's hand and continued in this fashion until they heard the order to halt. No. They would-n't be long now.

* * *

At two o'clock rations came along. These were handed down the trench from man to man. Bread, jam, tea. For three hours the men had been standing up to their thighs in water. O'Garra had loosed from his angry and tormented being a series of curses. Likewise Elston. All the men murmured. The orders were now known. Objective five thousand yards. On the right, the Aussies, on the left, the French. Centre body would make for the Albert-Roye Road. The barrage would open up shortly after five. Something approaching awe seemed to hang over the trenches. All was silent.

But soon the secret rage lurking in the ground beneath their feet would burst forth. The attack opened up on the very stroke of five. O'Garra was half drunk. He had very rarely taken his ration of rum, but Elston had used persuasion to such effect that O'Garra had drunk another soldier's ration as well as his own. A whistle blew. The earth seemed to shake. They were over the top.

And now every sound and every movement seemed to strike some responsive chord in the Irishman's nature. He hung on desperately to the Manchester man. For some reason or other he dreaded losing contact with him. He could not understand this sudden desire for Elston's company. But the desire overwhelmed him.

It was not the sound, the huge concourse of sound that worried O'Garra. For somehow the earth in convulsion seemed a kind of yawning mouth, swallowing noise. No. It was the gun flashes ahead. They seemed to rip the very sky asunder. Great pendulums of flame swinging across the sky.

In that moment they appeared to him like the pendulums of his own life. Swinging from splendour to power, from terror to pity, from Life to Death. More than that. There was a continuous flash away on his right. It was more than a flash. It was an eye that ransacked his very soul.

"Jesus! Jesus!"

The earth was alive – afire. The earth was a mouth, it was a sea, a yawning gulf, a huge maw. Suddenly Elston was drenched in blood. Like a stuck pig he screamed out:

"Oh funkin' hell. I'm killed. I'm dead. O'Garra. O'Garra. O'Garra."

"Shut up," growled the Irishman. "Can't you see that bugger behind you. You got a belt in the back with his head. See. He hasn't any now. That whizz-bang took head and arse off him at the same time . . . Phew! Everybody's mad."

"If ever I get out of this," screamed Elston. "I'll – I'll –"

Grundy came up.

"Shit on you. Get forward. What the hell are you fellows standing here for? You bloody cowards," he roared into their ears.

"What the bloody hell's wrong with you," growled the Irishman. "This fellow here thought his head was off. Everything alright, isn't it? We're going forward. Are you? You lump of shite. How long have you been in the line anyhow? When you've learned to piss in your cap, you sucker, you'll have room to talk."

And Sergeant Grundy thought to himself.

"I suppose he thinks he was the only one in the first gas-attack. H'm."

"I'll put a bullet in the first man who wavers," he roared out.

The men struggled forward. It was impossible to see, to hear, to feel. All the senses were numbed. O'Garra's face was almost yeasty with sweat. He spat continually, at the same time cursing Grundy, and endeavouring to keep this man from Manchester upon his feet.

"Oh hell!" he yelled. "Are you utterly helpless? Stand up."

With the speed of terror Elston screamed out.

"Yes. Yes. I'm frightened. Oh mother! Mother! Mother!"

"Shut it, you bloody worm," growled O'Garra, and continued on his way, dragging the Englishman after him.

"Where are they drivin' us to, anyhow?" asked a man from Cork.

"Towards the bloody objective of course. Where in hell d'you think."

"We fairly fanned his backside," yelled another man from Donegal.

The screams of the shells, the plop-plop of the gas-shells, the staccato drumming of the machine-guns, the shouts and squeals and blubberings, almost upset even a man like O'Garra.

"This is not so bad," he murmured. "The thing is – will these blasted sods come back? That's what we have to look out for."

"Come back," yelled a voice. "Christ, you'll want running pumps to catch the swine."

Then suddenly O'Garra stopped. He no longer heard the sounds of voices. True, the man from Manchester was at his side. But where were the others? And a thick fog was descending. For a moment he seemed to lose contact with the whimperer at his side. And O'Garra shouted:

"Elston. Elston. Hey Elston! Where are you? Something's happened. Can you see? Hey! Hey! Can you see? This bloody fog's thickening."

Elston blinked and stood erect. Then his face paled. He said slowly:

"We must have gone too far. Lost contact somehow. We must search about quickly."

"Too far. Too far," shouted O'Garra, and he burst out laughing.

Yes. There was the possibility of that. He had seemed to eat up distance after that scrap with the sergeant. And then he must have dragged this English coward some distance too. Before they were aware of it, the fog had blotted everything out. They were now conscious only of each other's presence. This fog had separated them from all that madness, that surging desperate mass of matter; that eyeless monster; that screaming phalanx. The fog became so thick it was almost impossible for them to see each other.

"We must do something," said Elston. "God knows where we landed."

"Maybe into his bloody line," growled O'Garra.

They both sat down on the edge of the shell-hole to consider their position.

They seemed oblivious of the fact that the attack had not abated. That to the right a team of tanks was shooting forward on to the machine-gun positions; that a thousand yards to the rear a mopping-up party was at work. Oblivious of war and life itself. A strange silence seemed to overwhelm them. O'Garra rested his head in his hands. Suddenly he sat up, gripped Elston by the throat, and said:

"I've a mind to choke you. To put you out of your misery. How funny that in the moment I first realized your cowardice, I became unconscious of my own strength. I must have pulled you a mile, you swine."

The blood came and went across Elston's face in a sudden gust of fear and passion.

"What good would that do you. Especially at this moment?"

O'Garra once more buried his face in his hands, and remained silent. Elston was thinking. What was wrong? And had O'Garra really dragged him a mile? And had they really lost contact? Where in Christ's name had they landed? And did this man really mean to murder him? By God, then the sooner they found the others, the better. Perhaps he had suddenly gone mad? By God. That was it. He had gone mad. Mad.

"O'Garra," called Elston to the man now seated on the edge of the hole. "O'Garra! O'Garra!"

There was no reply, for the Irishman had fallen asleep. This discovery petrified Elston. The consciousness that he was absolutely alone; alone, save for this sleeping figure, caused a kind of icy mist to descend upon his heart, almost suffocating him. He too, sunk his head between his hands. The action was profound, for it seemed to the man to shut out thought, action, all external contacts with the world. But O'Garra was not asleep for long. He opened his eyes, looked across at the huddled form of the Manchester man, heaved a sigh, then fell back again into a kind of torpor. O'Garra suddenly began to think, and to think deeply. This process he found painful, as it always is for those who have ceased to think over a period of years. His was an atrophied mind. But now the whole of his past shot across the surface of that mind. He asked himself, if he would not have been better off in Tara Street after all. Even those lonely nights, those fruitless endeavours beneath the clock in Middle Abbey Street, surely they took on a richer texture now. Surely all those common-place things achieved a certain significance. Those times when his mind had remained simple; when he had been wont to enjoy those sweet charities of life itself. After all there was something in it. Why had he come into all this muck and mud and madness. He could not find any answer to the question. Then again, there was that after the war question. Would the men be compensated for all the inconveniences.

All the inconveniences. All the men. Would they? He had a grudge. Only this morning he had had one against a foolish officer, and yet the sight of that officer's headless body had stirred something deep down in the bosom of his soul. He had borne a grudge. But that was forgiven. There were so many. Did not this state of affairs warrant some kind of vengeance? Perhaps it did. But how would a man get it? Everyone in the war must bear a grudge. But would they all demand retribution? Would they all wreak a terrible vengeance. Ah! – .

* * *

"Elston!"

"Yes."

"Oh! you're awake. I say, we must have slept a hell of a time. My watch has stopped too. This blasted fog hasn't risen yet, either. We'd better move."

"What's that you say?"

"What's up now. Got the bloody shakes again," asked O'Garra.

"Listen," said Elston.

Somewhere ahead they could hear the movement of some form or other.

"Let's find out," said O'Garra, and jumped to his feet.

"No need now," said Elston. "Here it comes. Look!"

They both looked up at once. Right on top of them stood a young German soldier. His hands were stuck high in the air. He was weaponless. His clothes hung in shreds and his face was covered with mud. He looked tired and utterly weary. He said in a plaintive kind of voice.

"Camerade. Camerade."

"Camerade, you bastard," said Elston, "keep your hands up there."

And O'Garra asked: "Who are you? Where do you come from? Can you speak English? Open your soddin' mouth."

"Camerade. Camerade."

"You speak English, Camerade?"

"Yes – a little."

"Your name," demanded Elston. "What regiment are you? Where are we now. No tricks. If you do anything, you'll get your bottom kicked. Now then – where have you come from, and what the hell do you want?"

"My name it is Otto Reiburg. My house it is Muenchen. I am Bavarian. I surrender, Camerade."

"That's all," growled Elston.

"I am lost, is it," replied the German.

He was a youth, about eighteen years of age, tall, with a form as graceful as a young sapling, in spite of the ill-fitting uniform and unkempt appearance. His hair, which stuck out in great tufts from beneath his forage cap, was as fair as ripe corn. He had blue eyes, and finely moulded features.

"So are we," said Elston. "We are lost too. Is it foggy where you come from? It looks to me as if we'll never get out of this hole, only by stirring ourselves together and making a bolt for it."

"That's impossible," said O'Garra. "True, we can move. But what use is that? And perhaps this sod is leading us into a trap. Why not finish the bugger off, anyhow?"

The two men looked at the young German, and smiled. But the youth seemed to have sensed the something sinister in that smile. He began to move off. Elston immediately jumped up. Catching the young German by the shoulder he flung him to the bottom of the hole, saying:

"If you try that on again I'll cut the rollocks out of you. Why should you not suffer as well as us? Do you understand what I am saying? Shit on you," and he spat savagely into the German's face. From the position the youth was lying in, it was impossible for either of the men to see that he was weeping. Indeed, had Elston seen it, he would undoubtedly have killed him. There was something terrible stirring in this weasel's blood. He knew not what it was. But there was a strange and powerful force possessing him, and it was going to use him as its instrument. He felt a power growing on him. There was something repugnant, something revolting in those eyes, in their leer, and in the curled lips. Was it that in that moment itself, all the rottenness that was his life had suddenly shot up as filth from a sewer, leaving him helpless in everything but the act he was going to commit? O'Garra was watching Elston. He too, seemed to have sensed this something terrible.

His gaze wandered from Elston to the young German. No word was spoken. The silence was intense. Horrible.

These three men, who but an hour ago, seemed to be charged for action, eager and vital, looked as helpless as children now. Was it that this fog surrounding them had pierced its way into their hearts and souls? Or was it that something in their very nature had suffered collapse?

One could not say that they sat, or merely lay; they just sprawled; each terribly conscious of the other's presence, and in that presence detecting something sinister; something that leered; that goaded and pricked. Each seemed to have lost his faculty of speech. The fog had hemmed them in. Nor could any of them realise their position, where they were, the possibility of establishing contact with other human beings. What was this something that had so hurled them together?

O'Garra looked across to Elston.

"Elston! Elston! What are we going to do? We must get out of this. Besides the place stinks. Perhaps we are on very old ground. Rotten ground; mashy muddy ground. Christ the place must be full of these mangy dead."

Elston did not answer. And suddenly O'Garra fell upon him, beating him in the face, and screaming out at the top of his voice:

"Hey. Hey. You lousy son of a bitch. What's your game? Are you trying to make me as rotten as yourself, as cowardly, as lousy. It's you and not this bloody Jerry who is responsible for this. Do you hear me? Do you hear me? Jesus Christ Almighty, why don't you answer. Answer Answer."

The young German cowered in the bottom of the hole, trembling like a leaf. Terror had seized him. His face seemed to take on different colour, now white, now red, now grey, as if Death were already in the offing. Saliva trickled down his chin.

These changes of colour in the face seemed to pass across it like gusts of wind. Gusts of fear, terror, despair. Once only he glanced up at the now distorted features of the half crazy Irishman, and made as if to cry out. Once again O'Garra spoke to Elston. Then it was that the Englishman opened his eyes, looked across at his mate, and shouted:

"O'Garra! O'Garra. Oh where the funkin' hell are you, O'Garra?"

He stared hard at the Irishman, who, though his lips barely moved, yet uttered sounds:

"In a bloody mad-house. In a shit hole. Can't you smell the rotten dead? Can you hear. Can you hear? You louse, you bloody rat. Pretending to be asleep and all the while your blasted owl's eyes have been glaring at me. Ugh! Ugh!"

"Camerade."

A sigh came from the youth lying at the bottom of the hole. It was almost flute-like, having a liquidity of tone.

"Ah! uck you," growled O'Garra. "You're as much to blame as anybody. Yes. Yes. As much to blame as anybody. Who in the name of Jesus asked you to come here? Haven't I that bastard there to look after. The coward.

Didn't I have to drag him across the ground during the advance? Yes. YOU. YOU. YOU." and O'Garra commenced to kick the prisoner in the face until it resembled a piece of raw beef. The prisoner moaned. As soon as O'Garra saw the stream of blood gush forth from the German's mouth, he burst into tears. Elston too, seemed to have been stirred into action by this furious onslaught on the youth. He kicked the German in the mid-riff, making him scream like a stuck pig. It was this scream that loosed all the springs of action in the Manchester man. It cut him to the heart, this scream. Impotency and futility seemed as ghouls leering at him, goading him, maddening him.

He started to kick the youth in the face too. But now no further sound came from that inert heap. The Englishman dragged himself across to O'Garra. But the Irishman pushed him off.

"Get away. I hate you. Hate you. HIM. Everybody. Hate all. Go away. AWAY."

"By Jesus I will then," shouted Elston. "Think I'm a bloody fool to sit here with two mad-men. I'm going. Don't know where I'll land. But anything is better than this. It's worse than hell."

He rose to his feet and commenced to climb out of the hole. He looked ahead. Fog. And behind. Fog. Everywhere fog. No sound. No stir. He made a step forward when O'Garra leaped up and dragged him back. Some reason seemed to have returned to him, for he said:

"Don't go. Stay here. Listen. This state of affairs cannot

go on for ever. The fog will lift. Are you listening, and not telling yourself that I am mad? I am not mad. Do you understand? Do you understand. Tell me?"

"Is it day or night, or has day and night vanished," asked Elston.

"It might well be that the whole bloody universe has been hurled into space. The bugger of it is, my watch has stopped. Sit down here. I want to talk. Do you see now. I want to talk. It's this terrible bloody silence that kills me. Listen now. Can you hear anything. No. You can't. But you can hear me speak. Hear that ucker moaning down there. They are human sounds. And human sounds are everything now. They can save us. So we must talk. All the while. With resting, without ceasing. Understand. Whilst we are conscious that we are alive, all is well. Do you see now. Do you see now?"

"I thought the bloody Jerry was dead," muttered Elston.

"Dead my arse. Come! What'll we talk about. Anything. Everything."

And suddenly Elston laughed, showing his teeth, which were like a horse's!

"Remember that crazy house down in Fricourt. Remember that. Just as we started to enter the God-forsaken place, he began to bomb and shell it.

"Remember? We both went out in the evening, souveniring. Went into that little white house at the back of the hotel. Remember that?"

"Well!"

"Remember young Dollan mounting that old woman. Looked like a bloody witch. I still remember her nearly bald head."

"Well!"

"And you chucked young Dollan off, and got into bed with her yourself."

"Was it a long time ago. In this war, d'you mean?"

"Yes. Are you tapped, or what. Course it was in this bloody war. What the funkin' hell are you thinkin' of, you loony."

For the first time since they had found themselves in this position, they both laughed. And suddenly Elston looked up into his companion's face, laughed again, and said softly:

"Well, by Christ, d'you know that laugh has made me want to do something?"

"Do something?" queried O'Garra.

"Yes," replied Elston, and standing over the prisoner in the hole, he pissed all over him. Likewise O'Garra, who began to laugh in a shrill sort of way.

There is a peculiar power about rottenness in that it feeds on itself, borrows from itself; and its tendency is always downward. That very action had seized the polluted imagination of the Irishman. He was helpless. Rottenness called to him; called to him from the pesty frame of Elston. After the action they both laughed again, but this time louder.

"Hell!" exclaimed O'Garra. "After that I feel relieved.

Refreshed. Don't feel tired. Don't feel anything particularly. How do you feel?" he asked.

"The same," replied Elston. "But I wish to Christ this soddin' fog would lift."

This desire, this hope that the fog would lift was something burning in the heart, a ceaseless yearning, the restlessness of waters washing against the flood-gates of the soul. It fired their minds. It became something organic in the brain. Below them the figure stirred slightly.

"Ah! – Ah! – "

"The ucker hasn't kicked the bucket yet," said Elston. He leaned over and rested his two hands on O'Garra's knees. "D' you know when I came to examine things; that time I thought you were asleep you know, and you weren't; well I thought hard, and I came to certain conclusions. One of them was this. See that lump of shit in the hole; that Jerry I mean. You do. Well now, he's the cause of everything. Everything. Everything. Don't you think so yourself?"

"Yes I do," said the Irishman. "That's damn funny, you know. Here is what I thought. I said to myself: 'That bastard lying there is the cause of all this.' And piece by piece and thread by thread I gathered up all the inconveniences. All the actions, rebuffs, threats, fatigues, cold nights, lice, tooth-aches, forced absence from women, nights in trenches up to your knees in mud. Burial parties, mopping-up parties, dead horses, heaps of stale shite, heads, balls, brains, everywhere. All those things. I made the case against him. Now I ask you. Why should he live?"

73

"Yes," shouted Elston. "You're right. Why should he? He is the cause of it all. Only for this bloody German we might not have been here. I know where I should have been anyhow. Only for him the fog might have lifted. We might have got back to our own crowd. Yes. Yes. Only for him. Well there would not have been any barrage, any attack, and bloody war in fact.

"Can't you see it for yourself now? Consider. Here we are, an Englishman, and an Irishman, both sitting here like soft fools. See. And we're not the only ones perhaps. One has to consider everything. Even the wife at home. All the other fellows. All the madness, confusion. Through Germans. And here's one of them."

"Ah! – "

Elston glared down into the gargoyle of a face now visible to them both, the terrible eyes flaring up at the almost invisible sky.

"Water – Ah! – "

A veritable torrent of words fell from Elston's lips.

"Make the funkin' fog rise and we'll give you anything. Everything. Make the blasted war stop, now, right away. Make all this mud and shite vanish. Will you. You bastards started it. Will you now. See! We are both going mad. We are going to kill ourselves."

"Kill me –"

"Go and shite. But for the likes of you we wouldn't be here."

"Water – "

In that moment O'Garra was seized by another fit of madness. Wildly, like some terror-stricken and trapped animal, he looked up and around. "Fog. Yes fog. FOG. FOG. FOG. FOG. FOG. Jesus sufferin' Christ. FOG. FOG. FOG. HA, HA, HA, HA, HA. In your eyes, in your mouth, on your chest, in your heart. FOG. FOG. Oh hell, we're all going crazy. FOG. FOG."

"There you are," screamed Elston into the German's ear, for suddenly seized with panic by the terrific outburst from O'Garra, he had fallen headlong into the hole. The eyes seemed to roll in his head, as he screamed: "There you are. Can you hear it? You. Can you hear it? You ucker from Muenchen, with your fair hair, and your lovely face that we bashed in for you. Can you hear it? We're trapped here. Through you. Through you and you bloody lot. If only you hadn't come. You baby. You soft stupid little runt. Hey! Hey! Can you hear me?"

The two men now fell upon the prisoner, and with peculiar movements of the hands began to mangle the body. They worried it like mad dogs. The fog had brought about a nearness, that was now driving them to distraction. Elston, on making contact with the youth's soft skin, became almost demented. The velvety touch of the flesh infuriated him. Perhaps it was because Nature had hewn him differently. Had denied him the young German's grace of body, the fair hair, the fine clear eyes that seemed to reflect all the beauty and music and rhythm of the Rhine. Maddened him. O'Garra shouted out:

"PULL his bloody trousers down."

With a wild movement Elston tore down the prisoner's trousers.

In complete silence O'Garra pulled out his bayonet and stuck it up the youth's anus. The German screamed.

Elston laughed and said: "I'd like to back-scuttle the bugger."

"Go ahead," shouted O'Garra.

"I tell you what," said Elston. "Let's stick this horse-hair up his penis."

So they stuck the horse-hair up his penis. Both laughed shrilly.

A strange silence followed.

"Kill the bugger," screamed O'Garra.

Suddenly, as if instinctively, both men fell away from the prisoner, who rolled over, emitting a single sigh – Ah – . His face was buried in the soft mud.

"Elston,"

"Well," was the reply.

"Oh Jesus! Listen. Has the fog risen yet. I have my eyes tight closed. I am afraid."

"What are you afraid of. Tell me that. There's buggerall here now. This fellow is dead. Feel his bum. Any part you like. Dead. Dead."

"I am afraid of myself. Listen. I have something to ask you. Will you agree with me now to walk out of it. We can't land any worse place."

"My *arse* on you," growled Elston. "Where can we walk.

You can't see a finger ahead of you. I tell you what. Let's worry each other to death. Isn't that better than this moaning, this sitting here like soft shits. That time I fell asleep I did it in my pants. It made me get mad with that bugger down there."

"A thing like that," O'Garra laughed once again.

"Listen," roared Elston. "I tell you we can't move. D'you hear. Do you? Shall I tell you why. It's not because there is no ground on which to walk. No. Not that. It's just that we can't move. We're stuck. Stuck fast. Though we have legs, we can't walk. We have both been seized by something, I can't even cry out. I am losing strength. I don't want to do anything. Nothing at all. Everything is useless. Nothing more to do. Let's end it. Let's worry each other like mad dogs. I had the tooth-ache an hour ago. I wish it would come back. I want something to worry me. Worry me."

"Listen! Did you hear that?"

"Well, it's a shell. What did you think it was. A bloody butterfly?"

"It means," said O'Garra, "that something is happening, and where something is happening we are safe. Let's go. Now. Now."

"Are you sure it was a shell?"

"Sure. There's another," said O'Garra.

"It's your imagination," said Elston laughing. "Imagination."

"Imagination. Well, by Christ. I never thought of that. Imagination. By God, that's it."

They sat facing each other. Elston leaned forward until his eyes were on a level with those of the Irishman. Then, speaking slowly, he said:

"Just now you said something. D'you know what it was?"

"Yes. Yes. Let's get out of it before we are destroyed."

"But we're destroyed already," said Elston, smiling. "Listen."

"Don't you remember what you said a moment ago," continued Elston. "You don't. Then there's no mistake about it, you are crazy. Why, you soft shite didn't you say we had better talk, talk, talk. About anything. Everything. Nothing. Let us then. What'll we talk about?"

"Nothing. But I know what we must do. Yes, by Jesus I know. D'you remember you said these Germans were the cause of the war. And you kicked that fellow's arse. Well, let's destroy him. Let's bury him."

"He's dead, you mad bugger. Didn't we kill him before. Didn't I say I felt like back-scuttling him? I knew all along you were crazy. Ugh."

"Not buried. He's not buried," shouted O'Garra, "Are you deaf? Mad yourself; are you?"

The fog was slowly rising, but they were wholly unconscious of its doing so. They were blind. The universe was blotted out. They were conscious only of each other's presence, of that dead heap at the bottom of the hole. Conscious of each other's nearness. Each seemed to have become something gigantic. The one saw the other as a barrier, a wall blotting out everything. They could feel and smell each other. There was something infinite in those moments that held them back from each other's throats.

"Not deaf, but mad like yourself; you big shit-house, can't you see that something has happened. I don't mean outside, but inside this funkin' fog. Savvy?"

"Let's bury this thing. UGH. Everything I look at becomes Him. Everything Him. If we don't destroy him, he'll destroy us, even though he's dead."

"Let's dance on the bugger and bury him for ever."

"Yes, that's it," shouted O'Garra. "I knew an owld woman named Donaghue whose dog took poison. She danced on the body."

And both men began to jump up and down upon the corpse. And with each movement, their rage, their hatred seemed to increase. Out of sight, out of mind. Already this mangled body was beginning to disappear beneath the mud. Within their very beings there seemed to burst into flame, all the conglomerated hates, fears, despairs, hopes, horrors. It leaped to the brain for O'Garra screamed out:

"I hate this thing so much now I want to shit on it,"

"O'Garra."

"Look. It's going down down. Disappearing. Look," shouted Elston.

"Elston."

"Let's kill each other. Oh sufferin' Jesus –"

"You went mad long ago but I did not know that –"

"Elston," called O'Garra.

79

"There's no way out is there?"

"Uck you. NO."

"Now."

"The fog is still thick."

"Now."

The bodies hurled against each other, and in that moment it seemed as if this madness had set their minds afire.

Suddenly there was a low whine, whilst they struggled in the hole, all unconscious of the fact that the fog had risen. There was a terrific explosion, a cloud of mud, smoke, and earthy fragments, and when it cleared the tortured features of O'Garra were to be seen. His eyes had been gouged out, whilst beneath his powerful frame lay the remains of Elston. For a moment only they were visible, then slowly they disappeared beneath the sea of mud which oozed over them like the restless tide of an everlasting night.

GREASER ANDERSON

I

"YOUR SUPPER IS LAID OUT in the kitchen," said the stout landlady of the boarding-house in Nelson Street. To which Mr Anderson replied that he would go in as soon as he found the paper he was hunting for. A reply that did not catch the good lady's ear, for she had already departed, leaving Mr Anderson to continue his rumbling among the papers in the tin box which was standing on a chair near the window. To himself he said:

"Yes, I will go in to supper, but first I must find this paper. First I must get my hands on it and read it."

Until this desire had been fulfilled he would not stir from the place. The idea that so suddenly had illuminated the darkness of his mind was peculiar in itself. Ten years was a long time. In all those ten years he had never given the matter a thought. The more he rumbled in the box, the more wild and urging became his desire. He felt that there could be no logical explanation for this sudden desire until he held the paper in his hands, until he had read it, every single word. That done the fever would die down; though the idea would expand, and that huge question-mark that appeared in front of him wherever he went, that too would vanish. He clung to this like a drowning man clinging to a rock. He was fearful of this idea, so suddenly resurrected, being as suddenly swirled away again into the dark fastnesses of his mind.

Mr Anderson was nothing remarkable to look at. In an age when Method was a tenet of modern philosophy one could not expect anything better than a standardised human being, so far as physical make-up was concerned in the matter, and indeed the mental arsenal was not above being influenced by this standardising process, for thought too was encompassed by this modern methodology. Mr Anderson emerged from that particular stratum where the mental temperature was standardised. Tall, rather thin, with a massive head, wherein eyes that seemed to water as freely as a ripe melon were set beneath bushy and straggling brows, Mr Anderson by his appearance and make-up presented the usual type of retired worker whom destiny has forbidden to plod further, for after all destiny was something over which certain men had influence. He was clean-shaven and his hair was dyed. His being clean-shaved was perhaps the one important thing about him, for it marked a definite stage in his life. He had eagerly followed the fashion that to shave clean was to look young, and to look young was of infinite help to the various Mr Andersons who plodded their varied ways about the world. It had indeed kept this Mr Anderson with a shipping company for nearly five years over the allotted time, he having decided to work ashore in the last years of the war. Then, too, the last year of the war had been a godsend to him.

War is not entirely indifferent to the souls it draws into its maw. To Mr Anderson it had meant more work, more overtime, more money. True, he had lost his only son in a rather bloody affair near Crônes Wood, and his son's wife, stricken by this trick of fate, had not long survived him. Fortunately for the old man there was a child. This child was now a boy of fourteen, a strange child, exhibiting all those characteristics manifest in children born during those dreadful years. He was highly sensitive, irritable, suffered from occasional fits, and bouts of bad temper, and now and then this was a burden on Mr Anderson's already overloaded mind – the boy was going into a decline. Altogether a curious and pathetic creature. The old man's mind was above these little things, however. He loved the child as his very own. It seemed indeed the last barrier against loneliness. The while he rumbled amongst the papers he thought of the boy, who was now upstairs, and sleeping he hoped, as he had put him to bed nearly an hour ago. At last, after nearly two hours' searching, Mr Anderson alighted on the much-longed-for piece of paper. A smile of triumph lighted up his features as he put his hand on it. He crushed it hurriedly into his pocket, then rushed off to the kitchen, only to discover that the meal on the table was already dead cold. He sat down, however, and enjoyed it in the kitchen, where, in the winter, he was allowed an occasional glimpse of the fire. The boy he generally saw off to bed at seven each evening. He hoped to warm the bed for him. After partaking of bread and butter, salt fish and lukewarm tea, he gathered up the remainder of the meal and went upstairs to his room. The boy was still awake.

"Aren't you asleep yet, Frankie?" he asked in a rather vexatious tone of voice. In the half-darkness he thought he saw his grandson smile, and now he replied: "No. Not yet, granddad."

Hungry boys do not make easy sleepers, and the boy was hungry. He devoured the remainder of the meal with a gusto that amazed his grandfather. The old man now lighted the oil-lamp and placed it on the table near the bed. Then seating himself on a chair he drew out the paper from his pocket with trembling hands, and opening it began to read. A draught came in through the open window, and the paper fluttered in his hand. Now whilst he read a dim consciousness stirred in his brain. This paper was a signal of power. This paper really meant that something possible might be done to get the boy away to a home where his peculiar illness might be attended to by experts. It would also be the means of blotting out this huge question-mark that appeared before Mr Anderson's eyes wherever he went. The paper was one he had received from his old firm in the last year of the war. It thanked him, Alfred Anderson, for his good work on their ships, two years of which had been spent on an hospital ship during the war. It also thanked him for his valuable work in the munition department of the firm, a war-time creation. Mr Anderson had spent the last year of the war there as a foreman. They hung a kind of halo over his devoted services and promised not to forget him. This last sentence shone like a kind of white fire before his eyes. "We will not forget you." Pause. "We will not forget you." Pause. "We will not forget you." Mr Anderson kept repeating the words like a form of prayer; the droning of his voice continued until he heard the boy say: "Aren't you going to bed, granddad?"

Well, of course he was going to bed. He was not going to sit there all night. For one thing it was much too cold for another there was a great thing going to happen to-morrow. There was a third thing to be done to-morrow. A task ahead and a duty to be done. Yes, he was coming to bed right away. He commenced to undress. In two minutes he had closed down the window, blown out the light, and was warmly tucked in beside the boy. They both slept soundly as though free from the weighted cares of the world.

II

Mr Anderson had not visited the company's offices which were situated on the Pier-Head, for over five years. The offices were sandwiched in between those of Hastie & Co., General Carriers, and Hunger & Want, the big shipbuilding and repairing firm. Consequently, when on this rainy morning he caught the tram and jumped off at the corner of Water Street, he was somewhat astonished not only to find the original building grown in size but that others of like stature were ranged alongside it, the building with the dome standing out especially as a kind of architectural accident rather than design, a form of hugeness and greatness that concealed rottenness, harboured energy, and measured its greatness by each exacting sweat-drop. Mr Anderson was bewildered. It was just after nine o'clock. A continual stream of black-coated clerks and gaily dressed typists were hurrying towards this giant of a building, wherein they disappeared, not to appear again until evening. It was like a tremendous mouth, ever open, that day after day absorbed so many thousand fragments of human consciousness, and drained them, and dried them up.

Mr Anderson walked slowly down Water Street and crossed the road. The middle of this road was now lined with cars, belonging to officials, major and minor, of the company. Ahead of him he saw the huge swing-doors for the first time. He approached warily, as though he were a felon bent on some dark deed. When he reached the steps – there were twenty of them – he stopped and looked up. The terrific size of the building at once made his own relationship with the universe painfully obvious. He was a mere pigmy, a unit, a fragmentary part of this huge body. He felt outside, lonely, terribly lonely. He wondered if there was anybody in the office whom he might know. He had had at one time, and the offices were much smaller then, the daily job of walking down from the dock to the office with the daily returns of work aboard whatever ship he happened to be working by. He knew one or two people who might still be in the same position in the office. He secretly hoped they were still with the company. They could not fail to recognise him. With this thought dominant in his mind, and the precious piece of paper clutched tightly in his trembling hand, he slowly mounted the steps. Already the big man at the door had seen him. He glared at him. Just as Mr Anderson was going forward to let himself in, two clerks, evidently late for their work, pushed ahead of him. There was an immediate jam. The doorman came to the rescue. Finally, Mr Anderson found himself standing in the long cold-looking corridor, though he could not understand how he had managed to arrive there. The big man was looking down at him. Mr Anderson was too busy watching the hurrying clerks disappearing round corners and into lifts to notice that the big gentleman was speaking to him. Suddenly he found this man's face pushed into his own, and a voice asked in a gruff manner: "Well! Who d'you want to see, eh?"

Mr Anderson was so astonished by the business efficiency the modern world was displaying that for a moment or two he remained tongue-tied, during which few minutes the doorman had taken stock of him, from his rather worn hard hat, down to his cheap blue serge trousers, with their frayed edges that told their own particular tale. He found his tongue at last. "I want to see the director," he said somewhat sharply, a remark that merely made the uniformed one stare harder at him than before.

"You what?" he exclaimed with a gasp.

"I want to see the director," repeated Mr Anderson and the tone of his voice was not so commanding now.

The big man merely laughed. He placed his hands on his hips, looked long and closely at the new arrival, then commenced to laugh again as though he had heard the greatest joke in the world. One could hear the huge voice echoing all over the building.

"So you want to see the director. Eh! HA HA HA! So you want to see the director, eh! Ha ha ha!"

Mr Anderson stood gaping at the big figure of the doorman, speechless with astonishment. Suddenly an idea occurred to him. He asked the big man if a Mr Ledgeworth still worked for the company. There was a momentary silence after he put this question. Again the big man laughed.

"Are you sure it's not Mr Ledgeworth of the sanitary

department?" asked the other in a rather sarcastic tone of voice.

"No. Ledgeworth who used to be runner for the ships at one time." Mr Anderson was suddenly angry, and he added quietly: "You know damned well who I mean." That made the big man appear to grow bigger still. He said:

"I don't give a God damn if you wanted to see the King. You wouldn't get past me after that. Who d'you think you are, eh? You're one of these bloody old-timers, always hanging round the company's doors, always on the bum. I've seen crowds of you fellers before to-day. Get to hell out of this before I boot you into the bloody street. Quick now – you cringing old devil."

Mr Anderson was going to say something in reply, but again his tongue refused to move, and in the same moment his hand went hurriedly to his pocket and he pulled out the precious piece of paper. He brandished it in a frantic sort of way before the eyes of the doorman. And brandishing it thus he suddenly found his tongue again.

"I want to see a director. Any director. I've a paper here. It's signed by a director of this company. Don't you bloody well forget it. Look! Look! Look!" And swiftly unfolding it he drew nearer and showed it to the doorman, though he took good care to retain his hold on it, lest the doorman might suddenly fancy to tear it up and kick him into the street.

"Look! Look! Look!" repeated the now desperate Mr Anderson. He saw his chance of getting into the office slowly disappearing. He made one last advance. He shouted at the top of his voice: "Christ! Why, it's signed, can't you see now? Look! It's signed by a director of the company. It's hard to read though, he is such a poor writer of his own name," and the big doorman leaned forward a little until his eyes rested on this oblong piece of paper, and what appeared to be a dirty smudge beneath the printed words. The smudge was the signature of the director in question. The big man tried his best to conceal a smile that was slowly threatening to stretch from ear to ear, for what the old man was holding out for his inspection was merely a printed sheet of paper, thousands of which had been duplicated and given to the workers of the company at the end of the war. It was of no value whatever.

The man whispered in Mr Anderson's ear: "D'you know what I'd call that? Hell! Don't make me laugh again. Will you? Why, thousands of bloody men got those things. Even the King had millions printed, but they're no bloody good. You ought to know that by now."

"But I tell you if you let me in this director will see me," urged the old man desperately. "Good Lord, man! Read it. Says: "We will not forget your valuable services." The King never had forms like that printed, did he? Please let me go through. I know that he'll see me if you only let me in."

"What's his name?" asked the other quickly.

Mr Anderson took his spectacles from his pocket, put them on, and looked closely at the paper. He looked up a second later at the big man, his features pleading a strange and pitiful helplessness.

"It's so hard to read the name," he said. "Can *you* read it?"

By this time the other man was getting very bored and he replied:

"What's his bloody name? If you don't know his name, what's the use. What d'you want, anyhow?"

"I want to see the director," answered Mr Anderson.

"The place for b— like you," growled the doorman, "is out in the bloody street. Come on. Leg it." Without another word he seized Mr Anderson by the collar of his coat, half dragged and half carried him to the swingdoors, moved it slightly, pushed the man through, and then returned to his usual place. Mr Anderson found himself in the street. It happened that at the moment of his ejection another man should be walking slowly in his direction. Mr Anderson suddenly found himself embraced by a long and very muscular person named Rafferty.

"Well, by God! Is it you, Anderson?" exclaimed Rafferty. "Come and have a drink, man It's years since I last saw you. How are you? What are you doing with yourself these days?"

Mr Anderson did not mention his very forcible ejection from the near-by shipping office of the company, nor the fact that he was down on his luck. He shook Rafferty warmly by the hand. Together they walked off into the town until they reached the "Legs o' Man." Here they entered and

Rafferty suggested a parlour where they could drink and talk in silence. The barman ushered them in and Mr Anderson found himself comfortably seated in the cosiest corner of the room. He rubbed his hands cheerfully.

"Well! What are you doing these days?" asked Rafferty once more. But the other immediately put the same question to Rafferty. The latter said he had just returned from a six-months' voyage down the West Coast of South America. The barman brought in two whiskies and Rafferty said:

"Add a gin and it for both, will you?"

They began talking again.

"I've never been to sea since the war finished," said Mr Anderson. I was doing shore work for Maclean & Ledgeworth for about a year and three months. The bloody firm has joined up with another now. Half the damned men sacked. I've given up all idea of ever getting a ship now. Still, one can't complain. How are you doing yourself?"

"Oh, I'm great, boy," said Rafferty, and began to laugh. "I'm simply doing great. Drink up and have another. We've plenty of time. It's only just turned a quarter to twelve and they don't shut till three. Drink up, for old time's sake."

III

Coady, the Superintendent's chief clerk, was writing rapidly on a yellow printed form that looked like an allotment note, when suddenly he looked up, for eyes of Super were upon him and he had felt them. Super spoke. Paused. "Where is this confounded fellow?" he repeated. "Have they seen him off? What does he want?"

Coady looked into his chief's eyes and replied: "Anderson was hanging round here for hours. Was trying to get up here an hour ago to see some director." He continued with his writing.

"Oh," said Super, and began licking his lips like one who prepares to sit down to roast chicken and apple sauce. He moved restlessly in his chair. Rose and walked up and down the room. He breathed heavily. Suddenly pulled himself up. His clerk went on writing. This action was strangely irritating to him and he called out abruptly: "Stop! Stop writing." Was not right, he felt, that he should be worried when an ordinary clerk was not. Barked at him now. "What are you working at there?"

"Allotment notes for S.S. *Hadrian*."

"Oh!" A long silence. Outside this room tap-tap of many machines could be heard, a sea of murmuring sounds, feet scurrying up and down stairs, along corridors, the hum of the lift dynamos. Occasional coughing, for there was much 'flu about and all in that building were feeling fed up. Through the whole of this building many noises expressing energy of men. Long corridors were lined with oil paintings of directors who had made the company in past years. There were many rooms where men spoke to girls who typed quickly on to their machines. Great gusts of wind whirled through the building, for the company was very busy, and busy meant huge doors swinging open, shut, all the time. Some people coming in were important and these were saluted. Others not very important as they were poor people. Sometimes the sun shone through a window but none saw it. Too busy and company working hard and men serious all the time. It was a great city was Liverpool and reputation to keep up and figures and alphabet were bread for many people. Reputation must be kept up, they said. Hurry and scurry and bells ringing all the time. Even assistant Coady worked convulsively as though every minute were his last in mortal life. He was terribly busy with the great pile of papers on his desk. He heard the Super muttering about some "damned Captain doesn't know his business," and he crouched low over his desk. He was afraid. No questions asked, none answered. Always people moving in and out of rooms, rushing here and there, from and to lavatory, up and down lifts that were run by men with one arm, as all ex-soldiers were given work – or how could they help to pay taxes to treasury of Government in order that cries of Victory bond-holders might be appeased. Bondholders and others for whom men with one arm had fought in the war that was far off in the memory. Mr Anderson knew a man who had half an arm and who was sacked promptly. His wife had been confined and he had sat all night by the bedside watching her, and so was tired and slept in. He lived in next house to the old man and used to buy the boy candy on Saturdays. He was ten minutes late for his work and came rushing down sweating and huge building frowning on him like a monster. In the lift he said to his mate:

"I'm sick of this bloody life. One friggin' arm and trying to look after my wife and bastards here tick me off for good because I was a few minutes late. Slept in. Fed up that's all. After fightin' the bloody war for them."

"It's hard lines," Mr Anderson had said, and that was all, for the man was found hanging by his braces in his own closet. Mr Anderson imbibing drink upon drink had forgotten such things, and as for the Super and his clerk they had their own worries to think about. A wind was blowing outside. The Super crosses over to the window. Looked out. The sight of a passenger liner lying at the stage reminded him of something. He rushed up to Coady:

"Get me Mr Finnegan at once," he ordered.

Mr Finnegan was a little man well worn in the service of the company. He worked on the bottom floor of the building. When the clerk went out, Mr Gorman, the Super, started swearing in a loud voice.

"This damned fellow is getting on my nerves scrounging round the place, and then this blasted skipper late again for the tide. Damn him. Wonder what this fellow wants anyhow. What kind of a paper has he that he says

has a director's signature on it? I suspect it's one of those
things we issued out to the men after the war." He laughed
then for he remembered the war was a long time ago and
men like Mr Anderson were old and done with and forgotten. Mr Anderson, in short, was worrying Mr Gorman the
superintendent. He must be kept off the premises. That
doorman wanted sacking. Did not know his job. He would
soon fix that matter. The man could be warned by the
police about pestering people like that. So he rambled on.
The truth was that the doorman had done his best and
could do no more. And it was not his fault that Mr
Anderson, still obsessed with the idea of interviewing a
company director, the piece of paper now a pulpy mess,
from the sweat of his tightly clutched hand; it was not his
fault that the old man should elect to enter the great building by anoher door. And this time staggering just a little on
his feet. He passed slowly along the corridors, through a
continual stream of office-boys, typists, porters, messen-
gers. He hiccoughed. Every now and then he stopped,
stretched himself to his full height, as if the feeling were
upon him that each minute he must grow taller and taller,
more commanding. His breath came short. In the middle
of the corridor he stopped again. Then in a loud voice,
stammering and gesticulating with his right hand, he said:

"I'm greaser Anderson. That's who I am. And don't you
bloody well forget it." He surveyed the small crowd of
interested people who appeared on the thresholds of the
various offices. It was obvious to them that the gentlemen

with the funny hard hat was a little drunk, which was true, for Mr Anderson had just left the very convivial Mr Rafferty, and he none too steady on his own legs, which is the result of long voyages and forced absence from old shipmates. Mr Anderson did not appear able to comprehend the position he was in. In fact, long afterwards he marvelled how he had ever got into the building at all, for the figure of the big doorman was one that engraved itself very forcibly upon his mind. He again shouted at the top of his voice: "I'm greaser Anderson. That's who I bloody well am. Worked for this company afore half you b— knew what yellow looked like. Greaser Anderson. That's me." He patted his chest. There was a chorus of titters, whisperings. Luckily as yet Mr Anderson had not caught the attention of the man at the swing-doors. Just then a tall important-looking individual came walking in the greaser's direction. Mr Anderson with a dramatic movement of the hand, reminiscent of *Othello*, Act II, took two paces forward and pulled the individual up sharply, saying:

"I'm greaser Anderson. That's who I am. Where's the director? I want to see the director." The gentleman gave him a withering look, turned to a passing office-boy, and demanded that the porter at the door be sent for immediately.

"Yes, sir," said the boy, and hurried away.

But Mr Anderson, the smell of whose breath was beginning to fill the corridor, was not yet finished.

"I want to see the director. Please. Which office is it? Worked in this bleedin' company afore half of you were born. We won't forget you. By God, they better hadn't. Anderson's my name. Everybody knows me. I want to see the director."

Again a chorus of laughter. Suddenly Mr Anderson beheld a flight of stairs ahead of him, and immediately advanced on them. The crowd followed two or three at a time. Slowly he dragged himself up the first flight, then the second. Unconsciously he was approaching the Super's office. The crowd crept behind. At the top of the second flight Mr Anderson collapsed and lay on the floor, a strangely huddled heap, with many strange sounds issuing from his mouth. Some thought he was in a fit, though all felt he had had a little too much beverage. Mr Anderson sat up. His voice thickened, as standing on his legs with some difficulty, he remarked: "Must see this director. Company can't do a thing like that. Got a bloody paper here anyhow. Must see him. Little lad at home. 'Won't forget you,' that's what they said and it's on this piece of paper. God love me Charlie. Years I was in this company too."

Passers-by caught such phrases as: "Director. Must see him. Big dog. Ten years. Mean devils."

Mr Anderson turned on his heel and walked the full length of the corridor, and began a ceaseless knocking at every door, murmuring continually, "Bastards – too lazy to see me. I'm greaser Anderson, I am." He stopped an office-boy and questioned him in a rather incoherent manner. The boy hardly noticed his condition, or even smelling his thick breath, promptly informed him that there were ten directors, he thought. Which one did he want to see? Mr Anderson did not know. There was the signature of a director on this piece of paper he held in his hand, though the writing was so bad that he could not make out the name at all. No. He did not know which director he wanted. The office-boy grinned. In a desperate moment he blurted out that any director would do. The office-boy then referred him to the director on the ground floor. Mr Anderson pricked up his ears.

"Yes, quite OK," said the boy, still grinning. "You'll find him there all right. Standing by the swing-doors. Wears a long blue coat with brass buttons on it," and the boy passed on. Mr Anderson felt more bewildered than ever. He started to ascend the next flight of steps. By this time all interest in him had ceased, and those who had satisfied their curiosity returned to their offices and work. Meanwhile in the Super's office the clerk Coady had returned and at that moment was wading through a pile of ship's papers. The Super was sitting at his own desk, his hand on the 'phone. He asked once again:

"Who is this bloody stutterer?" following it up by spitting into the grate.

The clerk looked up at his boss and replied:

"His name is Anderson. Says he was a greaser in this company for years. Wants to see a director. He doesn't know which one. Has a paper with him. Is an old servant of the company. Sailed in the first ships that ran for us. Thirty-seven years, he says. The doorman put him out twice this morning. He told a boy below that he had to see a director as it was most important. It seems he's had this paper since the 'war. A kind of printed sheet with somebody's duplicated signature on it."

The Super laughed then, HA HA HA! and said the whole idea was ridiculous. Hundreds of men had had such papers in their pay-envelopes.

"He keeps going from one office to another complaining about the way he is shuffled about by people. He's drunk most of the time, so Evans says. Says he has a right to be interviewed. Something about the company won't forget him."

The Super did not make any remark, for just then the bell rang and he picked up the receiver. He looked up half a minute later and remarked: "Did I tell you that bloody ship has missed the tide? She has though. That's twice in nine months that Wilson has failed us. A clear nine hundred extra in wages, by God, without talking about the rise in harbour dues. Blast him." He became silent. Then suddenly there came to their ears what appeared to be a low murmuring, that now as they listened carefully resembled a kind of musical monologue. The clerk went to the door, but did not open it. They could hear quite well without doing so. Greaser Anderson was outside talking to himself. His inability to find somebody to talk to had resulted in this decision to talk to himself. The Super got up from his chair and listened by the door. He said:

"Is that him? Why he must be fairly soused all right. He's singing, isn't he?"

Mr Anderson had managed to reach this door after much struggle and climbing of steps. He had enough sight left to be able to read OFFICE OF THE ENGINEERING SUPT. PRIVATE, set in the frosted glass panel of the door. In his endeavour to knock at this door he had slipped and fallen helplessly to the floor. He was now sitting with his back to it, uttering all kinds of queer remarks in many different sounds, that made the Super say to Coady: "Open the door. Just a little."

And clerk opened the door a little "just for a lark." Mr Anderson babbled away. "Bloody company always kidding us up that's what they are won't forget. Won't forget you. Years wasted messing about in their old cockle-shells of boats. Hear 'em talking, lot of liars that's what they are don't give a God damn they don't and me and the poor kid stuck there stiffen them anyway. Brave lads we are oh aye off to sea in their old boats all right during the war though b— you now – "

"He's quite drunk," said the Super, "you might 'phone down to Jeffers and tell him to come up and take him out of the building altogether."

"Yes, sir."

"Cheer up they say we won't forget you must see director company can't do these things lousy sods all new fellers here I expect don't know me fellers like me made this bloody company by Jesus they made their promise how can they dodge it? Ugh! they're mean devils. Ugh! they're mean they are. Kick him out. Muck on him who's he? Only a greaser. Damn and blast them war's over now and everybody has forgotten by God – "

Mr Jeffers came round the corner then. Mr Anderson did not see him. Before he realised it he was pulled roughly to his feet. His bleary eyes looked up at this huge person standing over him, and once more his tongue was tied. Mr Anderson was dumb. It seemed that like Moussorgsky's Idiot he was empty. He was done. He had said his say. Nothing more to be said and nothing more to be done. The big man began shaking him.

"Wodderwant! Woddyerwant? Who the bloody hell are you anyhow?" He started to drag Mr Anderson by the collar of his coat, but with some little instinct left him, and a little determination, Mr Anderson suddenly clung tightly to the handle of the door. He shouted out in a loud voice: "I wanner see the dir – ec – dir – ec I wanner see the direc – c – "

"You're drunk," said the doorman angrily, and he was himself smitten with fear that some official of the company might discover him in this rather embarrassing position, and that might not augur well for his future.

"I wannersee Mr Ledge–. I wanner see Mr Ledgeworth. Mr Ledgeworth knows me God blast you let me alone will you I wanner see him, why can't I see him, eh?"

Mr Jeffers felt there was only one thing he could do. He would carry this drunken, worrying, interfering person outside the building in his arms and deposit him safely into the arms of the nearest policeman. The man was helplessly and hopelessly drunk.

"Mr Ledgeworth knows me sailed with him in the old *Ionia* Christ why don't you give a feller a chance why don't you-you lousy-you-muff-you – "

"Nobody named Ledgeworth," said the doorman angrily, and picked up Mr Anderson in his powerful arms.

"There is. Saw him yesterday. It's his name on this paper. Look at it. Says we will not forget you well I'm an old servant of this company what the hell – "

"Outside you go," said Jeffers quietly.

"Good Jesus man listen to me this paper and everything's all right I know him well please let me see him you think I'm drunk but I'm not – "

"OUTSIDE," commanded Jeffers, beginning to move. "You're not drunk. I know that. You're bloody crazy."

In that moment Mr Anderson managed to free his arm. He banged on the door. The chief clerk went to open it, when the Super said:

"All right! I know who it is. I rang down for Jeffers before.

Coady said: "It must be that worrying fellow again,

"See who is *there*," said Gorman.

Coady approached and opened it a little more.

Immediately a volley of words, pleadings, threats, taunts and curses met him.

"What you want?" asked Coady gruffly, as he saw Mr Anderson securely fastened in the doorman's grasp.

"I wanner see the director damn you who are you bleedin' cringer sucking round here all your life what about us fellers fought in war I wanner see the director can't lie here's his bloody name look at it on this paper Ledgeworth. D'you hear me? Thirty years in this firm I tell you. Said they wouldn't forget me. Where's the director?"

Coady whispered in Jeffers' ear: "Hold him a second," and disappeared into the office again. Mr Super was on the 'phone loudly declaiming and cursing Wilson's having missed the tide, and calling down the wrath of the gods on the Harbour Board who would not reduce their dues. Coady crossed over and spoke to him. The Super was pale, for he felt angry. He did not reply to Coady, merely nodding. When he put down the receiver he asked Coady if the working returns for the *North Star* had been handed in by the time-keepers. Coady opened his mouth to reply when the door was burst open. The clerk rushed across to close it on account of the draughts coming in when the Super said, "Open it wide. Yes. Right back."

The door swung back. Jeffers was standing there with greaser Anderson tucked safely in his arms. Mr Anderson gave one look at the Super and his mouth once gaping like a fish out of water now closed like a trap. It was as though this man had suddenly dealt him a smashing blow in the face. He glared at him. Mr Anderson was silent. He still stared like a lunatic at the Super when that individual shouted in a high-pitched voice:

"Forget you! By heavens we will never forget you. Throw him out. Hanging round here like a confounded dog. Throw him out" – he almost screamed now, for he had not forgotten Wilson missing the tide. "Yes. Into the street." This was done.

A PASSION BEFORE DEATH

I

And whilst sentence was being passed, the man crumpled up. It appeared as though the very thoughts stirring in his mind had overwhelmed him. The tendency of this train of thought was fitting to the occasion. There was the judge, and what was he? And what had he done? Well, there was a current of feeling between himself and the public in the court. An incessant mental telegraphy. When he looked at the public they sensed immediately the power that was his; not by right of the fact that he *was* judge, and the man in the dock the condemned, but by the fact that the look in his eye revealed to them that they must surrender themselves. Whether he liked it or not the judge could not help but absorb all that which came from the public body both in looks and in feeling. So although the man in the dock hearing sentence of death passed upon him, sat there hunched up, and could not see the judge distinctly, he was nevertheless conscious of his power. He could not stand to receive sentence, having lost one leg below the knee in the great war. Behind him this sea of people appeared to have suffered change. The sea of people was a kind of wall, a high wall, and gradually it seemed to be moving nearer and nearer. He felt conscious it was pushing him, nearer and nearer to that judge. The twelve men in the jury box had become indistinctive too; he could not see the various faces, and though he were able he would have seen nothing. For like the public they had emptied themselves both of thought and feeling. Suddenly the man in the dock raised his head. Looked around the court. Only one face appeared to stand out. The Judge's. He was staring at him now. He in turn at the judge. They spoke by silence. A warder tapped him upon the shoulder. He turned. Gave a last glance around the court. *She* was not there. He went below. An hour later he was sitting in a cell, a quite different one from that which he had occupied prior to his being sentenced. All was quiet now. Two warders sat in the cell with him. They sat directly opposite. The man sat down on the bed and placed his head in his hands. He began to think. It is a trick of fate that in such moments and in such circumstances human thought should surrender itself to an intensity of feeling, that words having lost all power, the feeling should manifest itself through the medium of the body. And whilst Carter sat thinking of the act that had reduced him to this sad state; certain phrases had flitted across the surface of his mind. Such phrases as: "Will you help me!?" or "Can you save me!?" or "Please for the love of God don't hang me!" or merely the two words "Save me!" These words seemed to suffer from a strange impotency, yet they had attained a terrifying significance. Terrifying only. So that at one moment he would be thinking of how by a single stroke of fate he had been denied the consummation of his marriage, he would suddenly murmur: "Oh Christ save me! All! I ask. Please save me."

These murmurs were to himself. Already a certain phrase had destined to reveal to him the terrible power of words. GUILTY. This barrier was very high and very strong. The warders looked at him with the dull stare of cows. He removed his hands from his head in order to blow his nose. The sudden change in the features might mean nothing to them, though after all, communication through words being futile, and these same words urging and pleading utterance, had revealed their message and their power through his body. The eyes had lost their light and sparkle, even their colour was unimportant now. Also they had shed the terror and wonder of a few hours before. They were dull and that was all. The jaws had sunk slightly, and perhaps this revealed the almost crushing power of the thoughts he dwelt upon. The mouth also had resolved itself into a certain shape or attitude. Its very shape spelt finality. Just as that word GUILTY had spelt finality. The hands too. These had gained something. The hands of a deaf and dumb human are a thing for wonder. So too were Carter's. Not only through movement or gesture did they serve to convey to the world what lay at the pit of his thought, but also through shape they seemed to signify a certain awareness. There are moments that confound reasonings and philosophies, when the most commonplace object transcends itself into something powerful and overwhelming in significance. One has seen a Cathedral, and how through time it has at length surrendered itself to a certain subsidence of the earth. We see the first brick crumble. And soon the stone falls. Until finally the edifice collapses. Was there some secret power lurking in the ground? It is not beyond reason to suppose it. Beyond wonder there is nothing. So with Carter. It was their very gestures, their attitudes that gave power and urgency and something vital to their shape. Again he placed his hands to his face and again the warders looked at him. Then he dropped the hands again, rose to his feet and looked towards the window of his cell. When he rose the warders rose too. Carter said to them: "What time is it?"

"Eight o'clock," they replied as with one voice.

"When will they hang me?"

"To-morrow."

"But why to-morrow. It is very soon."

"We cannot say. And please ask no more questions of that nature. "

Carter sat down. So too did the warders. The man thought:

"Now *why* did this happen? And *why* am I here?"

And again: "Why did *he* come?" and "If only he had *not* come. Where was *she* now? And where is *he*?"

Later *he* became *Him*. And in all his thoughts when the name Johnson came to his mind. Johnson was the name of *Him* who had tried to rape his wife on their wedding-night. But why had he tried to do so? Why in the name of God had *he*, Carter, killed him?

His brain was afire. His thoughts were forever passing in and out of furnaces. Each time they passed through they seemed to gain added strength. In time they were tempered to a white heat that blurred his conception and knowledge of external things. The whole universe had disappeared in a great white cloud; even as it had collapsed and passed from his sight when the expression upon the judge's face, and the look in his eye, had tended to show that the one sweet charity of life had been absorbed through *him*, and all other things robbed of their power in consequence. He was aroused from this torpor by hearing one of the warders say:

"Would you like a game of cards?"

"No," he replied, and added: "Why are you hanging me to-morrow?"

The other warder immediately explained that the law had been altered owing to public agitation against men having to wait three weeks and sometimes a month before the sentence was carried out. The warder who had asked him if he would play cards then said:

"Everybody agrees it is more human."

"To hang people?" enquired Carter.

"Yes. And to do it quickly." There was a moment's silence. Then the elder of the two warders asked:

"Is there anything you want? You can have anything you desire."

"I want my wife," said Carter slowly and deliberately.

For a moment this reply was not understood by the warders. And when the man repeated "I want my wife," there was a greater insistency in the tone of the voice, and now they realised what he had asked for. They were both dumbfounded because in all their experience no condemned man had ever asked for his wife after the final interview. Not in all their years at the prison. The silence was broken by Carter.

"I want my wife I tell you."

The elder warder saw how impossible the whole thing was.

"We can't help you that way," he said quietly.

The effect of the man's reply upon Carter was overwhelming. And now, repeating to himself the words "We can't help you that way," he realised in a flash that he *did* want her. This desire became more urging and more intensified; it was a flame slowly spreading, burning up all his thought. He *must* have her. Let the whole world be devoured, dried up, hurled down into the bottomless abyss – he must have her. He recalled a certain tormenting thought, that, under the stress of the circumstances and occasion, had been smothered beneath more conflicting ones. And now it had forced its way to the top.

"I want my wife! I want my wife I tell you."

He hardly realised that he had spoken aloud, until the dull monotonous tones of the elder warder's voice awoke him to the fact that he was periodically talking aloud, and as though to an audience, though there were but two men in the cell with him Again and again he spoke, now raising his voice to a high pitch, now by various inflections portraying in a powerful way the terrific desire consuming him. The elder warder crossed over to him and sat down on the edge of the bed. Carter's head was sunk upon his breast, his two hands clasped together and resting idly in his lap.

"My dear fellow," said the warder. "We cannot help you that way."

The words had no effect upon the condemned man; they might well have been strange sounds from some nether world. He put the self-same question again.

"I want my wife. I want my wife I tell you."

The words gained power through repetition, the voice of Carter became more highly pitched, then settled down to a definite musical monologue, for he kept repeating:

"I want my wife, I want my wife. I want her I tell you."

Now he uttered the words in a rich bass voice, now in a highly pitched tenor; and to every word he appeared to give a variety of tone inflections. But the men sitting opposite might well have been deaf or dead. They stared at him, and yet not so much at him as through him, and this seemingly unconsciously. Carter suddenly burst into a fit of weeping. As suddenly he stopped and there was an oppressive silence for five minutes. A strange and intense silence. Then once again he began to sing out in the same way as before.

"I want my wife. I want her I tell you."

The elder warder whispered into his companion's ear

"The crazy devil! What's he talking about? And him half way there already. The damned fool."

His companion replied by saying:

"It's hard lines."

Three words that spelt for the elder man a certain horror. Filling his being with suspicion and misgiving. Once again he whispered into the other's ear:

"What do you mean?"

"That it's hard lines," repeated the warder, and the words lost all their meaning now. They fell from the man's lips like so many leaden pellets. His companion looked him full in the face.

"Dickson!" he said. "You should not talk like that." And still more softly he added: "You know very well how dangerous it is for people like ourselves to become sentimental. Now, if the Governor had heard you. Do you know what he would have said?"

"What?" asked the warder, and he looked attentively at his companion.

"Well, he would have said two things. 'Disgusting and insulting.' It is not right to remind any human being who is under sentence of death, of the debt he owes and must pay in full to society."

"To society?" queried the warder, in almost a whisper. Again silence.

The elder warder, Carruthers, had served in the prison

for twenty-one years. He was a medium sized individual with a face that experience had tempered into a mask, expressionless, without feeling, it was just a mask and nothing beneath it. The younger man, Dickson, had served in the prison for seven years. He had witnessed three executions, his companion eleven.

"Yes," continued Carruthers, "to society. But look! Now he has fallen asleep. Don't disturb him. He'll get over that crazy idea of his after a good sound sleep. Listen! I haven't finished yet. Just now you said to him: "It's hard lines." Because, although you were addressing me, you were consciously or unconsciously addressing him in feeling. Feeling is like poison and a certain kind of high explosive. We, as warders, have our duty to do. It is not a nice duty, but still it's our job, and you ought to remember that feeling must be left outside altogether. It should be something that can be used and unused, if you understand what I mean. Like something you can remove and replace in a pocket."

"What the bloody hell are you talking about?" growled Dickson. "Feeling! Feeling! Christ! Look at him now. Look at him lying on the bed."

Both cast a glance towards the bed. Carter was lying across it. His one sound leg and stump stuck out grotesquely like the branches of a tree whose life has already been determined. He lay on his face. His two arms were clasped in such a way as to reveal to a close observer the fact that the last thought before sleep had determined that position. Carter was in fact embracing the bed. If he could have spoken it would certainly have been a key to the position he was now lying in, and the reason for it.

It might be that he was saying to himself: "I want her now. This very instant. My wife! My wife!" or "I must and I want to plunge down to oblivion," or "I must hide myself. I must allow my desire to suck me down." From a world of delirious thought where words and not looks or gestures spelt finality and futility.

Suddenly he woke. The two warders became aware of this by reason of a terrible scream from Carter, who suddenly sat up, looked all about him, and commenced to shout at the top of his voice:

"I want my wife. I want my wife. My wife. Wife – wife – wife – wife."

"Listen my dear fellow," said Dickson, who had crossed to him, and was now endeavouring to pacify him. "Listen! Be reasonable. You know how we feel about these things, don't you? Can't you see that what you ask is impossible?"

And Carruthers interrupted in a slow and drawling voice:

"Get the cards Dickson, we'll have a game of nap."

"Will you play nap?" asked Dickson of the man on the bed, and he looked him full in the face.

"Cards! Get out of my sight with your cards. O Jesus Christ Almighty! Bring my wife here. Bring my wife here."

He fell back upon the bed, turned over on his belly,

stretched wide his arms, and his position now indicated what he thought in feeling. He continued to scream:

"Bring her. I want my wife. I want her. My wife – my wife. Oh! Oh! Oh!"

"Dickson," whispered Carruthers, "come here a minute."

Carruthers was sitting in a chair situated on the left hand side of the cell door, his feet stretched out before him, a look of utter boredom upon his face. Dickson went over to him.

"Well!?" he exclaimed.

"This man is going mad," said Carruthers. "You know what is the matter with him, don't you?" he asked, and the very tone of his voice appeared to veil the meaning of the sentence.

"Know what's the matter with him? Yes. Before – but he . . . I won't tell you. No! I won't tell you. But listen now. We'd better bring Mr Cheesman here. Now. Right away."

"Ring then," said Carruthers, and Dickson went outside and rang.

Immediately somebody appeared in response to the ring, and that somebody was informed that Mr Cheesman must be brought along at once. Yes. At once. A man was going mad. Hurry!

Mr Cheesman at that very moment happened to be playing a game of dominoes with his wife. When he received the urgent message a frown clouded his features, enhancing as it were its usual gloom. He got up, saying to Elizabeth who was his senior by ten years:

"I suppose this Carter will confess now. I shan't be long."

Meanwhile Carter had jumped upon the bed, and had begun to tear off his clothes, with all the strange antics of a monkey. Carruthers and Dickson fearing he might injure himself and so insult not only the majesty of the law but that of his majesty the king, ran over and laid hands upon him. They held him down upon the bed. Carter's face was almost black with sweat. Though the lips seemed hardly to move a stream of words poured forth from them:

"Hell! Man alive! Jesus! Jesus! Bring my wife. I tell you that you *must* bring my wife. You say I can have anything I want. Then for Christ's sake bring her. Now. Now. Do you hear. My God! My God!"

A silence then as if in that very moment Carter's thought had been washed out by the powerful tide of feeling, as if words had ceased to be useless, and with no place in human language. Even their sounds were alien for it mystified both the men now holding him. Dickson was nearly in tears. He was afraid. Not of the man (he was of a religious turn of mind himself, and not the one to begrudge Death all), but of himself. His head was lowered, almost caressing Carter's breast, so that Carruthers could not see the spontaneous drops from his eyes that were immediately absorbed into the condemned man's shirt, as raindrops are absorbed into the parched and hungry earth. Also there was another reason to be afraid. He felt he was losing something of himself through the powerful feeling of Carter. One moment a fit of fear was upon him. It came like a sudden gust of wind. In the next moment he was his ordinary calm self again. He spoke to his mate:

"Where the hell is this fellow Cheesman? I can't stand this. I'm going to ask to be relieved. Oh, Good God!"

There was the sound of footsteps in the corridor, and then a key was heard fumbling in the lock.

"Thank heaven," exclaimed Carruthers.

"Thank God!" echoed Dickson.

Still holding Carter down they both half turned to meet the steady and somewhat vacant stare of Mr Cheesman.

"What is the matter?" asked the chaplain.

And Dickson replied: "I think he is going mad."

"Is that all?" asked the Chaplain.

"All, sir!" interrupted Carruthers. "No sir. Not at all. He whispered something into my ear half an hour ago. Do you know what he said?"

The look of utter boredom upon Mr Cheeseman's face now changed to wonder.

"That he was guilty," remarked the chaplain.

Carruthers laughed. He said quietly:

"The poor wretch is asleep now and won't hear what I tell you. He wanted me to sleep with him."

The chaplain's face altered its expression. The colour of the face was darker, as though the blood had rushed there in a fit of anger.

"Is that all you brought me here for? To hear a dirty story?" He glared at Carruthers.

"Carruthers," he continued, "but for the fact that a night like this is most trying to a warder, I would report you instantly."

Certainly the chaplain was angry. He felt keenly about this disturbance of his game of dominoes. And he realised also how a condemned man has, for an allotted time, a strange power; a power to see in the most trivial things an overwhelming urgency and importance. But it was not so much that as the power that the condemned had attained over certain words. Mr Cheesman took a handkerchief from his pocket, and blew his nose so vigorously that it disturbed Carter who for the past half hour had been in a deep sleep. Yet it was more than sleep. An excess of sleep. A kind of premature death. When even the sense of aware-ness is gone, and the world of reality sucked down into nothingness. The figure on the bed suddenly stirred. The first slow movement was the forerunner of movements more convulsed. When the winter of anguish descends upon the spirit of a man. The two warders still held him securely.

"You say he is awake?" queried Mr Cheesman.

The reply that Dickson made could not be heard for it was devoured by a shout from Carter, who making violent movements flung off the two warders, and when the chap-lain looked towards the bed, the condemned man had arched his back like a cat. He seemed a kind of humped beast as he knelt there, naked save for shirt and boots and socks. Mr Chessman beholding the sight experienced a physical revulsion stirring in his blood, and turned his head away. And the man shouted again:

"Jesus Christ! My wife! My wife! Bring my wife here when I tell you. You say I can have anything I desire."

Mr Cheesman spoke rudely now. He thought of his waiting wife and the unfinished game of dominoes.

"The trouble that some people create," he murmured. "And it is always a hewing from the same rock. Fear. They fear their God. The trembling cowardly wretches. And this man," he thought. "He wants his wife. Was he trying to hide from God behind his wife? All these murderers were the same. Cowards all. As if anybody could hide from Him," he thought. (Mr Cheesman was a High Church man and a true believer.) "Why he can see into everything. Not only into man's heart, but into his letters, his bank-accounts, his pigeon holes, his desks, but especially his bank-accounts (and this was a matter that always occupied the chaplain's mind. The interest in the bank might be a mean four and a half per cent, but in the bank of Heaven it was a matter of thousands per cent). The chaplain said aloud:

"Sit him up. Turn him round. I will talk with him. But hold him just the same. Both of you please."

Mr Cheesman drew a chair across the floor, and sat down facing Carter. With the first glance at the doomed man's face, he thought:

"Good God! This man is a prison in himself."

For those features appeared devoid of life. As though the whole body had been hewed out of granite. The eyes glared, communicating nothing. The acts and thoughts of a condemned person are as so many weights that crush him. Mr Cheesman now felt that all murderers were without kindness, without feeling, without heart, and in his long experience as High Heaven's ambassador, devoid of soul. The man's mouth suddenly began twitching. The chaplain immediately thought: "Fear." And perhaps he was wrong. True, the mouth twitched, and such movements can reveal what is locked in the brain. FEAR.

But when Carter's mouth twitched it meant that slowly and surely words were ceasing to have any meaning. Perhaps very soon he would be unable to form words. The power was going. So the lips continually twitched, like a fluttering candle flame that surrenders its life to a sudden draught of wind, or a breath as soft as the trembling of a leaf.

"My dear man," began Mr Chessman. "Come! Make your peace with God. My dear fellow, in a few hours you will be in eternity."

"My wife! My wife! Bring her here. Bring my wife. My bloody wife. My beautiful wife. Bring her. Bring her. Bring her."

"You cannot see your wife," fell from Mr Cheesman's lips like a shot from a gun.

The coldness of the reply made Dickson shudder and he said to himself: "The fool. The big stupid fool."

"You saw your wife yesterday," continued the chaplain. "Come! Make your peace with God."

"Bring my bloody wife, now, right away. You damned scoundrels. Hear me. Do you hear me?"

These words had little effect upon Mr Cheesman, for he said:

"Get this man something to drink."

Both warders refused to move. How could they tell what might happen if they loosed their hold upon him.

"Dickson! Ring please. This man must have something. I think he is suffering from delusions."

Carruthers let go his hold of Carter and ran to the door. Instantly, as though a great weight had been lifted from him, Carter lunged, and in so doing flung Dickson to the end of the bed. In the same moment he had propelled himself upon the chaplain. Both fell to the floor in a heap. One hand of Carter's was upon Mr Cheesman's throat, the other was vainly endeavouring to tear down the chaplain's trousers.

"Bring my wife here at once or I'll tear your heart out. Bring her. Bring her I tell you," moaned Carter. "Do you hear me. Jesus! Jesus!"

He continued screaming whilst a cold sweat broke out upon the chaplain's forehead. He shouted at the top of his voice:

"Help! Help! I believe the man is mad."

II

Mr Cheesman had never felt so startled in his life. In the moment when Carter's vicious design had manifest itself in so real a way, the chaplain was seized by terror. It seemed to make vital one single thought that in itself shut out from his sight the external world. It was not: "Why was the man in the cell?" or "What made him commit this murder?" or "Will he confess his guilt upon the scaffold at the last moment?"

None of these things. A something entirely new had caused this terror to flood his heart. He had realised in a flash, had discovered some knowledge of the human soul. As though he had dug deep down into the human abyss, and had returned with fauna and flora, strange and terrifying. The first thing he became aware of was the fact that a new strength had come to him. A physical strength only. And he had thrown this man from him. Had himself lain upon Carter and stared into his face. There was a something that he saw there. A single thought appeared to gather up all his feeling. He now beheld in Carter's eyes a something that moved him to abject pity, that turned his own fathomless heart into a living lyre. He felt that all the agony and despair, the hopes and desires and longings, had become alive and vital. Through shape they were fingers continually strumming across his heart. He could not help or prevent it, but the tears flooded his eyes, ran down his cheeks, and so dropped one by one upon the condemned man's face. He saw in Carter's eyes a look born of despair and wonder that speaks by silence alone, and though he tried to shut out the thought, he could not, and his lips moved slowly in a strange murmuring: "I do not understand. I do not understand."

The warders stood motionless. Neither seemed able to comprehend this strange scene, the chaplain kneeling over Carter, the latter's one leg and stump stuck between the chaplain's knees. Not a sound in the cell now save the agitated breathing of the men upon the floor. Dickson's hands were clenched. He stood staring down at them, whilst Carruthers kept shaking him, pulling at his sleeve, and whispering:

"Dickson! Dickson! Ring again. What is the matter with them? And what is the matter with you?" Dickson would have run then had not a voice arrested their attention. It was not Carter speaking, but Mr Cheesman. He had risen to his feet and was staring at Dickson in a strange manner. Then his gaze turned on Carruthers. He looked at both of them as though they were complete strangers whom he had met for the first time in his life. Carter himself lay very still. His eyes were closed. The chaplain said:

"Lift him gently upon the bed. I am going to see the Governor at once."

"But the Governor has gone into the city, sir," said Carruthers. "He won't be back until after eleven."

Mr Cheesman looked at his watch. He watched the two warders lay the man upon the bed.

"It is time to see him. I am *going* to see him. Remember you are both responsible for this man's safety."

"Yes sir. Very well sir," replied Carruthers, and touched his cap to Mr Chessman. As soon as the chaplain had gone Dickson turned upon his mate.

"Listen here!" he said. "I am going to apply for relief. As soon as the Governor comes here I am going to speak my mind. Do you hear me? Ah! Don't laugh. I feel I should go mad myself if I had to remain here another hour. And what good is that? Carter is mad, but then he is going to die. I would still be alive and the memory of this night colouring all my thought. Do you understand me?"

"You fool," exclaimed Carruthers, "when you have served as long as I have you will have a different idea of things, a different sense of values. Ssh! Here's somebody coming now."

At that moment the door opened revealing the chief warder. Behind him stood two other warders. The door closed on them.

"Dickson! Carruthers!" said the chief warder. "You are both relieved of your duties by warders Hope and Ferguson. You will report at the Governor's office after nine o'clock tomorrow morning."

The two men addressed stood stiffly to attention. They looked at the chief then at each other. Not a word was spoken. Carruthers and Dickson left the cell. The two new men had already taken up the seats lately occupied by the relieved men. They sat and stared at the wall in front of them, which was the beginning of their vigil. They sat side by side.

"Hope! Ferguson!" began the chief warder. "Dickson and Carruthers having been relieved of their duties, I wish to add that they were lacking in necessary precaution when the chaplain had to complain, not only of their strange behaviour, but of the prisoner's conduct. I understand that Carter tried to do something to Carruthers. Be careful. Have no words with him, only when strictly necessary. It is only a matter of a few hours and you will both be relieved. To-morrow there will be an enquiry, not only into all that passed between Dickson and Carruthers, but also what passed between Carter and the chaplain. If he should wake up and speak to you, do not answer him. I may possibly be stretching a point in asking both of you to observe this rule which is only an extra precaution on my part, and taking into consideration, not only the responsibility and anxiety resting with you, but also of the prisoner's nature. I understand that Mr Cheesman thought the man mad. Ignore this. It is merely good acting on his part, and an endeavour to awaken pity in us as human beings. But as men of experience, of good character, allied to common-sense and a belief in justice, you will see how dangerous it might be to get into conversation with him. There was a period when he might have had anything he wanted, but that has happily passed, though it will not deter him from certain privileges in the morning. If he should ask for anything within reason however, ring. But again I ask you to be careful. He has been worrying the last two men almost to distraction. Take no notice of that at all. Remember it is only a matter of a few hours. All correct?"

"All correct, sir," they replied as with one voice.

The door closed upon them. Hope, a little man with a drooping moustache, began twiddling nervously with his fingers. He began talking in low tones, not so much to Ferguson as to the floor, as though some secret lay hidden beneath it.

"I wonder what all the fuss was about?" asked Ferguson in almost a whisper. He drew his hand across his face and let it sink heavily into his lap.

"That's what I'd like to know," replied Hope. "I could hear him shouting before, though I could not understand what he was saying. I think he was shouting: "White. White. White." It's strange, isn't it, how a condemned man changes. In himself I mean. He becomes something so mystifying. I wonder sometimes what they really are thinking; how they feel, and what their thoughts must be as the last minutes approach."

"Perhaps he was thinking of the white cap when he commenced shouting like that," said Ferguson.

"Perhaps," replied Hope.

They became silent, and one could hear the laboured breathing of the man on the bed.

"What time is it?" asked Ferguson

Hope looked at his watch and replied slowly:

"A quarter after ten."

"Strange they haven't brought him anything to eat," remarked Ferguson.

"That," said Hope, "was purely a matter concerning Dickson and his mate. In any case he might wake up and ask for something."

"Did you notice the look on old Cheesman's face as he went down the corridor?

"Yes. He looked hellish. Didn't he?"

"I should say so."

"Carter's not very old, is he?"

"About thirty-four I should say."

They both looked across at the condemned man.

"God! What a sight!" exclaimed Hope suddenly.

"Yes," said Ferguson, "he lost a leg in the great war."

"Hard lines alright," remarked Hope.

The man on the bed stirred slightly.

"Suppose he wakes up," said Ferguson, as he watched Carter's arms move slowly outwards from his body.

"Well!"

"Oh, nothing!" drawled Ferguson. "Nothing. God! Nothing. I'm tired. Aren't you?"

"Not very," replied Hope, "but if you want an hour I don't mind keeping my eye screwed on him."

Ferguson smiled.

"Good," he said. "I'll try and get an hour. I'm fair beat. I should really be going off duty now, but I was sent for at the last minute to relieve Carruthers. I suppose they'll be up before the Big Fellow to-morrow."

"I suppose so," said Hope.

Ferguson settled himself down comfortably in the chair. Closed his eyes. Hope looked intently at him. In five minutes he was fast asleep.

Hope immediately gave his attention to Carter. The man had moved towards the end of the bed. He suddenly woke. Sat up and opened his eyes widely as though he were a child waking up to all the wild freshness of the morning. Hope was thunderstruck by the expression upon the condemned man's face. To him it was the expression of a man, to whom, in his lifetime something terrible has happened – who had forgotten it for a long time, and then suddenly remembered it. The look expressed neither awe nor wonder, pity nor terror. The whole face seemed to have been seized and set in a stare wholly vacant, and yet owning this expression, the like of which Hope nor any other man has ever seen upon a human countenance. Immediately Hope began saying to himself – and as these thoughts took possession of him he lowered his head, and that very act seemed profound – began putting questions to himself and vainly endeavouring to answer them.

"*How* did that happen?" and "Whence came that stare?" and "*What* was he thinking of in the moments that this expression hewed itself as it were out of some vital part of his being?" and "*Why* did he look such an idiot?"

Hope himself had a heart, and even prided himself on having a soul, and yet there was nothing in his nature, no chord whatever that could strike a response to the look upon Carter's face.

"Now I *wonder* what he is thinking of," continued Hope to himself. "And why in God's name is he looking at me like that?"

For the condemned man had now settled his eye upon the new warder, and again those eyes shifted furtively from himself to his sleeping partner. Hope could not understand. It was not the terrible tragedy in the last few hours of a human life; it was not the tense atmosphere in which they sat; it was not the consciousness of being hidden away from the world with all its swarming life, its rhythm and feeling and beauty. Hope began to fidget in his chair. Once or twice he heard Carter murmuring: "My wife. O Christ! My wife."

It dawned upon Hope then, that what he had really heard in sound down the corridor, was the word Wife. The word was continually being murmured now until it was a tragic note, and to Hope gaining power with each utterance.

"Ah!" he thought. "I know now. He's hungering for his wife. Poor devil. Less than six hours and all the wives in the world will be useless. Poor devil."

A terrible sense of shame followed on this last thought. Shame, not so much for the whole tragic business, the sending down to death of a human life; not so much that as his own utter helplessness. And the more he thought it over in his mind, the more intense his feeling grew, the more monstrous the whole thing became. He murmured:

"Almighty God! Not I alone, but all humanity must feel ashamed. All. With no exceptions, and Pity herself flung out into the darkness. Why Pity? No pity needed here. How revolting to prostitute a charity in itself. How awful. Futile! Futile! Futile!"

The warder's mind now resembled a smouldering furnace – there was nothing in its essence that might fan a flame into life, and so endow him with that quality which is the richness and strength of the human spirit.

Nothing whatever. In condemning a man they had condemned themselves. But Hope thought:

"That in itself is not the real tragedy – the very real tragedy that plucks at the heart. No. No. Not that. But the utter helplessness. The horror of having brought into being the very machine they were helpless to smash. Futile! Futile! Nothing to be done.

The more the thought forced itself upon him, the more aware he was of a sickness, mental and physical. Guilty.

Again he began murmuring in almost a whisper: "Guilty. Guilty. Guilty. Horrible. Horrible. Oh futile. Futile!"

The power of the word. All the evil of men personified in it. He muttered:

"Now that for the first time in my life I have envisaged this horror, I feel I want to probe deeply; to remain unsatisfied until I have looked it wholly in the face."

Like a flash it occurred to hint to shout aloud. Which he did. He roared at the top of his voice:

"Guilty! Guilty! Guilty! O you murderer. O you foulness. O you horror. O you Succubus. O you – you – "

The outburst awakened Ferguson.

"Christ! What's the matter?" He demanded, and looking at Hope, he said coldly: "Are you another too? Come, shake yourself. Brace yourself together. It's only a few hours more."

"A few hours," said Hope slowly. "A few hours. Really! Or is it not rather a few eternities? A few eternities of time wasted – rotted out made poisonous by our distorted conception of humanity. Ugh! the foulness. Listen you! The past hour has been for me an hour of waking life. Do you understand what I am saying to you? And all the pity that rode my blood; all the futility of these nightmare hours; all the farce we have created; all the foulness we feed; all the rottenness we sustain and maintain. There it is. There it is. All in that man. All vested in him. What meanness. What utter meanness. Oh Jesus! For twelve years I have been a warder. I cannot tell you, why at this moment, a terrible sense of shame should visit and over-whelm me. I cannot tell you. If I have thought more in your sleeping hour, than I have ever done in years. How helpless I am. How helpless we all are. We are so rotten that even in the last extremity Pity should deny us one drink from her cup. And now – "

"Shut your bloody mouth. What's wrong with you?" growled Ferguson.

"I'm trying to tell you. I'm trying to tell you that this

man is in agony," continued Hope. "And do you know the worst, the most horrible thing about it? No. You do not. The man's own heart has imprisoned him. Do you see now? Listen?"

The two men sat quite still and listened. Carter was lying upon his face, mumbling, and the words were impossible to understand. Hope continued:

"Don't you see now? He has been struck dumb."

"Dumb! What in heaven's name are you talking about? Dumb! You fool. Come! What the hell are you talking about? Tell me?"

"Words," replied Hope. "Words. The word Guilty. The word Futile. The word Men. The word Humanity. The word Life and the word Death. This man has lost his understanding of them. Their own futility has robbed them of any meaning. I wish I could express to you what I really mean."

"I wish you could. I do that," replied Ferguson sarcastically.

Suddenly Ferguson jumped up, and lowering his head, glowered into his companion's face.

"Are you drunk?" he asked. "Are you crazy? Forget all this. This silliness. After all how would you feel if you were a woman, and a man came along and murdered your husband? Or even your own brother?"

"And you," said Hope. "How would you feel if you were a man, and somebody tried to rape your wife on your wedding-night? But don't dote on that. Dote on something else. How would you feel when the word was drummed into your ear – when the word was pronounced for you? GUILTY. Tell me that. You could not. You could not. All words which express feeling, remorse, pity, horror, wonder, terror, misery, hatred; all these become and are subordinate to that one word GUILTY. Truth itself is a kind of twilight that few of us see. But when we do see it, it seems more terrible than the impenetrable darkness of despair. Oh! I'm not being poetical. Don't think that above anything. Not that. No. I'm too ashamed. Too ill – too – Oh Christ! It's awful. A machine. A machine. A million cogs. Cogs. And do you know this? Those millions of cogs must move millions of other cogs, millions of times, before we are capable of realising the crime we have committed. In him – that man – we can see all our foulness made manifest in a most terrible way. It makes a man shiver to feel and to know how near he lies to destruction – how near to inevitable nothingness – that he must go down forever into darkness, without a word of protest, without a little glory even. Hard. Hard. But watch that man. Watch him. His mouth opens and shuts like a fish. His eyes have beheld something, and we lack the power to visualise it. The more I look at him, the more wildly my blood stirs, the more powerful the pluck of this huge hand at my heart, so that I feel – I feel through every fibre of my being, that I should jump up – that I should fly from this cell, which is the living expression of human idiocy – that I should run screaming down the corridors, that I should run to the Governor and the Chaplain, and scream aloud:

"Idiots! Idiots! Idiots! Not wretches but idiots. Not anything save idiots. See now. He looks at both of us. His mouth moves."

Ferguson had gone down before this flow of words. He could not understand. He felt he had been lifted up and flung down at the same time, and finally hung perilously upon the edge of a precipice. The precipice of his own mind. Every thought pained him. For him, and he rarely thought to any length or depth, his thinking was like the beginning of a woman's labour which ends up in the consummation of agony and ecstasy. He shook Hope by the shoulders.

"Listen Hope," he said. "I don't understand a thing you've been talking about, and I don't want to either. Get that right now. Now listen. There is a pack of cards here. Will you play?"

"No I won't."

"There is a draught-board. Will you have a game of draughts?"

"No. No. I tell you I won't play anything," he replied, and anger coloured and darkened the tones of his voice. He thought to himself: "Draughts! Good God! And here, quite coolly, quite coolly, we play a game of draughts with the body and soul of a man."

"No. No," he repeated, and in an instant he too was upon his feet.

He crossed over to Carter, and turned him over. He took the man's hands in his own and pressed them convulsively, as a result of a spontaneous thought that flashed upon him. "Feel for him."

The next moment he felt something like a stab in his heart, and he realised the uselessness of feeling. "Too late. Too late."

Yet he held the man's hands. His whole being surrendered to a power that made him kneel at the man's bedside, and bury his head upon his breast. He felt debased and crushed; the awful consciousness of the uselessness of protest appearing like a tremendous weight that crushed the breath out of him. He wanted to kiss the man, he wanted to abandon himself, to atone and cry out With power and grandeur, the inhumanity of men.

But if this sudden sense of abandonment had rendered him so helpless as to make him embrace the man and hold him close – as though there were something profound in the action of the hands themselves, shutting out from the condemned man's sight, his approaching doom; he had forgotten that he had contacted himself with something more than a man, and at the same time something less than a man. Carter was a mass of feeling. All thought had burnt out; the tremendous concentration on the word GUILTY; upon the word HOPE; upon the word WIFE had eaten up his thought. Everything had surrendered itself to feeling. And he felt now the warm contact of a body, Hope's body, and so feeling it, had awakened something. This something was movement, physical movement, symbolising all the poetry of his body. Before he was aware of it, Hope's trousers had been partly opened by Carter. Ferguson had dozed off in his chair; his wrist-watch exposed to view showed a quarter to twelve by it. No sound save Ferguson's steady snore, and the convulsive-like breaths of the condemned man. Hope suddenly felt all his power deserting him. Though he was conscious now of the man's hands groping at his trousers, he did not move. As if exhausted Carter suddenly fell back upon the bed, and Hope heard him murmur two words:

"My wife."

Their utterance petrified the warder. He fell away from the bed, dragged himself to his feet, and then collapsed into his chair. He *wanted* to wake Ferguson and he didn't want to wake him. It was now mid-night by his own watch. His eyes opened and closed periodically for it was not so much tiredness as a certain ennui that held him in thrall. Carter suddenly commenced to worm his way from the bed to the floor. He reached it, then crawled to the end of the bed, and began to embrace it, and through movement only expressing the poetry and urgency of his feelings. Hope was dumbfounded. He could not understand the immensity of the occasion, the terrible hunger of the man, the overwhelming desire to give something of himself to the world, to play some part in the realm of human activity. The warder turned and looked in Carter's direction. He was not near the bed. Instead he was slowly crawling towards the door. Even had he realised the man was attempting to escape (though the door was locked),

Hope knew instinctively that he could not have moved. He watched the man drag himself up against the door on his leg and stump, raise his shirt, and for a moment stand staring very stupidly at the lock. There Hope saw the man try to express his feeling; to do it, and he seemed a helpless child, through the medium of the key-hole. All feeling concentrated between the thighs. It spread like fire. He pushed and thrust himself against the door, and continued the movements he had made up on the bed. The very action of the man was overwhelming in its meaning. Hope could stand it no longer.

Saying to himself: "God help you!" he picked Carter up and carried him back to the bed. He laid him down and pulled off his shirt. He drew back the single blanket, saying half-aloud:

"I have never done such a thing in my life-time, but I do it now. It is not you who owes the debt. But I. I. All of us. O Lord Christ!"

Calmly he stripped himself naked, and joined the man in the bed. He stretched his limbs, embraced Carter, and murmuring, "There! There!" like a mother suckling her child, he yielded himself.

NARRATIVE

I

THE SUPERINTENDENT ROARED AT THE top of his voice: "I won't pick a single hand unless you cut this bloody row out."

Pandemonium. A veritable forest of hands high in the air, each hand waving frantically a blue book. The man standing on the barrel could not make himself heard. He picked up a megaphone and roared through it:

"God damn you all! Are you going to cut this confounded noise out?"

"You're all right, you big bastard."

"Shurrup!"

"Pull your bloody socks up and pick the men then. Don't stand there bawling through the fog-horn."

"Are you going to quieten down?" roared the Superintendent once more. Shouts, oaths, curses, threats. Three hundred hands, three hundred men. All shouting and pushing, cursing and whining. They moved in a solid mass towards the man on the barrel. Suddenly this individual roared out:

"Only seven men wanted. Only seven men."

"By God The lousy swine! Getting us down here! Having us hanging round this dump for three hours! I –"

"ONLY SEVEN MEN. ONLY SEVEN MEN."

More pushing and crushing and cursing. The huge cargo shed resembled a circus. At that moment a man rushed down the gangway of the ship. He was without a hat, a high official of the company. He looked worried. He said to the master-at-arms standing at the foot of the gangway:

"Can't you do something? What in the name of Christ are you standing there for?" Then he bent down and hissed into his ear: "What in God's name do we pay you for, eh?"

The master-at-arms did not reply immediately. He looked at the angry face of the Marine Superintendent and then said in a tremulous voice: "Can't do anything, sir. They're out of control. Half of these fellows mutinied on the *Teutonic*. Remember, sir?"

"CALL THE POLICE."

At that moment there happened to be a mounted policeman patrolling the dock-road, and as he passed the dockgate the officer on duty there called out: "Hey! You're wanted down the shed there. Dirty business on, I heard." The policeman immediately wheeled his horse round and without a word rode down the shed at full gallop. Being alone he did not draw his baton, but sat erect upon his charger looking ahead at the angry crowd of men whom the shipping company had kept waiting in the cold for three solid hours in the hopes of getting a job. And now this big man on the barrel had informed them in no uncertain manner that there would only be berths for seven men. Seven men out of three hundred. The crowd seeing the policeman galloping towards them suddenly became dangerous. They started once more hurling oaths and threats about, cursing the police, the company, the Superintendent, and everybody within sight. Suddenly the master-at-arms roared out: "Clear the shed! Clear the shed!"

Obviously the sight of another uniform helped some vestige of his authority to return to him, for he kept shouting at the top of his voice: "Clear the shed! Clear the shed!"

But the crowd would not move. He went up to the officer on horseback.

"Can't get these fellows out at all," he said. "Unruly gang. Only seven men wanted here. Traffic held up and everything upside-down since nine o'clock this morning. Can you do anything?"

The police-constable looked at him and grinned broadly.

"Can I? Can you! Can *we* is what you mean, isn't it?"

"I don't care if you bring the whole bloody army out," replied the master-at-arms.

"They ought to be in the Army," said the officer.

And whilst this conversation was going on something happened which altered the whole situation. The crowd pushed steadily forward, a pair of arms shot out, and the next minute the big man on the barrel was upset and in a flash he had disappeared beneath this army of legs that

trampled and crushed him. The officer shouted out: "Get
out of here." The men took no notice. Then a piece of
brick caught the horse on the nose. The officer drew his
baton. He wheeled round and charged. The crowd fell
back. CLEAR THE SHED. CLEAR THE SHED THERE.
CLEAR THIS BLOODY RABBLE OUT."

Different voices roaring themselves to be heard, frantic
endeavours of the men now to board the ship, a veritable
army of men at the top of the gangway trying to hold them
back. Danger of the gangway giving way and propelling
the men on it into the river. The officer on duty at the
dock-gate was telephoning for more men. A score of
policemen ran at full tilt down the shed and drew their
batons. But by this time the men on the gangway had been
beaten, and the unruly crowd were already clambering
aboard the ship, some up the gangway, others up the cargo
shoots, others up the wire ropes that moored the ship to
the bits. A wild, howling, uncontrollable crowd. Three
hundred men. And only seven berths. They ran along the
deck in the direction of the bridge. Some sought the chief
officer, others the bosun, others the second engineer.
Every mouth was agape with wonder, every eye was pregnant with enquiry, a seeking, a hunger and desire. Then
somebody shouted along the deck: "Second up on the
boat-deck. Second engineer up on the boat-deck." A wild
rout. Legs and arms flying up the companion ladder, a
forest of legs and arms. A frantic scramble along the boat-
deck. The man in uniform with three gold braid bands and

one purple one round his sleeve looked up suddenly on hearing the terrific row, dropped his pipe in consternation, then rose to his feet, drew himself up to his full height and bawled out:

"What's the bloody game"

The answer he received was certainly not one he expected. A veritable shower of books appeared to descend on him. Men were calling out their own names, beseeching, urging, begging, worrying, until the engineer did not really know whether he was standing on his head or his feet. He heard a medley of cries, of many voices shouting, and that was all.

"I sailed with you in the old *Norwegia*. You know me. Look at my book."

"Mr Traynor. Mr Traynor. Remember me. Fired for you two years ago. Remember."

"I've a leading fireman's book, sir. Have a look at it. Union all paid up too."

"Name Coady, sir. You know me. Good Jesus, give us a chance."

So the remarks and questions and beseechings went on. But by this time Mr Traynor told himself he had had quite enough. He climbed up into a ship's boat, and immediately the crowd surged round him. He roared out:

"Quiet, men. Quiet, men. What's all the bloody bother about? Good Christ! I can't do anything for you no more than the rest of them. Listen to me. I can take two trimmers, a fireman, and a greaser. That's all. No more. Not a single one. Now let's see your books."

In that moment the second engineer regretted what he had done. He was literally suffocated, smothered, hemmed in, bombarded by hands and books, he was conscious of the nearness of many faces, shaved and unshaved, all manner of expressions upon these faces. It was like a full orchestra of the emotions – anger, dejection, sorrow – and he knew that his job would be no light one. He knew these men. He knew them like an open book. He had worked with many of them. They were all of them good workers who knew their jobs. He did not blame them cursing the company. He had cursed the company himself scores of times. He was a little more patient than the man on the barrel had been. He explained at once the impossible situation. The men quietened down immediately.

"I ask you fellows, how would you like the job I've got? To pick four men out of hundreds. Can't be done. God, men, I don't know! I don't know. Now stand well back. I'll call those I want. Back. Right back now."

The crowd started to retreat. When they had gone back about ten yards the second engineer called out four names – Connor, Morgan, Smith, Newton. Four men came forward and presented their books. The light of hope shone in their eyes as they stood shivering and waiting. The engineer said:

"Steward's room at two o'clock." Not a word more. Then he relighted his pipe and walked along the boat-deck The remaining men stood silent for some time. All were staring in the direction of the engineer. Suddenly one shouted: "He's a mean kite, anyhow."

"He said it wasn't his fault," said another.

The four men who were picked drew closer together. Somehow their instincts were harmonizing – they sensed in some way a coming danger. They walked away towards the funnel. Stopped. Not a single man spoke. Still the other crowd stood staring. It appeared as though they did not believe the evidence of their eyes and ears. Then slowly they drifted away from the boat-deck, one by one, until all had gone down the ladder to the saloon deck, all except- ing the four men. The departure of the unlucky crowd served to open up a conversation amongst the remaining four. Two of these four were merely youths; one was middle-aged, the other was old, seemingly very old. All had some good points, otherwise the engineer would never have picked them. And now the youngest amongst them suddenly spoke. He looked from one to the other of the three as he said slowly: "By heck! That was a near do, eh? That was a lucky bloody do all right."

"By God!" said the old man. "I would have been very much surprised if Traynor hadn't picked me."

"Why?"

"You wouldn't understand," replied the old man grinning. "You wouldn't understand."

"Why are you well in?" asked the middle-aged fireman.

"Well in," continued the old man, laughing, "I should bloody well think so. Why, Traynor knows me all right, and so do I know him. Or by Crikes, if we didn't, then there'd be a hell of a mess on both sides."

"What the hell are you gassing about?" said the young man.

"You wouldn't understand," said the old man. He pulled out a gun-metal watch from his pocket, and looking at it exclaimed: "Ten minutes to two." The four men had now been waiting over four and a half hours. They decided to go down off the boat-deck and into the alleyway amidships and stand around the steward's door until somebody called them in to sign. Not one amongst them showed any anxiety for a drink, for a meal. Hunger and thirst were things very far off in the memory. Everything was willed to the present moment, to the next ten minutes. All four were keyed up to a high pitch of expectation. They would not be otherwise until they had heard the articles read out and had actually signed. The conversations between men in such circumstances were strangely absent from this group now. There was no talk about the ship, what she did, what she was like – nothing. All waited in stony silence. They seemed like dogs nosing around a huge kennel, one kennel being the steward's room, and the door itself appeared to have become animate and threatened to bark at them at any moment. Again the old man pulled out his watch and said slowly, and with more hope and confidence in the tone of his voice: "A minute to two. We won't be long now." And again he was not answered; the remaining three pairs of eyes were glued on the magic door. They knew it must open soon. They could already hear a hubbub of conversation going on inside the room.

The old man was in the act of pulling out his watch again when three more men came round the corner of the alleyway and made for the steward's room. On seeing the four there they pulled up, and one of them asked:

"Is this where they're signing?"

Again it was the old man who answered, for this silence of the others appeared more than a silence. "Yes, this is the room. Wish to Christ they'd put a move on. I've had nothing since seven this morning."

It was then that the youngest, who was shipping as a trimmer, remarked:

"Hell! You're not the only one, mate. Not the only one."

The door opened. The face of the second engineer appeared. The mouth moved. The voice uttered two words, "In here," and the seven men disappeared like a flash. The door closed again. The room was full of men. Three engineers, two officers, bosun and his mate, ship's steward, two shore skippers, Marine Super, and the seven men engaged for the voyage. These latter lined up in front of the table. They doffed their caps, almost stood to attention, whilst the long thin individual at the table called out in a drawling tone of voice:

"Answer your names as they are called." He proceeded to call out the names of all seven, and when he had finished he stopped and appeared to give an individual stare to each one, to probe each person as though he were intent on opening them up, body and soul, to see what lay behind such peculiar faces, such peculiar figures, such strange and differentiating expressions. The men stared at this man as though they knew instinctively that all was not yet done with, that the tremendous danger of being turned down still remained. One among them was already asking himself why they had not been asked to go before the doctor. But he was soon to learn that the company had not forgotten. There was nothing going to be left undone. The man said: "Listen carefully to the articles as they are read out to you."

Not a movement among the men. The engineers went outside. The bosun and his mate did likewise. Then the two officers disappeared. Only the man at the signing-on table remained with the shore skippers and the steward, and the seven men. He proceeded to read as follows in a slow monotonous tone.

"The S.S. *Corinthian*, 20,000 tons, bound for unknown destination. Sails on receipt of sealed orders. All ratings serve for six months or longer as required by the Admiralty. Firemen will receive eight pounds ten per month, sailors eight pounds. Trimmers six pound ten. Greasers nine pounds. Deck ratings are liable to be called upon to work coal in case of listings or any other causes that make it necessary for bunkers to be trimmed. The ship will cease from this date to bear her usual name and will henceforth be known as transport AO.2 under Government orders. In cases of emergency ratings will be required to give their services wherever required and on whatever occasion the captain deems them necessary. No member of the crew must give the whereabouts of his ship during the voyage. Any man deserting will be liable to be dealt with in accordance with the rules affecting desertion of ratings under Government orders during national crisis. The question of disputes will differ greatly, and no member of the crew can refer to his union regarding food or accommodation. Under these conditions men are signed. The ship is liable to be in service more than six months. All ratings will join the ship at eight o'clock on Saturday in the South Hornby dock, where she will be berthed." The man stopped reading and looked up. He suddenly asked: "Have any of you men seen the doctor?"

All answered as with one voice: "Not yet, sir. We have not passed the doctor. We were told to come right down to this room at two o'clock, sir."

"Take these men to the doctor," he said, turning to the steward.

"Very good, sir," replied the steward, and turning to the men he said: "This way. You fellows follow me." He led them down the alleyway until he reached the officer's mess-room. He told them to stand outside until he called them. The seven men waited. The first one was called. His name was Connor. He was the eldest of all the seven. His hair was snow-white, he had a little round red face, and the small eyes were grey and penetrating. He was quite stocky and strong for a man of his age. He passed through to the doctor. The ship's doctor was a man even older than Connor. He was thin, his hands trembled violently, and he was completely bald. His face was almost flat, and the rather high cheek-bones gave one the impression they were trying to push his round blue eyes up into his head. He continually snorted and grunted like a well-fed pig. He turned on hearing the man enter, and at once sized him up. He knew Connor. He merely said, "Open your shirt, Connor," which the old man did immediately. The doctor put the stethoscope to his chest, and listened. He drew away, sized up the man carefully, and asked bluntly:

"No diseases, Connor?"

"No, sir."

"All right," said the doctor, and Connor passed out.

The next man came in. His name was Michael Brady. The doctor looked hard at him. "How old are you?" he asked sharply, and the young fellow looked up. He was a bold, hardy type of youth, one evidently who had roughed most of his years about the docks. He looked the doctor straight in the eye.

"Eighteen," he said.

"Eighteen what?" bawled the doctor.

And the fine hardy youth said meekly: "Eighteen, sir."

"That's better," said the doctor. "Drop your trousers down." The youth did so. He examined him all over.

"You've been a scaler or trimmer before?"

"Yes, sir."

"Passed," said the doctor, and the youth left the room. "What is your name again?" called out the doctor.

"Brady, sir."

"All right," he replied. "Next man."

The next man was the middle-aged greaser named Morgan, tall, thin and wiry. He had a scar down his left cheek. He had recently been in hospital with hernia. The doctor looked at him, recognized him at once, and said: "All right, Morgan." Morgan immediately left the room. The men Newton and Smith appeared. The doctor looked at them. He said: "Hold out your hands."

The two men held out their hands. He studied them carefully and said: "Right."

The seven men now returned to the signing-on room where each man as he was called out signed the paper, drew his advance or allotment note, and quickly left the room. And each one knew that he was in for a long voyage. Each one knew that he must be aboard ship at eight o'clock prompt, as ships could not afford to lose a tide. The man Morgan was walking slowly up the shed when the youth Brady came up behind him and said:

"That was a bloody near do, eh?"

Morgan affected a certain surprise and replied: "Near do. Didn't think so myself. My bloody job in her was a cert anyhow. Traynor knows me well."

"Are you that well in?" asked the trimmer. "Jesus! Oh boy!"

"Don't be so bloody impudent or I'll crack your jaw

for you," said Morgan. He was a quiet inoffensive man. Married and three children. He was feeling light-hearted now that he could return home and say he had signed.

His wife was like many other wives of seafaring men. She went in continual dread of her husband being seized by the military police and being forced to join the army against his own will. She remembered her own brother. He was an able seaman on a cargo boat running to South America. He had been away for fourteen months, carrying horses from America to Europe. On the morning he went down to the South Home in Canning Place to draw his money he had a rather surprising experience. He was standing with many other men from the ship in the long room waiting to be called up to the counter to sign for and draw his money. Suddenly the three doors in the room opened and half a dozen Red Caps rushed into the room, locked the doors and practically as much as told the men waiting there that they would have to show cause why they were not in the King's uniform. Mrs Morgan's brother saw at once that he was in danger of being dragged up, and as quick as lightning he opened the window and jumped down into the court below. It was later explained that a new order had been issued by the authorities to the effect that merchant seamen if ashore from a ship over forty-eight hours were liable to be called up for the Army. As Johnny Morgan had a distinct dislike for the King's uniform he decided to make a bolt for it, which he did to good effect. So one was able to understand

the anxiety she felt whilst he was out. Morgan reached the
top of the shed and before leaving the trimmer remarked
casually:

"You won't really need a bag this time, matey. Just
bring your braces. That's all you'll ever require." A remark
that made Brady laugh, as he already had his bag packed,
and even a piece of string tied round his toilet box to
remind him about the pair of garters his young lady
wanted. The ship was now loading ballast. Sand only. She
was painted a French grey; her name had disappeared,
and in its place on the bridge was erected a huge board
bearing her number as supplied by the Admiralty, AO.2.
She had one gun fitted up on the poop. Nobody knew
where she was bound, when she really would sail,
whether she was going to carry horses or become part of
a trooping convoy. She might be fitted up in some obscure
port as a queer ship or a dummy battleship. Everybody
was profoundly curious. The phrase "sealed orders"
covered a multitude of meanings, at least for the crew. But
amongst this crew there were already men who had been
on ships that had been torpedoed, blown up, rammed, run
ashore, burnt, and for some this strange ship with no
cargo but a ballast of sand, with her six-inch gun mounted
on the afterdeck, her whole physical appearance changed
by grey paint, bespoke adventures – adventures perhaps
that no man had ever experienced before. The few
dockers who had been working down her hold remarked
as they sat in the various pubs in the evening time "that it

looked a queer bit of business all right." What with her empty holds, and the cavernous tween-decks, that had a ghostly smell and ring about them, it was enough to expand the weakest imagination and set it careering off to the most unheard-of places in the world of the mind. Some of the crew indeed never allowed their imagination to get the better of them. Here was a ship, they were members of it, and that was all. There might be what the Admiralty called a national crisis existing, but to such men it meant little or nothing. They were earning their living and that was all. There was something of the Stoic in these particular men. And certainly amongst them as a whole there was a desire for action, an urging for doing, for being up and out of it, away. Two days and that ship would be under way. All seamen cursed sailing days, but generally after the Channel had been encountered they settled down to the usual monotony that is an inseparable part of seafaring life. And all these seven men had experienced something that morning. Each one of them had realized something. It would not be easy for them to forget how miraculously they had fared. Three hundred-odd men. All hungry and eager for work, the riot, the frantic endeavours, the struggle with the police and officials, the boarding of the boat *en masse*. And from that three hundred-odd men they had been chosen. There seemed something singular about it. When Morgan arrived home his wife was waiting for him at the door. She wore an anxious expression, which he quickly dispelled, and now the ghost of a smile crossed her pale face as he told her he had signed and was sailing the "day after to-morrow."

"God's good," exclaimed Mrs Morgan, and started to prepare the tea for her husband. The two young children were sleeping upstairs. Mr Morgan went up to their room. He bent over the bed and kissed them affectionately. He loved his children with a deep passionate devotion. He smiled as he saw the chubby pairs of hands clutching the bedclothes. There was a new joy in his heart. No more walking about; the dread fear of being forced into the Army, which he hated, had disappeared now.

"I might possibly be away twelve months or more," he remarked to his wife as they sat down to the evening meal.

"That's a long time, isn't it?" she replied.

"What about it?" he said. "Better than the Army where you never get home at all. By God, I was a lucky man this morning all right. Just imagine. Three hundred bloody men all fighting for a job in that ship, because she's going for a long trip. Old Traynor spotted me out of all that lot, though. The Government's always changing orders. Still, but for that I mightn't have got the damned job. They signed on a few extra men. The whole of the dock road must have heard the shout that Super gave. Only seven men wanted. What a riot! When I got to the shed it was black with men. I thought all Liverpool was gathering for a fete or something. You never saw anything like it, Rosie. The row they kicked up too. I'm a lucky devil all right," he concluded, and went on with his meal of sausages and bacon.

Mrs Morgan's imagination ran riot for a few minutes. "I was only thinking yesterday," she commenced. "If you got a long trip I would be able to send Peter to that man for lessons."

Mr Morgan sighed. "Don't start all that over again, Rosie. You know that I haven't even started yet."

The light went out of her eyes for a moment. "Well, thank God anyhow. Twelve months is a long time – still – "

"I'm tired," said Mr Morgan, "and I'm going to bed. You won't be long, will you?"

"No, Andy, I won't," she replied.

Morgan went up to his room. He had a sudden desire to undress as quickly as possible and get into bed. There seemed a greater security in bed. He had such a lot to think over. He could think best lying stretched out on that bed.

Before the light was blown out he turned to his wife.

"Well, aren't you really glad, kid?" he asked.

"Of course I am. Of course I am. You know that. God bless you," she whispered in his ear.

She blew out the candle. They fell asleep just as the moon outside appeared from behind a bank of cloud and filled the room with a palish glow of light that illuminated the features of Mr Morgan, whose head was facing the window. The features expressed calm and peace.

II

"That's a funny ship you've signed on," remarked Mrs Brady when Michael came downstairs. He was dressed up in his best suit, and had a new white muffler tied round his neck. He had had his hair cut, sported a new pair of brown shoes, and was altogether quite a different Michael from the one of a few hours previous. He stood in front of the mirror evidently admiring himself, when Mrs Brady remarked casually that Elsie had called. The youth turned suddenly and asked: "Called? She called? Why?"

The mother affected surprise. She placed her hands on her hips and said:

"Why? Well, good God, that's a queer question for you to be asking at this time of day. Why shouldn't she call? You're going to marry the girl, aren't you?"

"Marry her. She might as well marry a leg of mutton as marry me. Every man who has signed on this ship has signed for the duration of his natural life. Queer ship. I should think so. Sticking a couple of dummy funnels on her."

"But that's nothing to do with the girl, is it? Good God, you'll have me disgraced before you're finished."

"Me! Not me. Not a bit. You'll hear a pretty tale just now about that little scut."

"Michael!" exclaimed Mrs Brady. "Michael."

"Well, isn't she? Actually caught in a bloody ship's boiler with that fellow Farrell."

"What! What's that! Oh dear God!" said his mother.

"What's the use of talking, mother? Is my tea ready? I'm going down to see the Maughams at seven o'clock. Besides, Johnny Maugham is sailing in her, too."

"That fellow," said Mrs Brady. "Fancy that thing getting a job."

"He's alright. A real good sailor too. Take my word for it. Well, where's the bloody tea? I'm hungry, and I'm in a hurry."

Mrs Brady set his tea on the table whilst she thought all kinds of things. They careered round and round her brain. She stood over her son and watched him wolfing his meal. She placed a hand on his shoulder. He looked up. He saw the amazement, the enquiring look, the dawn of a certain sadness crawling like a mist over the brown of her eyes. He touched her hand. Held it tightly in his own, and by the feel of it he knew she was trembling. "What's the matter with you, mother?" he asked her.

"Nothing," she said, and then to his complete surprise she burst out crying. "I was dreaming about you last night, Michael. It reminded me of a similar dream I had one night before your father sailed away on one of those China boats. Oh, I've been so worried all day. Tell me, Michael, it's nothing dangerous. Mrs Morley was telling me this afternoon that everybody is talking about the ship. Nobody knows what she's going to do or where she's going to sail. Not a thing. Listen, Michael, I'm afraid. Can't you back out of her?"

He almost scowled then. "Back out, and finish up with six months in the bloody clink. Can't be done. This ship is under the Admiralty now. If she still was chartered by the Eastern Line it mightn't matter so much. You don't understand, mother. It's almost like being in the damned Navy."

"Oh, Heavens!" said his mother. "You surely haven't joined the Mercantile Marine Reserve?"

"Not at all. Don't worry and everything'll be all right. Here, sit down and get something to eat. And let me finish my tea. That fellow's sure to be waiting for me even now. I expect he's at the top of the street this minute."

A silence fell between them. Mrs Brady felt that if only she could say the right thing, the correct thing, she would be safe. But she couldn't think just what to say. A fear seized her. If only she knew what to say. And her son was sailing soon. She half-murmured a prayer that God would guide her to say the right thing. She could not afford to lose him, her Michael. He was all she had. She had lost her husband five years ago when his ship had run on the rocks off the Canadian coast. The thought of the youth setting out on such a dangerous voyage filled her with this fear, almost to suffocating-point. And if this dream had disturbed her it had not affected her son in any way. He laughed about it, and later made a joke of it with all the other men in the ship. They laughed too, knowing, as men do, that women know nothing about sea-folk.

"Well, I'm off now," said Michael. "I'll be in soon after eleven. Bye-bye."

"Don't be landing in here after midnight like you were last trip," warned his mother as she commenced to tidy up the table. She crossed to the window, drew back the curtain, and stood there watching him walk down the street. She heaved a sigh, turned to her task, and having cleaned up the kitchen she went upstairs to her own room. Here in the silence and peace of it she knelt down by the bedside and prayed. No, she told herself, she could not stop him from going. But she asked God Almighty to guide him safely home again. She got to her feet and sat down on the edge of the bed and commenced to meditate. Her head dropped lower and lower. She fell back from sheer tiredness on to the bed. Half an hour later she was snoring.

Meanwhile her son had reached the pub, where he was joined by a few more of his friends, and now all were seated in the back parlour. The conversation was deviating continually from such things as football-matches to billiard handicaps, when a fellow named Duncan started up the talk about the AO.2.

"Strike me!" he said, "that was a queer do this morning. I was watching the crowd from the monkey bridge where I was trying to get a shine on the bleedin' binnacle. What a riot! By heck, you never saw anything like it."

"She signed you fellows yesterday then?" remarked another man named Macormack, who had shipped as lookout man.

"Yes."

"How long have *you* been on her then?" asked Brady.

"Twelve months this June."

"Where'd she get to last trip?"

"Round Marseille, Yonkers, New York, Saint Nazaire, Salonika, all over the bloody place. One minute you're carrying a thousand bloody mules and the next minute you're taking Aussies up to Alex and Cairo. Then we carried a crowd of the Fusiliers up to Salonika. By Jesus! They were the boys all right. The bosun of our ship netted a cool two hundred out of those guys with his crown and anchor board."

Michael drank his beer, lay back comfortably and looked up at the ceiling. He began dreaming. He had never been to any of these places before. The only part of the world his travels had taken him to had been the States and Canada, with perhaps an occasional run to the West India islands. Now he visualised a real adventure. Here was something for which his whole heart and soul had longed from his very boyhood. He could not believe his good fortune.

"Queer ships all the same," went on Duncan. "Can't write a letter home saying where you are, can't go ashore in half the ports, all dead-lights down, and black crowd compelled to work six-hour shifts in times of emergency. Wait till she gets under way. Then you'll see something.

I had a great time last trip though. This trip nobody knows where she's off to. Sealed orders. Might go for troops. Might be turned into a base or supply ship.

I had a mate who was on the supply ship to the Gallipoli adventurers. Told me all about the special cases of oranges from Jaffa for Hamilton, the head serang up there. By Jove! he's a great boy that, all right. Special ship for him no less, carting him about from one corner of the Meddy to the other."

The four persons seated round the table in the bar-parlour laughed. And one of them remarked casually: "Have you ever seen him bathing near the breakwater up there?"

More laughs, and the man concluded with a "looked more like a bloody accident than a commander-in-chief. Ah well! That on him and all his rummy gang," and there was a sudden flash of spit from his mouth, that was almost the shape of a wolf's. Brady still looked up at the ceiling, blowing out great clouds of smoke from his mouth. He lit one cigarette after another. But his thoughts were very far away from that bar-parlour. Farther than there and farther than home too. They were wafting about the blue skies and blue seas of the Mediterranean. He was not alone. There was a young woman sharing his thoughts. None other than Janet Maugham, whose brother was now sitting opposite him, a tall pasty-faced young man who was a fireman. The sereneness, the evident content sitting upon Maugham's face might have been violently disturbed had he been able to divine the thoughts occupying his shipmate's mind. For Michael Brady had an eye on Janet, a rosy buxom girl of twenty-one years, who worked in a local draper's shop, and who had at some time or other smiled at Michael. It was the first cause of that strange eruption in his blood, which had caused a certain distance that existed between Elsie and himself to lengthen itself. Elsie, who was a good-looking girl, had been hoping to seal a matrimonial pact with young Brady, whose mother she had rather got to like of late. So far nobody had heard of the strange occurrence in the boiler of the *Media*, though in some way or other Michael himself had heard of a scaler who had lured Elsie upon the boat after dark, and with the same cunning and adroitness had lured her down the engine-room ladder. Eventually she ended up in the boiler with the scaler, who quite calmly proceeded to possess her in no uncertain manner. But to Michael such an incident in his life was small. It possessed no significance whatever for him. His shock on hearing of the occurrence was as brief as his remembrance of it, and now there was but one thing he wished to do before he sailed away on the Saturday. He wanted to know Janet Maugham, but how this was to be achieved he did not know. Nor did his brain and all the arsenal of thought embedded there help him to arrive at anything. He suddenly lowered his head and looked across at Maugham. "A penny for them," said Maugham, grinning so that his ugly mouth almost stretched itself from ear to ear. Michael laughed.

"Worth much more than that," he replied. "Have a bloody drink, mate."

At ten p.m. when all four left the pub they were decided upon one thing. They would stick by each other through thick and thin, they would none of them let the other down. They would be good mates all through that trip. Two of them caught a passing tram, whilst Michael and Maugham set off in another direction. Maugham said he was going straight home and would be leaving Michael at the corner of Stanley Street, to which Michael replied that he felt like a bit of a stroll and would go right on pass his, Maugham's, house. It was merely an excuse with Brady, for a few minutes later, when they were actually turning into Stanley Street, Maugham exclaimed suddenly:

"Well! Why not come in anyhow. You pass the damned house. Come on!" Which was what Michael had been hoping for. When they entered the house they found that both Mr and Mrs Maugham had gone to bed, leaving Janet and a younger brother who was at school in the kitchen to await their brother's return. On seeing Michael Janet smiled, a smile which Brady immediately returned. There was something almost naïve in the way he approached her and shaking hands exclaimed: "Pleased to meet you, Janet," and her reply to this greeting was one that almost upset the youth. It was so charming. There was certainly something about Janet, he told himself, that left him quite helpless. There was so much he wanted to say to her, and now the tongue in his mouth held firm and he was helpless. The girl placed a chair up to the fire for him and he sat down, her brother meanwhile having gone into the back-kitchen to bring in supper for all three. The conversation commenced about the ship that was sailing on the Saturday, and the girl remarked that she heard from the office where she worked that it was going away for two years. Maugham smiled.

"Might go away for five years, never mind two, mightn't we, Brady?" And he looked across, at Michael, whose attention was drawn by a pair of socks hanging on the line. They were full of holes, and he said:

"Are they yours?"

"Yes, they're mine," replied Maugham laughing. The conversation took a somewhat delicate turn then, for he started to talk about Elsie. It seemed half the street already knew how she had been led down to the dock and practically forced into a ship's boiler to help pass half an hour away with a scaler who had a spring feeling. "Didn't you hear about it, then?" asked Maugham. "Why, everybody knows about it now."

Brady remained silent. He did not relish talking about Elsie when the only girl he was anxious to talk to and know was Janet. Maugham was not blind to certain glances and expressions upon his sister's face. When Brady finally left about half-past eleven he said to her in quite a blunt manner:

"What was all the bloody winking going on between Brady and yourself? Good Lord, you ought to know better. Haven't you heard about the other one he was carrying on with?"

Janet replied that she hadn't, whereon her brother began to give her all the details about Elsie, which made Janet raise her eyebrows.

"Well, there you are," he exclaimed; "now you know what kind of a fellow you were winking eyes at."

"I'm going to bed," she said, and she rose from her chair, placed it back against the wall and crossed to the door. "Good night," she said.

"Good night," her brother replied. When she left the kitchen he drew the big arm-chair up to the fire, and stretching out his legs he allowed his mind to wander down certain virgin paths from which they periodically returned with a certain mental jerk. He was thinking of Brady and his own sister. He knew Brady well because he had sailed with him often, and not only that, he had spent most of his school years with him as a chum. He did not like Brady enough to accept him as a future brother-in-law without qualms. He turned the idea over and over in his mind until he at last got up, started to pace the kitchen backwards and forwards, and there was an expression of anxiety tracing a line upon his forehead. He was not afraid of Brady. He vowed that he could hold himself against Brady any time. It was not the thought of what might happen, but what might have happened already. He put out the light and went up to bed in a disturbed state of mind. He could not sleep. This sudden fear on his part appeared like a shot from the blue. How had it come about that in a few minutes he had learned to hate one with whom he had spent most of his working life? He said aloud:

"How do I know? How does anybody know what has happened? Perhaps she's in the family way now. How does anybody know? By God, if I thought – "

He fell asleep cursing the man with whom in two days' time he would be working in the stokehold. He snored.

III

Newton and Smith were drinking in the pub opposite the Brocklebank dock. Newton was turned forty years of age and had at one time been a ship's carpenter, but through drink and neglecting his duty he had been given a bad book. Now he was glad to be able to get any job, and when he was signed on as a fireman for the transport he went almost delirious with happiness, for he never knew he would get the bad mark in his book erased. He was a single man, living in lodgings with an old Irishwoman who had been boarding sailors ever since her husband had died abroad of malaria. Newton was a small man, with a straggling sandy moustache and a nose that appeared wrinkled at the end as though it had once been caught in a drum-end. His brown eyes rarely showed the light of a smile. He was silent, morose, pessimistic, hated company of any kind, though not when there was free drink to be had. He was an inveterate gambler. His companion Smith was only twenty-two years of age. He too was a fireman, but he held his job against older men with greater experience by reason of the fact that he was a good worker, never complained, and was always willing to learn from people, and never afraid to ask questions. He was ten months married and had one child. His wife went out to work in a jute factory whilst the Corporation looked after the child in the daytime. Both men had been drinking freely, and like all men who have reached that stage in inebriation they talked of their forth-coming voyage. Newton, who was banging his fist on the table and declaiming against the men being forced to register with the RNR, had been drumming into Smith's brain for almost an hour the information that the AO.2 was going to be turned into a cruiser and that before a member of the crew had time to get his bag on board he would find that naval officers were there instead of the ordinary ones. Smith only grinned, as so far the information had failed to make any impression upon him. But when at the top of his voice Newton shouted that "once you get in the confounded Navy you're goosed for ever," Smith lost his grin and the good-natured expression upon his face suddenly turned to one of consternation and astonishment.

"Christ! Are you sure about that, mate?" he asked suddenly.

"Sure!" exclaimed Newton. "Why, I was never more sure in my life."

"And that means," went on Smith, "that means we'll be put on bloody naval pay. Well, by God, I believe I'll back out of her. No Navy for me. By Heavens, no. I've seen something of the Navy. D'you remember Higgins?"

"Jack Higgins" queried Newton. "Yes," I know the fellow."

"Well, he's been on one of those damned cruisers The old *Eldon*. Turned over to the Government. Used to carry passengers out to Canada. You know her."

"Yes," said Newton, "I know the ship all right. I once trimmed in her."

"Well, last trip this fellow Higgins was telling me that they do nothing except cruise up and down the North Sea, in bloody cold weather too. He came up off watch one afternoon. Black as the ace of spades. Gets to his hammock and picks a cigarette and lights up. Bloody master-at-arms comes along. Says – 'Higgins. Wanted in chief artificer's room at once. Show a leg quick there.' Master-at-arms beats it. Higgins sits down on deck and thinks. Bloody position he was in. If he went to the fellow's room right away without changing he'd get bloody cells for crossing the quarter-deck in his dirty clothes. If he changed and washed and then went to the fellow's room, he'd get cells just the same for being late in obeying an order. Those bastards don't understand anything I tell you. Treat you like a blasted dog. Well, poor Higgins tried to think it out in a couple of secs, and so he decided that he had better chance it, and off he went to the artificer's room. Result, told off. That's not all. Ninety days bloody cells for crossing quarter-deck in his working gear and leaving a trail of coal-dust on it. Bastards! That's all they are. I tell you this, that the first time I hear that she is going to come under the reserve, well, I'm off. You bet your life. I don't care a hang where she is. She can be in Timbuctoo. I don't give a God damn, I'll clear out of her."

"But it mightn't be that bad," argued Newton. "Have a bloody drink and forget it." He called out to the barman that he wanted two Guinnesses and a lemon-dash. This was brought almost immediately. Newton started talking then. He leaned his head on his hand and, looking right into his companion's eyes, he said:

"All you say might be correct. Good! But Christ Almighty, we're men, aren't we? If they start that bleedin' caper we know what to do, don't we?"

Smith laughed and replied: "Aye! So did the fellows on that bloody heart-and-soul burner – the damned *Teutonic*. Why, you heard about it, didn't you?"

"Heard something," said Newton. "I was up the Meddy at the time."

"Why, the whole black crowd, sailors and all, came off her at the stage. Protested against the rotten grub. Nearly a bloody riot. What did they do? Bloody admiral or somebody came down. Men assembled. Says he:

"'Men! Back to your ship! Men! Back to your duty. We are in a state of war. If any man deserts this ship he is liable to be shot. The question of rotten food will be gone into.'

"Bloody trimmer walked out from the crowd and said to this fellow with enough braid on his hat to make a patch-work quilt: 'You're all right, you big-bellied swine. How'd you like muck for grub, eh!'"

"Phew!" exclaimed Newton. "I didn't hear about that."

"Who did? The poor bastard got two years' hard labour. Navy. Navy," he exclaimed in derisive tones. "All my bloody eye. Not a decent man among the lot. A confounded lot of Cissies. All they're good for is polishing brass knobs."

The manager appeared behind the counter.

"TIME PLEASE," he shouted at the top of his voice. "TIME PLEASE."

The two men got up from the seat, and ambled their way towards the door. Outside they looked for a car. A tram was coming down the road. They boarded it, and all through the journey remained strangely silent.

"Must get off here," said Smith, as the car reached the end of Oberon Road.

"Alright. See you to-morrow. I'm going straight home to kip. Good night, old timer." He waved a hand, the car passed on, and Smith made his way towards his lodgings. He was feeling tired. He was going to have one good long sleep before the trip commenced. As he walked along he kept pondering over certain rumours he had heard, and the dominant fear in his mind was that the ship would go into the reserve forces of the Navy.

Smith's fear of the ship ever going under Naval orders was quite a genuine one. It was based on some experiences he had had, together with nearly two years' association with naval men. He could not stand them. He often said, and quite emphatically that all naval men were a pack of washerwomen, a gang of old women who did nothing but polish and wash clothes and toe the line to every individual who had the fortune or misfortune to wear a piece of gold braid on his cap. Amongst these individuals there were men known as stewards whom Smith could not stand. If he saw one he immediately gave vent to his opinions of them, which were certainly not praiseworthy, but rather of an insulting kind, and this weakness of his for loathing these men had been brought about not through any every-day hearsay. Smith knew them like no other man. He had rubbed shoulders with too many of them in his time, although that was not a very long period. He had drunk with them in foreign ports, argued with them in foreign pubs and hole-in-the-corner places, and always they annoyed him by a certain smirk, a certain servility in their make-up that more than all else Smith loathed with a persistent hatred and savage condemnation. He was certain they were not men at all. Even when the seas were finally cleared and peace once more reigned over lands as well as oceans, Smith never forgot all he had seen. To mention the Navy to him was to incur an insult, or a volley of oaths that came spontaneously to his lips, that sprang from some inner part of his being that had registered the events, the experiences, the moments and the hours when the Navy had hit hard against the traditional pride he had in the merchant service. But that was not a weakness that applied to Smith alone. It applied to all merchantmen, whose hatred of naval men and methods was a genuine and full-hearted hatred. They hated servility, they hated uniform, they hated old women's work, they hated swank.

When he returned to his lodgings he was hungry, and made light work of the big dinner which his landlady had kept heated up in the oven for him. "Your supper was burnt to a cinder last night," she remarked.

"Aye!" he said. "I had one or two too much last night. That was a real fine dinner," he concluded, and he got up from the table and went to the corner, where he commenced taking everything out of his canvas bag.

"I thought you'd finished packing," said the landlady

"Quite! I'm just going through it to see there is nothing left behind. I'll tie her up now, and she'll be all ready for the fellow who calls for it to-night. Now I'm going to turn in; I'm rotten tired, and I don't want to be called at all."

"But your breakfast?"

"Oh hang that," said Smith. "Don't disturb me."

When he got into bed he smoked cigarette after cigarette, the while his thoughts criss-crossed and swept his mind, a mind that had never been used to deep thinking. Once he spoke aloud: "Yes! If that ship becomes a cruiser or anything like it I'll clear out as sure as I'm lying in this bed to-day." When the landlady looked in an hour later she found him still half-dressed lying stretched on the top of the bedclothes, and a pile of cigarette ash spilt upon his shirt front. She said to herself: "Poor fellow! It's a hard time they have these days, what with these dirty Germans and all kinds of new rules and having to have their photographs taken. Poor fellows! They must see things these times indeed. Glad I am that my old man slipped his cable long ago. Thank God! Some of these poor fellows just want to make me cry when I see them. Never know when they'll be flung into the water and have to fight for their lives. Poor lads! Poor lads!"

She closed the door softly and went downstairs. She looked at Smith's bag lying on the floor near the front door. She put her hand on it and stroked it as though it were a cat or dog; the very act awoke in her a sympathy not only with her young lodger, but with all men who went down to sea in ships, especially when in her lodger's case they had to face the perils of submarine and hidden mine. But these were things that in the ordinary sense did not worry Mr Smith. Aboard a ship a man's mind is usually occupied with but one thing – the idea of getting back home for a grand bust-up. With such men it was not a matter of having any objective, of questioning this or that motive, or even thinking about the war. Immediacy came only with thoughts of pay, of good food, of a decent ship and a decent boss to work for. The AO.2 captain was well known to everybody in the port. He had been a training-ship boy himself and was indeed a member of the Reserve. He treated men as men, not sops or old women. He was only five foot two in height, and in bad weather when the dodger was up his tiger had to bring his special stool out on to the bridge, upon which he climbed and generally puffed and blew if a head-wind came in his direction. He was a man afraid of any kind of fog, any kind of fuss, any kind of ceremony. He honoured and obeyed the company for which he worked. From his men he expected loyalty and good work. He was even a little pious and hated men going ashore and getting drunk. Such men he generally logged if they stepped beyond the bounds even by an inch.

He was known amongst the seamen as "Foggy" the man who turned back from the Fastnet to the Pool instead of getting on to Cape Race as per orders. Now the war had seen him transferred to this one-time passenger ship; she was twenty thousand tons and had a speed of nearly seventeen and a quarter knots. For the past year she had been traversing the waters around the eastern coast and nobody save her crew knew what she was really about. For the past seven weeks men had been working on her day and night. It was current throughout the length and breadth of dock-land that strange alterations were being made in her, though what these alterations were really meant for nobody could understand, much less get to know. At night one could hear for miles the terrific din as the riveters and plumbers and fitters and turners and carpenters changed her out of all recognition so that a former member of her crew meeting her in some port months later would never know her. Certainly she was not going to carry horses for the French Government, and no one could say definitely as to whether she would form a troop-carrying convoy, as no provision was being made for accommodating soldiers. The crew racked their brains, tried to solicit all kinds of information without result. It was said that the captain himself did not know where he had to go. He would take the ship into the Channel. He would have the sealed orders in his possession, but until he had reached a certain point like the Fastnet or the South Stack or the Lizard he could not break open the seal. He would then discover the secret order, inform the first mate and chief engineer, and the helmsman would be told to steer a certain course. But of his destination proper nobody was the wiser or would be until he suddenly found the ship pulling into some God-forsaken place like Oran, or Algiers, or Alexandretta, or even Northern Spain. There were a few members of a ship's crew who rarely bothered to ask information. If they had a certificate, then they generally could manage to dig up a sextant from the bag, and at noon could themselves go on to the deck and find out the ship's position, and guessing her position from the equator would very soon know just where she was heading for. But men like Smith and Newton and Connor, who spent most of their lives down the stokehold, rarely bothered to find out anything like that. If a ship was going to America she just was going, and they weren't interested further. If she was going to Lemnos, or right to the mouth of the Dardanelles itself, well, she was going, and that was all. They never concerned themselves further than that, though a certain anxiety coloured their minds as well as their expressions, their habits, their social life at sea. At heart they had a certain stoical quality, a quality that served them to good purpose in moments when a man is powerless and helpless and stands a stricken giant before destiny or the elements or God Himself. They did not love, they worked. They did not sing, they worked. They did not think always, but they worked. In the network of oceans they worked and in the dark pits they worked, and high up in the truck-top they stood and scanned the ocean wastes that men like themselves had charted, out of toil and agony and despair and high hope. Scanned into the night and on to the dawn without resting or ceasing, and saw through eyes that never closed until the mind itself closed them. Closed them against the rage of men and the rage of waters, and the rage of elements. Towards a high purpose, blindly. Ploughing through wastes and tracts and mountains of water, and at the end the crinkle of notes betokened the high purpose for which they had surrendered themselves. Newton's one ambition in life was to be able to earn eighty pounds in one trip with which he might have a Bacchanalian feast, Smith's that he might be able to buy a full-keyed accordion, Connor's that he might be able to buy his wife a new skirt with belted top. So with them all. Their purpose was their own. The ship was not theirs, nor the sea, nor any single star, nor any moment of time until finally she tied up in dock, her sides and bottom barnacled from strange flora and fauna of ocean depths. The froth on the glass was inviting, and the smile and flash of teeth of any girl was like the taste of strong wine. A few days. Away again. No star invited, no purpose called. The poetic rage of wind and wild waters touched no chord of their being. The work must be done. The bunk is warm after toil, and soon they will be home again.

The morning was bleak and cold. A certain tang hung in the air. The silence was suddenly stabbed by a burst

from the AO.2's whistle. She was getting upsteam. It was
very dark, few people were about the dock-road, but
gradually one and then two, and then a group of three
were seen coming along the ill-lighted road with their
bags upon their backs. The ship's crew were joining her.
In the various houses where they lived strange scenes
were taking place. Maugham, who had been up since five
o'clock pottering about the house, was now sitting to his
breakfast. His father had gone out to work. His sister and
mother were up too, the former polishing herself up in the
back-kitchen, as she had to be at her own work at eight
sharp, whilst Mrs Maugham was busy tying up a parcel of
soap and matches for her son.

"You're sure you have everything, Andrew?" she asked.

"Everything," replied the son, whose thoughts were in
that moment very far away from the kitchen and everything in it. His thoughts centred round Brady and his
sister. He pushed his plate away and got up from the table.
The mother looked anxiously at him. There was a certain
apprehension within her. She went up to her son and,
embracing him, said:

"I hope you have a good trip this time. Better than the
last boat you were in. It seems funny to me that they won't
tell you where she's going." In reply to which the son
said he thought they were going to Nagasaki for a cargo
of dolls'-eyes. And the sister shouted in from the back:
"D'you really think that's funny?"

He made no reply, but left the kitchen and went

upstairs. He came down a few seconds later with a mandoline under his arm. This he proceeded to wrap up carefully in brown paper. Mrs Maugham went upstairs to see the time, as she had forgotten to bring the alarm-clock down. The son almost ran into the back-kitchen then. He gripped his sister by the arm.

"Listen, Janet," he said, "there's nothing between you and that fellow Brady, is there?"

When she looked at him she saw an anxious and inquisitive brother looking at her. She smiled and replied: "Between Brady and me? Good Lord, what d'you think I am?"

"I'll know what to think and what to say, too, if you're kidding me up," he said savagely.

"Why!" she exclaimed, somewhat alarmed, "what's wrong with you? Haven't you slept well or something? Besides, you seem to take a very sudden interest in my welfare. Mind your own damned business and I'll look after mine too." She pushed her way into the kitchen just as her mother came downstairs. The son followed her in.

"Am going now," he said quietly.

"Are you. Oh dear!" said Mrs Maugham. "Can't we walk down to the dock-gate with you? God knows how long you'll be away this time."

"No! I can go down myself. I told you before I don't want anybody seeing me off or docking me when I come home. Good-bye." With a certain abruptness he embraced his sister, then his mother. He picked up his bag, slung it on his shoulder and moved towards the door. He turned as he lifted the latch with his free hand. "Goodbye," he said. The door closed. He was gone.

Long after her daughter went to work Mrs Maugham was upstairs kneeling by the altar praying for a successful voyage for her son, invoking the protection of all the saints in the calendar, whilst a stray tear fell on her cheek and for a moment glistened there, then trickled down until it disappeared in the folds of her fat neck. "God look down on him," she prayed. Pause. "God look down on all those poor fellows who have to go away on a day like this." Long after she had ceased to pray she knelt there as though some invisible force had rooted her to the spot. Meanwhile the son was swinging his way down the hill towards the dock. He coughed and spat.

IV

In the bedroom of Morgan's house the three children had been awakened. They sat up now rubbing the sleep from their eyes, staring in a bewildered way at their father who was standing over the bed. Apparently they wondered each in their own different way why such things as ships and wars and fathers going away should disturb them from their sleep. Mrs Morgan was standing at the bedroom window with a far-away look in her eyes. And Mr Morgan sat down on the side of the bed and took each child's hand in his. He talked to them, told them that he was going far away to a strange country and that he would always be thinking of them. When he was sailing for home he would bring each of them something nice. But they had to be good children and not worry their mother and not do any bad thing, else he wouldn't like them any more. They looked at him, and the look was one of wonder, whilst the mother, who had turned away from the window, looked from them to the man who was leaving her so soon. He was so interested in the chatter of the three-year-old boy Donald that he could not hear his wife saying: "It's nearly time now, dear."

When she came near to him, saying no word, but merely placing her hand on his shoulder, he knew his time was really come. He bent over and kissed the children, held their heads in his horny hands; then one last embrace and he left the room. Husband and wife walked slowly along the landing, she with her hand on his shoulder, he with his own arm round her waist. They went into the kitchen. His bag too was packed and lying near the door. The baggage-man had forgotten to call for it. Morgan was angry. Although he knew he owed the baggage-fellow about a pound, he felt mad about having to carry such a weighty thing down by himself. He stood now in the centre of the kitchen, holding his wife's hands. She said to him:

"And you don't even know where the ship's going. God! I felt so queer last night about it all. I mean you're getting the job so easily. It made me think things."

He laughed and told her not to worry. Everything was all right.

"God knows where we're going. But why worry about that, old woman? Lord! I've been to the queerest places on earth in my time, and you never worried then. Why should you be worrying now? Don't. It only starts me thinking things too, and once you start thinking things – well, that's done it, so to speak. Look after the kids, that's all I ask you to do. Don't be thinking about anything. I'll write to you, of course I will. Don't forget that when you write you must send the letter care of the GPO, London. You won't forget that, will you now?" he said.

"No! I won't forget, darling," she replied, and suddenly before he was aware of it she was crying and tears were running on to his hand. He looked into her eyes, and the look in them was something that pulled at his heart, and

he murmured low in her ears: "God Almighty! You mustn't
be like that. Straight and honest, if you keep it up I'll back
out. I'll clear out! Why act like this? Listen to me! Listen to
me," he pleaded. She did not look up, and he raised her
head with his hand and looked long into her face, and for
a single moment he remembered a crushed flower he had
once picked up from his own kitchen floor, and the colour
of her eyes was the same, and the expression was that of
a woman who was being crushed even like the flower. He
released her hands and said:

"Darling, I must go now. Good-bye." He almost
strangled her in his embrace, as roughly released her
and strode across the kitchen and picked up his bag.
To himself he said: "Good God Almighty! Is this all that
one can offer a woman? A last look and a last embrace.
Be hanged to it. I'm sorry I signed in the blasted ship. And
what a lousy bloody day to sail – Saturday of all days.
And the confounded time they expect you to join her.
They'll have us messing about all day and then have us
pull her out by the night's tide. Why the devil they do mess
about like this I don't know." The bag was on his shoulder.
He turned round. "Good-bye and good luck. God bless
you," he said almost in a whisper. The woman did not
answer. She sat down on a chair and buried her face
in her hands. He opened the door, pushed himself out
bag and all, then banged it. He was gone. She rushed
to the door and opened it, stepped out into the street
and just saw him jumping a tram. She returned and closed

the door. Straight upstairs she went and buried herself between the soft curly heads of Donald and Sheila. They had fallen asleep. They did not hear her murmuring, nor any single sob. The room was very quiet. The sobbing ceased. She fell asleep. She had been up since five o'clock that morning. Mr Morgan was walking down the dock shed now. He could not forget that parting. It seemed so strange to him. He felt as if he were going to be executed. Never in his life had his wife demonstrated like that, never before had he felt such a pull at the centre of his being, never before had he poured out such love and tenderness to his children. He saw the long gangway running down to the shed through number three gate. There was a quartermaster standing at the bottom. Nobody was in sight except for him and a few dockers who had been working throughout the night. He dragged his steps as he approached the gangway. The quartermaster said, "Good morning," but he did not reply. He walked slowly up the gangway and disappeared through the huge bulkhead door. Here strange noises and many sounds of voices greeted him. And though on ordinary occasions such sounds were welcome to him, he felt different now.

The figure of his wife was before him always and he could not brush it away from his mind. When he reached the fo'c'sle he discovered that so far only half the crew had arrived. It was turned the hour now. Already rumours were afoot that the skipper had been aboard all night, that the ship was pulling out at nine forty-five by the morning tide. Everything seemed ship-shape and ready. Decks were cleared of cargo, lumber, ropes and shoots. Hatches were battened down, the derricks had been put into position again, the winches cleaned. The decks seemed strange to the men. Decks that on ordinary occasions were aquiver with life, passengers and stewards, and stewardesses. Now all was bare and bleak and hollow-looking. A group of sailors were standing by number one hatch, and the conversation was ever about the sealed orders, what they were going to do with her, when she was sailing and where to. But they were things out of reach of the ordinary crew. The Government were not concerned as to what an ordinary person thought or felt about the subject. And while they were talking they saw an engineer coming along through the well-deck alleyway. They all looked up as he passed, but he gave them a glare. No more than that. The air was ripe with soft curses and almost hidden oaths and remarks about the stuck-up son of a bitch who walked past them with the air of the Lord Mayor of London. He passed them again as he had to go up to the captain's cabin. Everybody seemed to slink about, there was a furtiveness about every movement. Suddenly a gang of firemen were seen coming down the alleyway. Then they knew at once that she was going to pull out by the morning tide. One of the sailors asked the firemen as they passed:

"Are you going down now?"

"Sure!" replied a fireman. "We're going down now, boy.

This old ship is getting under way at last." The fireman appeared so cheerful that it set the group of sailors on to another topic of conversation. In the firemen's fo'c'sle on the starboard side of her Morgan was sitting on his bunk talking to Brady the young trimmer. Brady was already changed and dressed for his turn below, although as yet no watches had been picked, and the scratch watch that had just gone below had been hurriedly got together. Later each watch would be picked in the ordinary way and the men assembled on the boat-deck for drill. Morgan was remarking to Brady that he thought the AO.2's fires were a bit of a mess-up, and that if ever she was chased they would never get eighteen knots out of her. This made Brady laugh, and he passed some remark about a ship he had been on. "A real bloody cockle-shell of a boat she was too," he said. "Supposed to do nine and a quarter. The bloody men got nearly fourteen out of her and that in a bloody rough sea."

"A submarine actually chased you in a rough sea" said Morgan, who was beginning to doubt the truth of what the trimmer said.

"As true as I'm standing here," said the youth. "We got away all right too."

"Well then, there's a chance for us if we ever get chased." Morgan stopped. The remark had remade him think of something he did not want to think about. There was his wife before him again, he could see her as plainly as though she were beside him. He lowered his head.

He was thinking something, something that manifested itself physically, his jaw dropped, the light appeared to go out of his eyes. Brady looking at him said suddenly: "Are you ill?" The man sitting by him appeared to shrink. The youth caught him by the shoulder, forced him up, looked at him, and said: "Well, Jesus Christ! Why, you've got the bloody jumps," to which Morgan replied with an emphatic, "Damn you," and walked out of the fo'c'sle and leaned over the rail, watching the men walking down the shed towards the picking-on stands. Watching the morning grow lighter, the surrounding atmosphere more noisy, the hoarse shouts and cries of the gangers, the stevedores, the winches singing their infernal song, the hooting of tugs, the long line of barges passing down the river laden with coal, the shriek of a ship's whistle. And leaning over the rail Morgan saw important-looking people descending and ascending the gangway, hurrying amidships, hurrying on to the bridge, rushing along the decks, a Superintendent examining hatches, bulkheads, derricks, masts, fenders, windlasses, winches. The captain's steward rushing along the bridge, down the ladder, up the ladder, and back to the cabin. One long ceaseless movement of men. Up and down, in and out, and the huge ship lying silent against the dirty stone wall of the quay, her sides thick with coal dust that soon a bosun's watch must wash off with a good power of water from the hoses, the decks likewise, and well aft a litter of ropes, lumber, chain blocks, blocks, a mass of debris, the result of seven weeks' work on the AO.2. Suddenly there was a blast on the whistle, and in the same moment the first officer appeared on the bridge. He put his whistle in his mouth and blew sharply. Four times. A quartermaster came rushing out of his room, skeltering along the deck and almost vaulting to the top of the ladder that led to the bridge. The mate was standing with his hands thrust deep into his jacket pockets. The quartermaster ran up.

"Yes, sir."

The mate looked at him, then suddenly he let loose, and the quartermaster listened, listened attentively, as all good quartermasters do. The mate said:

"Tell Mr Matthews to see me in my room in ten minutes. Warn the bosun to get his men ready. Stand by in five minutes to give the boat emergency signal. Inform Mr Marshall that the tugs will be attending us in half an hour. Tell the donkey-man that we want a good force of water in forty-five minutes. Tell the bosun's mate that the diver and eight men must wash down fore and aft as soon as she picks up the tugs. Four men will stand by on the poop with Mr Wilson. Number two and three derricks to be hoisted in readiness. Inform the gunner I wish to see him at noon prompt. Warn the gun's crew for drill in the afternoon. That's all now, Jenkins."

"Very good, sir," replied the quartermaster, saluting. He disappeared as quickly as he had come. In five minutes the orders had been communicated to the different individuals, and all the crew were in readiness. There were two long and one short blast upon her whistle and one knew the tugs were being summoned afresh. The first officer looked at his watch, looked from the watch out beyond the dock to the stretch of water and wondered if the tugs would be able to get her out into the river in time. In the captain's cabin three men were sitting with the skipper going through charts. One of the gentlemen, who had a round fat red face, and some gold braid on his shoulder, said to the captain:

"Of course you will follow this course until you receive wireless instructions, Mr —" Pause. Men of his station in life rarely called a man by his name, so with Mr — the skipper had to be content. The other gentleman, a long thin fellow, wore a monocle, and from time to time appeared to shut one eye whilst the other peered through the piece of glass at "Foggy," and the gentleman was wondering whether it was worth while to trust twenty thousand tons to a person who, though in his lifetime he had commanded big ships, was apt to be thoroughly upset by such things as fog. And he remarked to the captain, who sat there leaning his head on one small fat hand, that perhaps it would be better if he wirelessed Falmouth for orders as soon as he had cleared the Tusker. "Foggy" listened attentively and then replied in a slow drawling tone of voice:

"As you say, sir. Whatever you say goes, sir. I am entirely in your hands, sir," a peculiarly natural reply, and the skipper knew it to be, for he recollected that when ashore he was in his wife's hands, and in his daughter's too, a quite modern young lady who was doing her very best to help her King and country. And the captain felt that the men sitting in his cabin were very important indeed. The third gentleman, who had not spoken up to now, suddenly opened his mouth and said:

"I should think, Mr —, that your best plan in case of accident would be to wire Queenstown. We have the *Oroys* and *Hercules* lying there." And turning to his two companions, he asked, "What do you think, gentlemen?"

The gentlemen, whose thoughts happened to be elsewhere in spite of the extreme urgency of the occasion, and the fact that the Empire was in danger, suddenly condescended to look up at their confederate and reply as with one voice, "No. We don't, Commander Hughes."

Meanwhile the one man concerned with the matter in hand appeared to be taking a back seat during these important discussions, and he did not mind in the least. He said something to himself about these "footling old bastards trying to teach me my job, bloody relics of Queen Victoria's day," and, "can't ever forget the fact that Nelson commanded the *Victory*." Inwardly he cursed them for interfering nincompoops. As if he did not know his job. Why the devil, he asked himself, why the devil don't they clear out of it and let the confounded ship slip her ropes? At length with a great ceremonious effort the three gentlemen, who held high destiny in their hands, and the safety of the great port, too, rose from their seats, one even yawned, and then all three turned to the skipper. They held out a hand to him, shook it, which shake "Foggy" returned in his bluff and hearty style. Then one at a time they wished him Godspeed and good luck, for which he thanked them with the honour due to such important individuals and opened the cabin door for them to step out on to the bridge. Just then the steward came up. He had a note in his hand. The captain took it and tore it open. He read it, looked at the three gentlemen, who wore expectant expressions upon their faces, and said: "Gentlemen! There are five short among the crew. Two sailors and three trimmers."

"Oh! Very well, we'll arrange that for you, Mr —. Good-bye."

"Foggy" watched them descend the ladder, and waited looking over the top of the bridge until they should appear on the ladder leading down from the saloon deck. At length they came into view. He watched them descend the gangway, saw the quartermaster's hand go up in salute, though he could not see the latter's face. He returned to his cabin and sat down. He sighed. "Of all the interfering old women I ever saw in my life," he exclaimed aloud, "those damned fools take the biscuit. As if a man doesn't know his damned job. I'd see them in hell on any other occasion than this." He leaned back in his chair and looked up at the ceiling. Then he said half aloud: "Won't surprise me if they send another list of orders. Trust the

Government. Bloody war run by a pack of bearded ladies from London. Good God!" He put his hand to his head as though the latter thought were something over-whelming. Then he rang the bell on his desk. The steward came in. "Mr Wilson gave you the note, I suppose –" He stopped suddenly, for the steward interrupted with a "Oh no, sir. Shore Super handed that note to me. Said it was important."

"Thank you! I'm dining in the cabin here at noon. Thank you," and "Foggy" left the room and walked quickly off the bridge. He went into the saloon dining-room and saw nobody. He returned to the bridge and went into the chart-room. All quiet there. He pored over certain charts and maps. Then he shouted down an order to the engine-room. The second shouted up in reply to his enquiry that all was ready and the men were standing by for orders. The skipper grinned. They would be out of it soon and well away from interfering shore officials. All along he was firm in his conviction that if only the Country allowed experienced men to look after the situation everything would be all right and things brought to a quick and satis-factory conclusion. But whilst men like himself who knew their job through experience (and he remembered that he had had to pay well for such experience) were over-ruled by interfering people who had never seen a ship in their life, then he adopted a pessimistic attitude, and sighed only for the quick return to normal, so that he could pace his bridge and know that he was master, and not a person to be dragged hither and thither at everybody's beck and call. The mate came into the chart-room. He hurried up to the commander.

"We're short of five men," snapped the captain, to which the mate replied:

"Were, sir. Got them now. Men have just come on board. Were signed on in the shed."

"Had they books?" asked the skipper.

"Yes, sir."

"Good books?" snapped out the captain.

"Quite OK, sir."

The steward came in again with a telegram. It was from the head office. It read: "Proceed immediately on usual course and following usual position." Then followed in code what position he was to take after appointed spot had been reached. The skipper handed the wire to his chief officer, who read it, handed it back, and walked off the bridge. There was a sudden blowing of the tugs. The lock-gates were opening. They were coming through. The first officer's whistle could be heard blowing. One blow. Four blows. Two blows. He stood at the end of the saloon deck. First the bosun appeared. He did not ascend the ladder but stood on the flush-deck looking up, all attention, at the mate. The mate barked out:

"Order your men out, bosun. She'll be under way in half an hour."

"Very good, sir," and the bosun wheeled round and disappeared. The quartermaster came running up. He was an ex-naval man himself and apparently could not forget the fact that he had been in the Navy for twenty-one years as a signaller. Nor could he forget that he had had to do almost everything at the double. Having a very retentive memory, whenever he heard four blows upon the whistle he dropped whatever he was doing as quickly as though it were a red-hot poker and ran for dear life. Now he came up the ladder, saluted and stood almost to attention before the officer.

"Gurnan takes first wheel," said the mate. "Tell the lamp-trimmer to get the anchor lights ready and to have them on number two hatch as soon as he can get them fixed. Ask the carpenter for his eight o'clock report regarding the after-hatches and what she's drawing now. I want Sumner to stand by in the wheel-house aft. OK?"

"Very good, sir."

The mate watched him disappear like a flash of lightning and could not help grinning, as he returned to his own room. It was getting near lunch time and he was feeling a bit peckish. But for'ard matters stood quite differently. The men had been ordered aboard early that morning, though why they could not understand, especially when there was yet no sign of food coming from the galley. One of the sailors, a man named Garrett, was kicking up a terrific row in the fo'c'sle about the matter.

"The bloody swine get you on board and here we are muckin' about for five or six hours and no sign of anything. I wish to hell the skipper got fresh orders and we were put back for a day or two," and with this thought there was a visualisation of a royal feed at the Derby Arms together with a great pint glass of Falstaff.

A voice roared down the alloway. "Stand by on top! Show a leg! Stand by on top, men!" The men appeared to pour out of the fo'c'sle in a stream, the bosun's mate taking his watch aft to the poop. Pandemonium. Shouts, chorus of orders, the sudden rattle of the winches, the hissing sound of ropes as they took the weight, the almost volcanic tones of the voice that seemed to spit the orders through the megaphone. The man stood on the after-deck of the tug roaring through this phone.

"EASY THERE! HOLD HERE! LOOK OUT THERE! BLAST YOU! EASY SHE GOES. EASY THERE!" The great ropes hissed as they wound round the drum-end. Aft it was more difficult, as they were wire-hawsers. Men had to be careful as wire ropes were as slippery and treacherous as eels. The second officer stood there giving orders as calmly as though he were ordering lunch in a restaurant. The men worked hard, three sailors hauling in the rope, letting her go, taking in the slack, and now on to the drum end with her. Heaving and shouting and sweating. Gradually the huge ship veers away from the quay. More shouts, fresh orders, uniformed officials running down the shed as the ship takes her head with the tugs. More men running with heaving lines. Three men in a ship's boat down below rowing for dear life to get through the lock before the ship got well under way. Must get through quickly as powerful suction and draw of water by the AO.2 might drag them under. Figures dressed in gold-braid standing watching the scene. Figures in oil-skins and sou-westers, old shell-backs hurrying across the bridge before it was opened to let the big ship go through. All the officers excepting mate and second out on the bridge. The captain standing in the port shelter whilst the quartermaster rigged up the dodger. There was a wind rising, and the dodger must go up before she got into the river. Everybody straining, everybody sweating and breaths coming short. All busy until she drops the tugs and proceeds under her own steam down the river. Slowly she turned away from the quay, the tugs blew three blasts as a warning to river traffic to clear the way for the huge steamer coming towards the locks. The captains of the tugs at their wheels and looking very important. The pilot on board the AO.2 went across to the starboard side and started to chatter with the skipper. He remained silent, listening attentively to all that the pilot had to say. He felt it was best to say nothing. He wouldn't half be glad when they cleared the Bar Lightship. Such a conglomeration, such a network of officials, such a lot of interfering people they were. All telling him what he should do and what he had to do as if he did not know himself after thirty-three years at sea. He sighed as he listened to the conversation going on just below him. Two sailors were talking. He could not help smiling as he overheard. At least he knew that these were men, men whom he understood and who understood him.

Of course there was the question of his attitude towards them when in home ports. One had to be different with so many of the company's and Government officials knocking about, apart from an occasional admiral or shareholder in the company demanding to be shown round the ship, and ending up by asking the most ridiculous questions, questions which the officer or man generally answered to the best of his ability and without showing a trace of being ruffled. Yes, he, "Foggy," was fed up with their continual interference. Well, it wouldn't be long now. Being in this meditative mood made him forget for the moment that a gentleman known as the SHORE PILOT was addressing him. He wheeled round suddenly and replied:

"Yes. Thanks! I hope so too! Last trip wasn't so bad, Mr — Pilot."

The pilot smiled. "I hope you have a good trip this time too. She's certainly had a good overhaul. How long do you expect to be away?" he asked.

"About two years at the most," replied the captain.

"Good! Good!" said the pilot, and shouted an order to the helmsman.

V

Three-quarters of an hour later the AO.2 dropped her anchor in the river. The men went below to the fo'c'sles, the officers returned to their rooms, the captain to his cabin, accompanied by the pilot. The steward served them with lunch. Below in the fo'c'sles the peggies were busy bringing in the dry hash and tea for sailors and firemen. Most of the men had climbed into their bunks, apparently lazing the time away until they were called out on deck, when the watches would be picked. Some of the others thought it would be wiser if they buckled into their grub right away as they never knew the minute the whistle would go for boat-muster. Brady and Maugham were sitting side by side at the table. Before them the peggy had placed a dish of dry hash and a great mug of tea, together with a half loaf which Brady proceeded to tear with his hands as though it were a piece of paper. Curiously enough neither of these two individuals had spoken a word to each other all morning, apart from a rather conventional and gruff "Good morning." Then Maugham spoke.

"Well! What are you going to bring home for the Jane?" he asked. There was a queer expression upon his face as he put this question, though that upon Brady's face was even more curious still. Brady said:

"Which Jane? Which bloody Jane d'you mean?"

Maugham laughed and said quickly: "Why, Elsie, of

course." He watched the colour come and go in the trimmer's face. And Brady realised that what Maugham was after was to pump him for what he was worth and for what he could get out of the experiment, for that was how he looked at the matter.

"Elsie! Christ! Of course! A pair of Boston garters, I suppose."

"Nothing for anybody else, then?" asked Maugham, and he caught the other's eye at once.

Brady jumped to his feet, reached across and tried to push Maugham from the table, saying loudly: "That's enough, you bastard! What lay are you on, eh?"

Immediately there was a commotion. Other men who were sitting at the table let forth with loud oaths and much cursing, whilst both the young men contrived to push each other away from the table. A fireman lying back in his bunk raised himself on one elbow and said: "Why don't you two bastards get out on deck and argue there, instead of making a confounded rumpus here. You young fellows are all the same. Growling the whole damned time over bits of girls. Bloody men! Gerraway with you." He lay down again and drew his little curtain across to hide himself from everybody in the fo'c'sle. A man on Maugham's right had his tea upset. The man, a greaser named Dobson, suddenly jumped up and shouted:

"GET OUTSIDE, YOU TWO! GO ON. BEFORE I PUT MY BLOODY FIST DOWN YOUR THROAT." He drew himself away from the table, gripped Maugham by the collar and half carried, half dragged him out on to the deck. He flung him with tremendous force into the scupper, remarking, "Argue there, you noisy pair of bastards." He returned to the fo'c'sle. Brady was sitting to his dinner again, but without a word the man gripped Brady too, and, amidst a chorus of cheers, sighs and curses, dragged him out, and down the alleyway, where without the slightest compunction he flung Brady into the same scupper. He did not bother to wait and see where the fellow Maugham had crawled. He just returned to the fo'c'sle as if nothing had happened. He said aloud as he dug his spoon into the hash dish: "Bloody young swine! Give them a minute aboard and they're tearing at each other's throats for nothing at all."

"Don't let them interfere with your beauty sleep," remarked a man from a neighbouring bunk.

"Bet your damned life I won't. If they give much trouble here they'll get flung over the bloody side. You bet they will." The five other men continued their meal, none raising a head, or uttering a single word during this commotion. On the for'ard well-deck Brady and Maugham had stripped off, bare to the waist, and were busily engaged in hammering each other until the third mate, who happened to be coming out of the lamp-room, saw them and ran up, placing a restraining hand on Brady's shoulder, who certainly appeared to be getting the better of it. With a swing of his arm the officer almost catapulted Brady on to number one hatch, and remarked with emphasis that he was surprised to see two young men making such a disgrace of themselves. Turning to Maugham he said: "Why do a thing like that! Isn't it better to wait until she's well out in mid-ocean, when everybody is too busy with his work to take particular notice of young men's grievances. It's foolish. Wait till she's in the danger-zone and things are exciting, then you'll have something to fight about." He went over to Brady and remarked: "A big fellow like you on to a chap that weight. You ought to be ashamed of yourself."

"He started all the bloody row," growled Brady, without looking up at the third mate.

"Remember who you are talking to," said the officer. Then he said angrily: "Clear to hell off this deck. What in the name of Christ are you doing on the sailors' side, anyhow?"

Brady effected an immediate change. He slunk away, leaving Maugham wiping some blood from his mouth, with the third officer bending over him and obviously, so it seemed to Brady, giving him advice too. Maugham returned to the fo'c'sle ten minutes later. He had been and washed in the lavatory. He carried his shirt and jacket on his arm. He scowled as he passed Brady, who took no notice of him, but began attending to his own affairs. He started to make up his bunk. The other men were also arranging their bunks. In the midst of this the whistle suddenly went. Five short blasts on the ship's whistle and the whole scene was changed in a flash. From fo'c'sles and cabins and rooms and galleys; from wheel-houses, from bridge cabins, from stokeholds, from mess-rooms, from lamp-room and store-room and glory-holes men appeared in one long stream. All were making for the boat-deck. Orders were being shouted, falls were being examined, blocks inspected, boats' covers being whipped off at alarming speed, whilst the firemen and greasers and trimmers were lining up in orderly fashion, dressed in every conceivable kind of attire, whilst one or two of the sailors were in their bare feet. The officers and engineers, the wireless men, the cooks, stewards, butcher, baker, every man was standing-to. The sailors stood by for orders. From the bridge the captain watched the scenes of activity. He stood there with his hands in his pockets. He was meditating, reflecting, thinking. Each trip he had to stand there and see this drill gone through, which was most important, especially since submarines were making things awkward for them, and not only for them but for every ship that ploughed her way through sea and ocean, not excepting battleships and destroyers. There was something about a destroyer that a merchantman did not like, just as there was a certain quality about a naval man that they loathed, each in their own way. The first officer appeared and shouted, "Lower away, numbers four and five. Stand by numbers one and two. Numbers seven and eight and nine, man your boats." All the men had a brass number pinned in their coats as means of identification. Numbers four and five were started on the downward journey. Brady was in number five. He was standing at the helm of it and looking down from what he thought a terrific height. This height from deck to water was accentuated by the fact that the AO.2 was carrying nothing save sand ballast and she stood high out of the water. Brady gripped the for'ard fall, hanging on for dear life, for the boat was rocking in her davits, perilously to him, and he did not relish a fifty- or sixty-foot drop. It might have been a greater drop. At the moment it appeared to be that distance to him. Three sailors, three firemen, two stewards, an assistant cook, a quartermaster and lamp-trimmer were in the boat. Now all was activity and confusion. Boats were swinging, were being pushed out from the deck, were descending, whilst the rope falls were given a turn or two on the bits and men held by one powerful hand alone a full boat's crew. They hung in the air for a few seconds, then an order was given and the boat descended. As each boat touched the water the different members of the crew fell into their allotted positions. Brady was stroke oar. He had never been stroke oar before and was feeling rather nervous. An order came down to them through a megaphone that the second officer held to his mouth. He was standing at the extreme edge of the boat-deck shouting down the orders as follows:

"Veer off, numbers four and five! Steady seven and eight. Numbers two and three, point oars. Numbers four and five take your boat round the ship. Steady, numbers two and three."

On the starboard side of her the other boats were being swung out with the same promptitude and precision. Stewards were mostly on the starboard side. Morgan was placed in number nineteen boat. He was sitting in her fore-end talking to a mess-room steward. "D'you think they'll have much trouble this time out?"

"I shouldn't think so," replied the steward, a man named Costigan, who had a large family at home, a wife and nine children, which family in times of peace went off for annual holidays on the strength of Mr Costigan's tips, a thing that the steward sighed after now. Things were not the same in time of war. He remarked to Morgan that in peace time he could make on a monthly boat at least twenty pounds' worth of tips. Morgan, who had a sympathetic strain in him, a sympathy he appeared to extend to everybody he met, listened attentively to what the steward had to say. This man he told himself was a married man too. Married men were interesting to Morgan.

"Now," wailed the steward, "now. Well, there's nothing. One time I could wipe up a fellow's mess from the deck and probably get a dollar for it. Now you're wiping up bloody messes all the time. Wiping up fellows' guts, though it's not their fault, poor devils, but we have to carry them, half of them wounded and sick and ill and mangy and lousy. Sick and vomiting all over the confounded decks, spitting blood and Christ knows what. That's what we have to wipe up these days and all you get is your hand full of blood or some blasted kind of muck from them.

Why they don't discharge these poor soldiers I don't know, and I don't suppose God knows either. Aye! Give me the old times, mate, any old day. Us fellows don't make a bloody cent these days. I often think it might be a good plan to clear out first time a fellow gets into the States. Good jobs going on the Lake boats and plenty of good grub and tips. Besides, I hear that us fellows are liable to be called up for the bloody army! Struth, I do think I'll clear out as soon as we get to an American port." Morgan listened with rapt attention to this talk of the steward's. Immediately his own wife appeared before him, and this time with almost crystal clearness. And seeing her he could not but help see his own children. An idea suddenly occurred to him. Why if this steward had decided to get out of the country and get a decent job, free from danger, at least from that of mine and submarine, why shouldn't he too do the same thing? He was determined to have a quiet talk with this man as soon as she got well away from the port. Meditating thus with lowered head, that appeared at any moment as if it must fall forward and crash upon the oar he now held in his trembling hands, he did not hear the order hurled at him to stand up and take the for'ard fall in his hand. He looked up suddenly, a look of consternation upon his face, and saw the fall swinging towards him. He grabbed it in his hand and stood up. Another order and the boat gradually lowered herself into the water. By this time at least sixteen of the AO.2's boats had reached the level and were taking their different ways around the huge ship. By a quarter to two all the boats had returned to the ship and had been hoisted up again to their positions, though all were left entirely free of chocks as this was an order issued to all captains of merchant vessels. The men in the fo'c'sle, having done their share of work for the time being, lazed away at tables playing cards, or lay in their bunks thinking their own thoughts, though what they were might have been startling enough had they achieved expression. "Foggy" and the pilot had meanwhile enjoyed a good lunch. The captain had handed one of his best cigars to the pilot, who thanked him profusely, lighted it, and then stretched his legs out across the deck and started to talk.

"So you really think she is going to be used as a decoy ship. Just what kind of a confounded ship is that?" asked the pilot, blowing a cloud of smoke up towards the deck-head, following it with a great yawn. He had been up since three o'clock that morning and was feeling tired.

"So far as I can see," said the captain, "a decoy ship is one that follows a convoy at a convenient distance and when trouble is in sight sees to it that she shall be the target for any interfering submarine."

"I see!" said the pilot, like a school-boy receiving some rare and marvellous information, though probably he had seen long ago. It was a weakness he had for testing every skipper whose ship he had the good fortune to board, for isn't a drop of the best and a fat cigar after a really tasty lunch a piece of good fortune for any man whose business is to guide ships beyond the piloting point, in good and bad weather?

"Um!" remarked the pilot. "I see! So that's what she's going to be, then."

"How do I know?" protested the skipper. "You ask me a question and accept conjecture as gospel truth. Nobody knows where she's going, and neither do they know when she's coming back. I thought you knew that much, Mr Simpkins, anyway."

"You're delicate devils to approach any time," continued the pilot; "why, I would sooner go for'ard and ask one of your dirty trimmers."

The captain laughed. "And perhaps one of my dirty trimmers would give you the right answer, and quick enough too."

There was a knock at the door, and in answer to the gruff "Come in" the captain's tiger made his appearance to clear the table of dishes. He handed a telegram quite casually to the captain, and reported that the Port Commander's launch was coming alongside. The captain jumped up.

"Have they rigged up the accommodation ladder?" he snapped.

"I don't know, sir," replied the steward, who was endeavouring to pile a heap of china on to one arm, whilst the other picked up three empty bottles.

"Then go and damned well find out," he shouted into the man's ear.

The steward dropped his ware noisily on to the table and almost ran from the cabin. He decided to run to the saloon deck where the ladder would be slung into position. But he did not have to go far. The sailors had already rigged it up and made the ropes fast about the stanchions on the saloon deck. The tiger looking over saw the launch approaching and ran back with all speed to the bridge. He knocked at the door.

"Ladder is ready, sir, and launch now alongside."

"Very good," said "Foggy," and hurried from his room to meet the Port Commander, leaving the pilot reclining comfortably on the settee with a fat cigar stuck between his thick red lips. And as he walked down the ladder he said to himself that such people as Port Commanders were a "confounded bloody nuisance," and a lot of other things that if printed would shock the noble lords in London. Arrived at the spot where the ladder was rigged up he was just in time to see one of his quartermasters, a man named Rimmer, who had sailed with him in various ships in the past twenty-two years, helping the important-looking gentleman on board. "Foggy" gave a quick salute and the two men walked into the saloon dining-room. It looked bleak and bare now, without passengers, nor even a single child to soften the hard atmosphere of an otherwise warm and inviting place, though a member of the crew was never allowed to grace the atmosphere with his presence.

The two men, having selected a corner table, sat down, whereon the gentleman with the profusion of gold braid and profoundly expressive countenance proceeded as follows:

"Captain – Mr — er — ." Pause. The captain of the AO.2 looked up. The Port Commander looked a really important person now. "You will proceed at four o'clock, Mr — . You will take the course set, and on reaching the Tusker you will wireless Queenstown for your proper course. The orders handed to you this morning are cancelled." That was all. And the captain was wise enough and diplomatic enough to ask no further questions, to seek no further information. There was only one thing he wanted to do. That was to get out of the port as quickly as he could, he wanted more than anything else to see the last of this pompous-looking personage who had worried him no end during the past five days. The Commander rose to his feet, turned away towards the door and then stopped. "All correct, Mr — er — ?" he asked.

"All correct," replied "Foggy," and he watched the Commander being assisted again down the accommodation ladder. When finally the launch shot away from the ship, the skipper heaved a great sigh of relief and returning to his room on the bridge remarked as soon as he entered:

"That's the last of him and all his confounded tribe, too, for a good while, anyhow. Of all the interfering, footling, meddling old devils, he's the damned limit. When you get half a dozen talking to you at once as though you had never taken a ship out in your life, well, it gets rather exasperating."

He sat down and gasped. The exertion had obviously been too much for him.

The pilot sat up and helped himself to a fresh cigar: "I quite agree with you, Captain. I know something about the chaps myself. I always hated the job, though I still get one occasionally, of taking a confounded cruiser down the river. They do think well of themselves. I give them credit for that, though I hate their damned red tape." He lit up his fresh cigar and leaned back once more.

"I'm proceeding at four sharp," remarked the captain, who had now reached a frame of mind when he felt that one of his own cigars might be enjoyed, and he picked one too, cut it, and having lighted it, he, without a word, climbed into his bunk and lay back. In a short time the cabin was wreathed in great clouds of smoke, there was not a sound save the heavy steady breathing of the big pilot on the settee and the short sharp breaths of the captain, that resembled those of a child. All was quiet in other parts of the ship. There was a watch below. On number one hatch the lamp-trimmer had just bent on the anchor lights to a heaving line, preparatory to hauling them up before darkness was upon them. But an officer seeing this blew his whistle, and a minute later the lamp-trimmer was unbending the lights. "At last," he said. "Hooray."

VI

Rain fell. The skies became overcast. The AO.2 steered her way slowly down the river. On the bridge the pilot stood by the wheel-house from time to time ordering the helmsman to change his course. Slowly she approached the first, then the second lightship. The decks were being washed down. Fore and aft, in every nook and corner she was being swept clean. The great decks barren of life appeared ghostly, more gigantic. Ordinarily such a ship carried two thousand passengers, and at night the darkness would be stabbed with her thousand and one brilliant lights. Now all things had changed. She was a ship that rode the waters no longer proudly, but rather slunk silently, furtively away like a stricken giant. The derricks were in position again excepting for those over number one and two hatch. One or two of the hatch covers on each hatch had been loosened in readiness by order of the first officer, though the crew themselves could not understand for a moment why this was so, unless she was pulling into some port for a mysterious consignment of cargo. The watches had been picked, and already the four to eight were firing her. The sailors too had been picked, though now it was the dog-watch and the fo'c'sle was nearly full. Some had already turned in as they had to be out on deck again at eight o'clock. The remainder of them lazed about on forms or in their bunks. Some played cards, others passed, their spare two hours away by going through their mail, or emptying their bags and rigging up their bunks. This was going to be a long trip indeed, was the thought in every man's mind. In the fireman's quarters the same things were taking place. Men were sleeping, men were playing cards, men were arguing with each other. Aft a single quartermaster stood by in the wheel house. He had already lowered her log away. In the crow's nest the lookout man continually rang his bell as the ship was in the main traffic route of the Irish steamers, and they continually passed these steamers that were making both for Irish and English ports. On the port side of the firemen's fo'c'sle Maugham had rigged up his bunk. Brady had been placed in a different watch. They had not spoken to each other since their fight on the for'ard deck, though one of the men, Connor, the man who had been signed on with him, had endeavoured in his own special way to get them to make up to each other. This Brady would not do. He vowed persistently that Maugham was trying to get one over on him, and Maugham in his turn had accused Brady openly of trying to get the better of his own sister Janet. Brady was now down below with the eight to twelve watch. Maugham was sleeping in his bunk. All was silent the only sound being the chorus of heavy breathings of the sleeping men. The fo'c'sle was very hot and stuffy. The dead-lights had been screwed down over all ports as not only was there danger of a light being seen by an enemy ship, but there was the more important one of men being drowned in their bunks, for though they were sleeping above the water-line that was not very much. One single electric light served for one side of the fo'c'sle. There was another on the opposite side. In the middle of the fo'c'sle itself that was shaped like an apex stood a bogie in which some coal was now burning. This bogie was only in use during the ship's Western ocean crossing, but now the men had decided to light it, as not only did it come in handy for drying one's washing, but one was able to make toast at it for the evening or morning meal. Darkness crept gradually over the boat until finally it was swallowed up by this blackness, and nothing showed save her port and starboard lights as she nosed her way into the channel. In the captain's cabin the mate was receiving orders from "Foggy," who proceeded to advise his chief officer that certain orders must be issued to the crew first thing in the morning. What were those orders, the mate had enquired. And the skipper replied with an abruptness that surprised him that "the men must be warned against smoking on deck, even striking a match was dangerous." Also all dead-lights must be examined at sunset. All cabin lights were to be switched off unless covered with a curtain as also curtains must be rigged up against the doors of all rooms, the cook-house skylight must be covered with boat canvas. Nothing must be left to chance, as the ship was now approaching the danger-zone. The men below must be prepared in case of emergency to work six-hour watches instead of four. The lamp-trimmer must see that the lifebuoy lights were in order. The bosun was to take three men round with him first thing in the morning and see that the boat supplies were in order, contained sufficient oil and matches, the lamps and sails, the water and biscuits. The mate stood listening calmly to this recital on the captain's part. Then he quietly saluted and said: "Very good, sir. Very good, sir. I will see that those concerned are duly warned. What speed is she doing now, sir?" he asked finally, and the captain replied that he thought she was doing a round fifteen. Later when the mate had gone his way the skipper shouted down to the chief engineer: "I want your report as soon as you can send it up, Mr Pearson," and that gentleman replied that it would go up immediately by the donkeyman. The captain barked down the tube "Good," and then returned to take up his former position on his favourite stool on the port side of the bridge. Looking over the dodger he saw nothing. Looking ahead he saw nothing. Darkness final and complete. No sound save the incessant murmuring of waters washing her plates, the occasional ring of the bell in the nest, and the steady whir-whir of her engines. All this was music to the captain. He felt happy now that he was out of "the confounded authorities' hands." He had never hated so much in his life as he had in the past week. He breathed freely once more. It suddenly occurred to him, it had not done so before, that he ought to make some enquiries about the five deserters, and also some information concerning the five new men sent aboard by the company might be communicated to him. He therefore called to the third officer who was standing in the shelter on the port side of the bridge. The third officer went across to him. "Yes, sir," he said.

"Tell Mr Pearson and the bosun I want some particulars of the men signed on in the shed this morning. I want their books sent up to me also."

"Very well, sir," and the officer went below. The bosun was just turning in when the officer knocked at the door. He handed to the man the names of three sailors who had been last-minute signings. From there the officer went to Mr Pearson's room. He had just come up for a spell. He greeted the young officer with an affable "Good evening, Gregson," and in answer to the latter's question replied that two firemen and one trimmer had been signed on. He handed their books to Gregson, who immediately returned to the bridge. After delivering the books and bosun's list he went into the chart-room to examine the ship's log. In the moment that he was poring over this log there was a sudden clanging of the bell in the nest, a silence, and then clear upon the night air rang out the voice of the look-out man:

"OBSTRUCTION AHEAD SIR! OBSTRUCTION AHEAD, SIR!" Again a clanging of the bell and then dead silence. All was activity upon the bridge. The captain delved into the drawer of the locker by which he was standing and pulled out his night glasses. He peered through these, his hands trembled. Then he suddenly dropped the glasses, made one frantic stride for the telegraph and rang down the order to the engine-room.

"HARD ASTERN ON YOUR ENGINES. HARD ASTERN THERE, MR PEARSON." He ran to the wheel-house and shouted in to the quartermaster:

"HARD OVER ON YOUR HELM THERE! HARD OVER ON YOUR PORT HELM!"

The man gave her a full spoke. Looking aft one could trace the sudden change of the AO.2's wake. For'ard on the fo'c'sle head the bosun's watch were standing by. The men peered or tried to peer and stab that almost impenetrable darkness with their own poor vision. Many voices were ringing upon the night air. A man had already climbed the rigging to see if all was correct with the look-out man. Then, in that very moment that the human figure was silhouetted against the skyline, a huge black shape veered past them, almost seeming to scrape her sides, a miracle indeed that she had not been holed. The wind rose, the red and green lights of the passing ships loomed up clear and more clear from that abyss of darkness. They passed each other. Like the AO.2 the passing ship was in complete darkness. "Foggy" on the bridge breathed a sigh of relief and wiped the sweat from his forehead. Below in the stokehold where the men were now stripped to the waist strange conversations had been taking place and one saw in the eyes of the firemen stoking up their furnaces the dawn of a great fear. They shovelled and shovelled, their muscles rippled in the red glow of the furnace, and the second engineer had hurried down to cheer the men up. He had gone up to each man and given him a personal encouragement, and to all of them he stood and said in a loud voice that seemed to drown the very roar of her engines: "Men! We're in the zone. Push her for all you're worth, boys. Get her down to it. The old ship must get that twenty or we're goosed." No reply from the men. They bent to their tasks like the Trojans they were. They looked at each other in those flashing moments as they passed each other or when the trimmer shot forward from the dark alley that led from the bunkers and shot his load of coal up against the furnace. Brady was running to and fro, filling and tipping, filling and tipping, and his brain was clear, his mind stripped of the urgencies, the petty strifes and quarrels and jealousies, even his quarrel with Maugham was forgotten in the extreme urgency of the occasion. His mind was crystal clear, it was overwhelmed by the importance, the immensity of the situation, and like the others with whom he sweated he realised that on themselves alone depended not only human life but the life of the ship itself. Once only he stopped in his tracks with the barrow, and that was to steal a look at the engine-room clock. A quarter to eleven he said to himself. "Christ! I feel as though I had been down here a whole year." There was yet an hour and more than an hour before he went above. The heat was terrific. The smell, the aridness of the atmosphere was desert-like, it was difficult to breathe, to get a single breath of fresh air, unless unseen one rushed behind the boiler and was caught in the current of great draughts that poured through the cavernous opening of the bunkers themselves. Brady had tipped his barrow at number four furnace. The fireman put his hand on his arm, whose own was bare, and he felt the clammy touch of it, the warm clingingness of it, and it made him feel as though he must rush up to the deck and open wide his mouth, and breathe in hard and long, breathe in great columns of air, until his very lungs burst, until his whole body burst. The fireman gripped the youth's almost hairless arm.

"Sonny," he said in a kindly tone of voice, "how old are you?"

Brady grinned. "Just nineteen," he said. And the fireman said softly:

"Take my advice and keep away from the sea." Brady burst out laughing.

"Brady," roared the leading fireman suddenly, and the youth turned round to face the tall lean-looking man who had come up behind him.

"Yes," said Brady.

The man looked at him as though he were a piece of dirt and remarked dryly: "You look upset. What's the matter with you?"

"Nothing wrong with me," replied the youth. "What d'you want me for?"

"In ten minutes," said the fireman – he paused to look at the gun-metal watch he carried in his jacket pocket – "in ten minutes you must go up and call the watch. D'you understand?"

"Of course I do," said Brady. "I didn't know it was so bloody near seven bells though."

"Come on," growled the fireman, "get down to your muckin' job and not so much blasted lip out of you. One of these days you'll be sorry you spoke so quickly. Bastards like you remind me of an overheated boiler. You want to learn how to cool down," and he added as he scowled at the trimmer – "bloody well stay cooled down. That's what you've to do. Stay cooled down. Down! That's your muckin' place in life. Down! Down. All the bloody time down." He turned away, leaving the youth with a queer expression upon his face, now black as pitch from coal-dust, and the sour sweat had lined his face as though it were a human map. Brady put his hand to his forehead and wiped the drops off. He said to himself: "Well, by God! Fancy that! Never knew he was a bloke like that anyhow. Well, cheer up, you soft bastard, you'll get the better of all these old geysers one fine day," and he returned to his barrow, which he gripped with the fierceness that was urgent, and pregnant and chaotic within him. He looked round at the scenes. Saw in a flash a door fly open, the whole stokehold lighted up in a lurid light, that gradually as other doors were flung open resembled just one mass of flame. The faces of his companions he could barely see, and when he did see them in the fierce light of the fires, they filled him with a certain dread that sent a wave of apprehension surging through his body and his soul. In this light and this darkness, amidst this intimacy of human flesh and sweat, amidst this almost maddening heat, the almost suffocating air, in the midst of all this he felt strangely and sadly alone. He did not ask himself why. He knew, and, knowing, was afraid. He had never in all his three years at sea allowed his mind to be influenced either by men's talk or men's actions. He had never been afraid. And yet whilst he stood in this darkness and this light, he felt alone. Terribly alone. It may have been those words that had fallen from the leading fireman's mouth, it may have been a sudden recollection of his quarrel with Maugham. But Brady's thoughts were cataract, he no longer had any control of them. He murmured: "And I really loved his sister! Good God! Yes, I really loved his sister. And he says things to me, and he suggests things to me. It got my goat and I pasted him. Am I sorry? Am I sorry? For him or myself." He was meditating upon this when once more the volcanic tones of the leading fireman's voice caught his ear and he stopped dead and dropped his barrow. Without answering he strode towards the ladder which he commenced to climb. "Call 'em up!" roared the fireman after him. "Call 'em up! It's just on seven bells now."

The youth did not hear him. He was slowly reaching the top, and down this ladder the air swept as though it meant to devour him. He gripped the ladder tightly. He felt he must faint. The sudden change from heat to cold had gone to his head. He got to the top, stepped off on to the fiddley, and finally he landed in the alleyway. Here the heat was not much less than that down below. But a few yards and he was standing on the open deck, with a great head wind blowing in his face. He stood thus for some minutes opening and closing his mouth like a fish, filling his lungs with the clean air that swept from afar; and to the trimmer standing there, hot, clammy with sweat, and parching with thirst, the air seemed like wine itself. He went slowly for'ard and up the alleyway to the fo'c'sle. All was quiet within. For a moment he looked at the sleeping men and strangely for him he felt sorry for them. He looked at the various expressions upon their faces and said to himself: "What a bloody shame! To have to wake the poor bastards up." A second later he was bawling at the top of his voice: "SEVEN BELLS! SHOW A LEG THERE, MATES! SEVEN BELLS! COME ON, MY HEARTIES! SEVEN BLOODY MUCKIN' BELLS!" There were a series of oaths, groans, yawns, invocations, threats, then silence. High up on the bridge seven bells rang. Slowly and reluctantly the men climbed out of their bunks. Maugham said:

"Anybody bring the coffee in yet?" He sat up and rubbed his eyes. Brady took no notice of the question but went up to the bench near his bed and sat down. A greaser climbing down naked from his bunk said:

"If you want coffee go and get it your bloody self, though where you're going to find it God only knows.

Coffee! Won't you have ham and eggs, my chicken?" There was a roar of laughter from the bunk below Maugham's at these remarks. Now the men were hurriedly dressing. A man whose name was Larrigan, a fellow from the wild parts, suddenly shouted:

"Well, good Jesus Christ! Mean to say there's no coffee for the middle watch. By heck a bloody trimmer is supposed to make it and bring it in." He jumped down on to the deck, almost ran up to Brady and shouted in his ear: "*You* go and make it, you cheeky young bastard. That's your job. Every trimmer makes the coffee for the watch going down. Go ahead and make the damned stuff. What the hell d'you think you were sent up for, eh?" He pushed his face close to that of Brady and almost snarled in his face: "I'll break your bloody neck if you act the goat like that again," and spitting savagely on the floor in front of the now thoroughly frightened youth, he returned to his bunk and commenced to dress. In another bunk a fireman, a young man of thirty, was singing at the top of his voice:

> "What a life! What a life!
> It's worse than the Salvation Army."

"Shurrup! Put a bleedin' sock in it, mate. Chuck it! Pipe down." So the various remarks were flung at the individual who had had the audacity to break into song at the midnight hour. Now all were dressed. One bell rang as a warning to them to get ready. The men down below would be getting ready too, and waiting for the minute of twelve, waiting for eight bells to strike when they could mount the ladder, and like Brady fill their lungs with fresh air. Then to the galley to collect the black pan; coffee made and they would all settle down to a rare feast whilst the other watch carried on with the business, the very serious business of getting the ship to the Tusker light in time for her skipper to wireless the station for further orders. It was all a mystery to these men. It did not worry them they were concerned only with doing a certain amount of work every eight hours and then giving themselves up to sleep. Day after day and night after night they would fire down below, they would snore up above, and always they saw the end of the voyage, the crinkle of notes was the music in their ears. A round of drinks, and another round of drinks and the pay was gone. Dead and done with. The men were filing down the alleyway when the thing happened. There was a sudden shout from the man in the nest, a terrific clanging of the bell, a deafening explosion, a series of screams and wild shouts. The air seemed filled with strange sounds.

"Good Jesus!" shouted Brady. "She's been hit. Oh Mother of God."

VII

The ship lurched. The atmosphere throbbed with cries, shouts, curses. The sky above appeared almost starless, the very darkness itself seemed to stagger, as though this huge ship were rooted in that patch of water, out of which silently and secretly a secret rage had hurtled. Confusion. The incessant blowing of the ship's whistle. Hurrying and scurrying of ghost-like figures along alleyways and decks, up ladders, over rails, doors banging, crockery rattling with a terrific din that filled the saloon and the neighbouring cabins with strange sounds. The ship's whistle was no longer a whistle, for it was humanised. It urged, it called, it pleaded, seemed to speak by sound alone warning all human life that time was come, and above all this madness and chaos, this concourse of cries and curses, rattling of ventilators, the wild scream of the man on the look-out nest, who in a sudden frenzy had hurled himself from the nest into the black abyss, above all this there surged, roared tumultuously, swept and crashed the angry tons of water. The lights had failed. The emergency dynamo had failed. Darkness. Certain voices ceased, certain curses were caught as though the profundity of the moment had stricken men dumb. Again the ship lurched, heaved, was tossed up, was cast down. From the bridge came the roar of a voice through the megaphone, and the sounds were caught in the air that throbbed and seemed suffocated by the orgy of sounds and cries, and only faintly could one hear. "BOAT-DECK! BOAT-DECK." The ceaseless blowing of the whistle, the groups of excited figures performing strange movements with lifebelts, men half asleep flung crashing to the deck from their bunks, men naked, men hungry and tired, men babbling and swearing, all rushing, all hurling themselves through doors and flying along alleyways. On the boat-deck it seemed as though madness were let loose A wild scramble for the boats, that appeared to be torn from their davits as though by the hands of giants. The calm of the officer's voice as he rapped out the orders. The figures pushed, climbed, scrambled, hurled themselves towards the boats.

"Steady, men! Steady! Out boats from one to nine Steady there, you men! Plenty of time. Don't lose you; heads," and in saying this he saw once again the figure of the look-out man that appeared to catapult itself from the nest and go hurtling down towards the angry waters. On the bridge ceaseless ringing of telegraphs, buoys torn from their brackets and hurled down to the boat-deck. "Foggy" as calm and cool as ever he had been in his life. Speaking down the tube in those terrible moments, with calm voice and hope stirring in him as it had never stirred before.

"Are your men at the pumps, Mr Pearson? Report at once the damage to the bulkhead doors. Are your water tight doors closed? Stop your engines. Get your men ready. Stand by for any order I may send down to you. Ship listing badly. Port boats lowering now. Think she will float for an hour. Send up your log at once, Mr Pearson."

So the orders poured down the tube in a ceaseless flow, whilst the man standing there with his stern face knew that she could hardly float another twenty minutes. The carpenter rushed up to where "Foggy" stood.

"She can't hold out another ten minutes. She's holed from number three to four. Water coming in fast. Pumping useless."

"Thank you, carpenter," said the captain, without even looking at the man, though he was conscious that for some minutes after he had dismissed him the man had stood behind him, though for what reason the captain could not understand. A voice calling up the tube. "Holds filling rapidly. Men standing by. Fires clean out. Boilers threatening."

The AO.2 gave another lurch and almost heeled right over. "Foggy" shouted down the tube. "Every man for himself." He picked up the megaphone, and before roaring an order through it told the quartermaster to take his hand off the whistle cord. Then he bawled through the megaphone. "Every man for himself. Get your boats clear and jump for it."

He stood there motionless, a strange far-away look in his eyes. He thought of the wife and daughter who had controlled him in his weaker moments, and the ghost of a smile crossed his features when he imagined them looking at him now, in this very moment, on that bridge, that was no longer a bridge, that was part of nothing, a mere stepping-stone into eternity. Beyond the figures rapidly filling the for'ard boats he could not see. He saw something far beyond immediate things. His memory dragged him relentlessly along the years he had journeyed, the thousands and thousands of miles he had sailed, the thousands of men he had in his time commanded with the same efficiency, with the same sternness and justice and kindness as he commanded now. His hands shook. The ship was slowly sinking. He picked up the megaphone and called loudly. "Mr Stephenson! Mr Stephenson!" The mate came running along the bridge. He was bare-headed, his cap having been knocked off by an awkward boat's block. He stood before the skipper. For some time the captain did not speak. Then he said rather jerkily:

"Are your boats clear, Stephenson? Are the men up from below?"

"Not all. Not all, sir," replied the mate, and "Foggy" thought it was the saddest voice he had ever heard He stretched out his hand to the mate. "Good-bye, Stephenson! Try and get the boats mustered if at all possible. Keep together. There is every possibility of assistance, for we are right on the traffic route." He gave the mate the ship's position.

"Good-bye, sir," said the mate, and there was a lump in the man's throat.

"So-long," said "Foggy," as though he were merely

stepping from one bus to another. The mate disappeared. In a second he was swallowed up in the blackness. Below in the stokehold the men were trapped. The order had come down to the engineer too late. Pearson had appeared from the engine-room, minus everything save trousers and shoes. "Keep calm, men! Keep cool now," he pleaded with them. There was a hole as big as a house through which the water swirled and swept and smashed its way in. The bodies of two trimmers were floating in the water that was now reaching to the necks of two firemen who were fighting like wild beasts for their place on the ladder. The air was suffocated by clouds upon clouds of steam, an infernal hissing warned them that the boilers might go up. Pearson stood there watching the wild scramble for the ladder. He appeared powerless to help, he spoke no further word. He appeared over-whelmed. Suddenly a deafening roar told them that she was heeling over to starboard, and the expression upon the engineer's face was like that of a corpse, white, drained of blood and life and the last spark of conscious-ness surrendering to the blow, wilting beneath the power and the terror and the madness that surged all about him. The single light from a fire died out. They could not see each other.

From behind a boiler a human figure appeared, blood gushing from the mouth. This figure was being dragged through the water, there was a flash of white as the face stabbed this darkness, and a voice murmuring:

"O Jesus Christ! The bastards have got us. But hold on. Hold on, old man. I'll get you out of this all right." The speaker was Newton, the inert figure was that of Connor. He had been flung on the first impact hard up against his own furnace door, the water had swept him off his feet, he had been flung far away from his fire. Newton who had climbed a ladder leading to the gauge of the boiler he was attending, had by a miracle managed to survive. When he could hold out no longer he released his hold and dropped like a drunken man into the rapidly rising water. He struck a body, instinct told him to seize it. He had saved the old man Connor.

"God damn and blast you, make way there. Make way there." It was more than a shout, it was a scream, a scream that nobody heard. There was a murmuring, a curse, a sigh, a defiant laugh. The boilers burst. The waters roared, hissed, sang, lashed and swirled. The waters that had swung 20,000 tons of steel from one extreme to the other as though it were straw. The ship reared, her nose came up out of the water like that of a frightened animal, dropped again. The night was deluged by sounds. The sound of the wind that had suddenly risen, the patter of the rain upon the funnels and ventilators, the swish of many oars, and here and there a patch of darkness was swallowed up by a light. One, then two, then three lights appeared. The boats were veering away from the ship. The AO.2 shook from stem to stern, then with a tremendous roar the waters swept her decks. Slowly she sank, bow first until her stern appeared high out of the water, a something monstrous so it seemed that appeared to aim at piercing the very heavens itself. She sank like a stone, to the chorus of rumbling and hissing, the surrounding waters hymned hatred and defiance. "Foggy" stood upon the bridge. Not a sound. Once he put his mouth to the tube and shouted something down. No reply. He put his ear to the tube again. A dull roar greeted him. He looked up into the expanse of sky, from which the very stars appeared to have fled in terror, and now he saw the clouds sweeping across and darkening that sky. He gripped the rail. Bowed his head. He felt like one who stands stripped naked whilst countless blows are rained upon his body, and feeling this he saw as clearly as if through a mirror that his last gesture had been flung full in the face of fate. He heard a sudden dull roar. The waters were washing about his feet. "God look down on my wife and child," he said, and disappeared with the ship. The fury had not abated, the waters whipped themselves into a frenzy, boiled, bubbled, whilst great clouds of foam shot into the air. A sudden hissing, for a moment the waters themselves appeared to part. The boilers of the AO.2 had exploded. Half an hour later all was calm again.

Far off one saw the faintest glimmer of a light. The boats, ten in all, had so far kept together. In the first boat the third officer was signalling with a lamp to the other boats. The others answered these signals. In the boat with the third officer were the following men: MORGAN,

BRADY, CAMPBELL, AND MAUGHAM. Engine-room crowd. Jones, Peterson and Duffy. Deck department. Lamp-trimmer and third officer. The lamp-trimmer was sitting in the stern, the third officer stood in the bow. The others were rowing for dear life. They thought they would never get clear of those raging waters, with the powerful suction that could drag a town beneath their surface. There was now an anxious look upon the third officer's face. The wind was rising again, as though the disturbance of half an hour ago had angered the elements. He signalled:

"Each boat get its position. Best to cast off and separate."

Twenty minutes later the first reply pierced its way through to the first boat. The signal ran as follows: "Is that advisable. Cruickshank?" The officer did not know that the electrician had got into the furthest boat over which he had assumed command as there was not a single sailor or petty officer in number eleven boat. The third mate signalled back:

"ROUGH WEATHER AHEAD. ADVISABLE EACH BOAT CAST OFF AND MAKE OWN HEADWAY."

This order appeared to be ridiculous, especially to such an experienced man at boat work as the electrician of the AO.2. He did not know what to do exactly. His was a serious proposition. There were only five men in his boat two stewards, two firemen and himself. The idea of each boat casting off seemed foolhardy as there was a possibility of assistance coming any hour now, that was if the operator had been able to get in touch with a station or stations. The skipper himself had sent his message to the operator's room with the order that it had to be flashed to Queenstown immediately. But he never learned in time whether the message had gone through or not. Certainly messages had been sent out, urgent appeals for assistance must have been heard by some steamer in the tracks. But the operator had gone down with his ship, as indeed eleven men had gone down, trapped in her very bowels and suffocated. It was impossible to say how many of the crew had survived. Everything was against them at present. A heavy swell had come up, which was one of the reasons why the third officer was fearful of a boat being swamped and probably dragging other boats down with it. It was impossible to see any distance ahead on account of the almost black night, that appeared towards midnight to be deepening, and there was a fear in every man's heart that a fog might follow. If that happened they told themselves there was little chance. Amongst all the thirty-four men, distributed among the eleven boats, and the fact that they were spread over such a large number of boats was indication enough of the terrible panic this fear of fog dominated. Fog. Next to an iceberg that one can smell for miles, fog was the most hated and feared. As the wind increased the voices appeared to die down, there was just the splash of oars, the wind bellying itself into a jibsail or the low moan as it careered like a snake in and out from one boat to another as though there were a purpose and a wider significance in these boats being together, in being helpless in the middle of the sea, and as though the purpose and significance were something beyond human comprehension. Again the third officer sent a general signal to the other boats. Each boat was separated by twenty-five yards. In the broad light of day they might have appeared as a line of flats or coal barges peacefully ploughing their way towards some provincial port. But these boats were somehow different. The life in them was something that had been cast out, the ultimatum still rang in the air, and none knew what might happen if the waters suddenly decided to exact their due toll. But this experienced third officer realized that if things were to be improved they must separate. He for one was quite willing to cast off and make his own way. The one fear of a terrible storm arising, the subsequent panic, for there is a period when even seamen arrive at that stage, this one fear held him. The fact that one boat might drag all the others to destruction dominated his thoughts. He shouted to the man in the stern.

"Cast off there from number seven."

The man appeared not to have heard him. Again he shouted, this time cupping his hands. "Cast off that line when I tell you."

"But that is folly, sir," said the man in the stern.

"CAST OFF THAT LINE!" roared the third mate, and he saw the man set to it. By his watch it was well past two o'clock, but by the light of the lamp burning in the peak he discovered it had stopped. Nobody knew the time. The men bent to the oars, the boat itself seemed to hymn their energy, whilst all about them the darkness seemed to close in gradually, as though it were a huge black wall that threatened to shut out the external world from their sight, even the sky itself that now appeared weighted with those low-lying clouds that hid every single star from view. As they rowed it seemed as though there were a hidden pressure upon her from above and on either side of her, as if the elements were determined to crush and wipe out for ever this boat that harboured mere fragments of human life who flung out defiance to fate and destiny and the high gods. The man had cast off the line. He cupped his hands and called out:

"Cast off she is, sir."

"Good!" shouted back the third officer. He gave some orders to the men at the oars, one of which dumbfounded them, for the officer was practically asking them to turn her head right round and row as they had come. But here there was something different. Here there was a force that could override rules and laws and orders. The men pulled in their oars, one at a time, held them lank, and all as though one person looked for'ard at the mate.

"What bloody idea is this?" asked Morgan. "You have no right to cast off and turn her away from the other boats. No, sir, you haven't."

Morgan was just going to say something else evidently to explain the position finally, when his words were caught up by the wind and the next moment the dull flap of canvas told them that something was ahead. Instantly the men with the oars put them out again and without a single word bent to their task. They knew, as surely as they knew that night covered them, that this officer could save them.

"DOWN TO IT, MEN, FOR ALL YOU'RE WORTH!" he shouted. "WE ARE IN FOR A SQUALL. We must look to ourselves. My order should have been obeyed as this is the first boat." They saw him pick up the flash-lamp, and send a message. Morgan, who knew something of the Morse code, began to understand. Slowly he watched the flashes and whispered to the man at his side. "Here is the message!" The man turned to look at Morgan.

"Advise cast off and make way individually. Squall heading your way. Danger boats swamping."

One spoke and the words were seized in the belly of the wind and lost. One shouted and the words were almost drowned so that orders were getting more difficult to understand. Morgan leaned close to Duffy and said:

"Listen!" And when the man made no sign that he had heard Morgan said again, and this time as loud as he could possibly say it: "Listen! Can you hear, Duffy!" and the other's head turned slightly and two eyes glared.

"In the name of God, I wonder if we will be picked up. Christ! What a bloody game. What a sell. What a masterpiece. A submarine that nobody ever saw, a torpedo that none saw either, but felt." The man paused. He could not speak any longer. Morgan said: "That fellow in the front there knows his business. He will pull us out of this all right. Though, God Almighty, we'll be lucky if we ever make land with this storm coming up."

"Where are we?" asked Duffy.

"As near Jones's locker as ever you were," replied Morgan. Suddenly he shouted: "Look out! Watch the man in front." The man in front was Brady. He had started to bounce up and down in his seat as though he were riding on horse-back, the oar dipped and came up again, dipped and came up again. The officer in the bow walked slowly along the boat, looked at the youth, then clenching his fist he let drive at the youth's face with all the strength he could command. The body of Brady rolled from its seat like a log. The officer laid him down, took his oar and rowed.

"The first man," he said aloud, and to himself: "Mad."

VIII

"This senseless bloody idea," said Duffy to himself. Whilst the other continually muttered: "My poor bloody wife! My poor bloody children." The lamp in the peak flashed again but now there was no answering flash. Through the hours of darkness the wind raged, the waters tossed, thrust, swept the boat from stem to stern, and through those hours the men rowed and rowed, the sweat stood out upon their foreheads, ran down their cheeks and sometimes was swept clean from the countenance by a shock of wild spray, that was their salvation, for it kept them awake and stirred the slumbering power of the eyes to greater resistance. No word was spoken. One saw the heads of these men bent forward, some even sunken upon the breast, and in the darkness they resembled humped beasts. All life and all energy was in the hands that pulled, in the hands that gripped the oars. Already three men had been vomiting. Such rocking and pitching and rolling they had never experienced. Such wildernesses and plains of water they had never encountered with such close intimacy. The naked sky was something monstrous, the world of water harboured a contempt for the warm pulsating life, all powerful and all urgent. The gesture of abundant life that cruised so near to death. Dawn was approaching, and the first shaft of light to pierce the now rolling grey mists stirred the man in the peak. He stood up, whilst one hand gripped the mast, the other from habit went to the forehead and screened the eyes that tried to pierce the fastnesses wherein mingled the twin forces of light and darkness. He spoke, he shouted, he released hold of the mast and cupped his hands. He screamed. No answering voice, no sound. The waters were calmer. He turned round. Looked at the men, some erect, some bent, some sleeping.

"MEN!" he said. No sound or stir. "MEN," he repeated. Silence. No movement. He bent down and picked up a megaphone through which he shouted:

"MEN! Our other boats have disappeared. Are you listening? We must steer a new course. For four hours we have been pulling against a strong sea. We must steer a new course." He shouted to the lamp-trimmer: "Open the cask aft there and issue water to each of the men. See if your matches or wicks are wet. Open the box and issue two biscuits to each man." The lamp-trimmer in profound silence proceeded to issue one ladleful of water to each man. Slowly he made his way from one to the other, always returning to the after-end of the boat to refill. Then he took twenty or thirty biscuits from the box and gave each man two. He did not speak. All, excepting Brady and Duffy, sensed he was there. The hand was raised, the water was gulped and the biscuit grabbed. Brady still lay at the bottom of the boat. The third officer said quietly:

"Open that man's mouth and pour the water down." He then went aft and took his ladleful of water and his two biscuits. The issue of these rations seemed to cheer the men up. One at a time they assumed an erect position. Only Duffy and Brady did not respond. Duffy's oar was hanging precariously in the rowlock, the water played with it as it careered along, and there seemed a certain tumultuous glee about the way in which it played with it. The lamp-trimmer was bending over Brady in the bottom of the boat. Suddenly, as the water poured down the youth's throat, he began to murmur; the sounds were incoherent, the words impossible to understand. Maugham looked at this trimmer who only the day before had thrashed him on the deck, and there was a smile upon his face, that vanished when slowly the eyes of the youth lying in the bottom of the boat opened and peered up at the others. They fell on Maugham, whose feet practically touched those of Brady. But there was no light of recognition in the glance. The eyes wandered, now staring up at the expanse of sky, now slowly turning and fixing themselves in a vacant stare on each occupant of the boat. The third officer went to Brady. Spoke to him. Bent down, put his mouth to his ear. "Are you all right?" he asked, but there was no reply from the youth, whose eyes closed again.

"Have you any idea where we are, sir?" asked Morgan of the officer.

"Yes! two hundred-odd miles south-west of the Fastnet," said the mate.

"Christ!" moaned Morgan, and again fell to murmuring.

"My poor bloody wife! My poor bloody children." There was nothing about which he could think, nothing he could say but that. They appeared before him, and he remembered with pain the words of his wife when he kissed her good-bye that morning. So she was right after all. She was right. What a fool he had been to join her. A damned death-ship, he told himself. A death-ship. And who could tell his wife and family of his plight? None but God Himself. He shook himself as though of a sudden an ague had seized him. No, by God! No. He mustn't start thinking of them now. He might go a bit potty. Yes.

"Like that poor bastard there," he said, half aloud.

The officer put his hand beneath Brady's head and gently raised him up.

"Come, sonny!" he said, as kindly as his feeling and the circumstances would allow. "Come, sonny! Pull yourself together. We'll be safe in Ireland in a few hours." He raised him up and supported him on his bended knee. The others rowed, not of necessity now. It was a move-ment of the arms, backwards and forwards, backwards and forwards, something habitual, part of their life. The expressions upon their faces were of three kinds. Sullen-ness, helplessness, determination, each in its turn a window through which it was possible to see and know the state of their minds and hearts.

Suddenly an idea occurred to Maugham. He said to himself: "By Christ! Brady! Brady! Might peg out, slip his bloody cable. Janet! By God! I never thought of that." He

looked down at the inert youth, whom the third mate had
lain down again in the bottom of the boat. "Yes. By God!
I never thought of that. It's funny though he never recognized me, me at least, out of all these muckers here."
He looked round furtively. The officer shouted: "Lay to
now," and one after the other the oars were pulled in,
and allowed to balance themselves in the rowlocks. It was
getting light. As far as the eye could reach, water. They
had lost all sight of the other boats. The officer swore
when he remembered that a lead-line, and there was none
in the boat, might have helped him to some estimation of
his position. Nothing on the horizon. Then suddenly rain
fell. At first it appeared merely as a shower of fine dust
that powdered the shoulders and heads of the crew,
then it increased in force. As one man the crew bent their
heads in submission to this new torment though the lamp-
trimmer immediately put two empty canvas buckets into
good use. Every hour a man laid to on his oar, rested, and
then another took his place. The boat made slow progress.
The water was blue in colour, its surface had the sheen of
silk; it looked inviting. The hours passed. The men were
hungry and thirsty again. Once more the officer gave the
order for rations to be handed out. There was a low
murmuring amidships. One of the sailors was cursing his
luck that he hadn't salvaged his accordion. It would have
been great, he thought, to have livened up this sorry-
looking gang of men. The circumstances had sharpened
his mind, tempered his thoughts, so that he felt he must

protest against this apathy, this growing despair. After all it was the bloody Germans' fault, not his. Suddenly Duffy flung down the fragment of biscuit in his hand and shouted at the top of his voice: "S'help my Jesus Christ! but this is bloody hell. Nobody knows where we are, not a blasted ship in sight, and everything a bloody muck up! Damn! Damn! Damn!" He ground his teeth. Farther ahead another man started to laugh, and that laugh awoke the officer in the peak to a realization, a realization that he could not afford, at the risk of his own life, to ignore. He must talk to these men, he must put the position quite plainly to them. They were in a terrible plight, but, he thought, is the position any worse than that of the others! Instinct, and something more than instinct that came like a flash from the unknown, told him that the other boats would never be heard of again. The more he figured this out in his own brain, that so far had failed to surrender to the sights and sounds about him – a brain that appeared to expand as the position became more hopeless, a brain that could sweep illusion and apprehension away by its own strength – the more he dwelt upon it, the more he was sure that they would pull through. But he had to be careful. Already, and even before the rations had been touched, a man had collapsed, and now lay a helpless heap of overwhelmed consciousness in the bottom of his boat. Yes, he must be careful. Those rations would not last for ever, and then – and then – Yes. He knew. He knew what would happen. They would drink sea water. That done his task was ended, courage would avail nothing, perseverance yield nothing. Yes, he must be careful. His own position was none too secure. He asked himself a question! Had he done the right thing by casting off as he did, in the darkness and confusion and chaos of that night? Had he done right in knocking this youth out? His own heart supplied the answer. There were moments in life he remembered when all knowledge and all belief had to abdicate in favour of staggering Chance. This was such a moment, and he counted on Chance. He sat and watched these men, and he knew just what his position was. In times of great crisis certain humans succumb to what is known as the inevitable, part of a reasoning and logical system, but here in this moment logic and reasoning were no part of the mental make-up of his crew. He turned his head round and scanned the horizon. There was nothing in sight. He said:

"Men! This is a time when you will be called upon to have courage. We are in the position of being nearly three hundred miles away from any possible help. If it were only possible to take a sounding I would know something at least. Remember that each man must stand by his mate. The salvation of us all depends on one thing. Determination. Soon the rations will be shortened. I now ask you to work in threes, whilst the others can lie down somehow and sleep. I do not think we can go another day without being discovered. The other boats apparently headed right into a squall. The lamp-trimmer will issue you something now." And the third officer said: "Issue water and biscuits."

"Why! Why in the name of God can't he find out where he is?" asked Duffy. "He is supposed to have a compass in the boat. A poor bloody man who can't find his way with a compass."

"But there was none in the boat. Everything was in it excepting the necessary thing," said Morgan. And whilst these two men spoke they looked straight ahead, their eyes focused upon the horizon, though nothing met their persistent stare. Maugham sat strangely silent. He had not spoken for hours. The man lying in the bottom of the boat was mumbling. And the third mate hearing his strange jabber said to the others:

"I think we shall have some trouble with that trimmer later on. He's in a fever."

And suddenly Maugham said to the officer: "And can't you do anything for him, then?" It was almost a snarl. The officer's face whitened.

"On board this boat you will obey me. On board this boat you will keep your mouth shut. On board this boat I am in command. Should you reach the same condition as Brady, I will put you out with a rowlock and quick."

"What's that?" shouted the lamp-trimmer. "You'll put a bloody man out. Who are you? Take care we don't put you out instead. With your bloody orders to cast off, and nobody knows where the hell he is. You don't give a damn. You're all right. What about – "

"I am no better or no worse than you!" said the third mate.

"God Almighty!" shouted Duffy. "Shut your mouth, will you? Shut your bloody whining mouth. D'you want to drive us all crazy, you bastard?"

Silence then. Each man scoured the boat from stem to stern with his eyes. And all looked at the officer in the peak.

"My poor bloody wife," said Morgan. "Fancy listening to that bloody argument and my poor bloody wife and kids waiting. Damn everybody. I've a mind to take a header and swim for it."

The entire crew laid to on their oars. It was just when the first signs of fog became obvious that the trimmer in the bottom of the boat confounded everybody, took everybody's mind off the urgency of the occasion, by talking. At first it was merely a mumble of confused sounds that fell from his lips and appeared to bury themselves in the bottom of the boat. Later the words were more intelligible, and the officer shouted: "Nobody go near him. He is all right; he will work that fever off. Look after yourselves. Point oars again." The oars were pushed out again into the water, blindly, aimlessly. And whilst they pulled on them they opened their ears to Brady.

"Brave lad, she said, off to sea like that and the bloomin' submarines after you and no beatin' about the bush and your Georgie up the Dardanelles and no crying either. Janet, nobody'll see you up in the corner not after ten o'clock at night how the hell does your Andy know I'm muckin' about. Your cousin Jack in the bloody Aussies Jesus wept saw those bastards up at Alex carried the bastards up to Lemnos five hundred Light Horse and Skipper said these men have to get put ashore at all costs. Aussies. Good lads and went ashore we tied up after in a bloody stinking place. Seven hours later – was it eight? – damned if I know back with your ship to the Mouth-bloody Admiral Double – You or some swine says that – Back there. Two hundred Aussies on board, three hundred Aussies, a bloody thousand. Lying on the bleedin' decks. Where's your confounded hose? he said to me and I was only just turning the damned hydrant on. Washing down how the name of Jesus can we wash down can't wash good soldiers off decks he said. That on you do as you're told – all working for the cause. Can't do it – can't can't – can't – bastard laughing there, bleedin' Aussies lying there all muck and s— and blood on their gobs sick on their tunics, doing it there as they couldn't move – skipper said too many men on this ship too many men. Soldiers everywhere like flies and bloody wounds festering how could we get the bastards into a port before their wounds did them in. Washing down at night, poor bastards couldn't move, best rations for Hamilton and his muckin' staff, special oranges in cases for those swine damn-all for the bleedin' troops. Too many men on the deck they said far too many. Middle watch washing down – how the hell can we do anything with these poor bastards

best thing bosun said – but the other order was the bloody
gear – other order was the bloody masterpiece. Take the
bleedin' rails off – she'll run up against it to-night bloody
accident if sea sweeps decks and some bloody soldiers
off too what about it only bloody Tommys six bob a day
saves time he said – saves work they said – who – all these
bastards running bloody war in Lemnos Salonika
Alexandria Cyprus never saw a bloody war in their life.
That long thin-looking pig too with his toothbrush whisker
and bloody medals running right round his tunic inspect-
ing bloody men before their breakfast old man standing
there – bloody fool he was too. Stand to attention this s–
said. Mind that though. Soft devil standing four hours like
a ramrod nothing in his guts and no fags on that ship
either and wind blowing down his neck for king and
country. Us God stiffen it we're bloody fools we are never
get a breath of air and subs dodging about all the time
same as they dodged after damned hospital ship with four
funnels and red cross on her sides hard-faced bastards
telling Germans and country we're British we carry
wounded liars when the holds full of muckin' shells.
Thought Jerry was thick was he hell. Knew hold had
shells and wounded on top messing about and emptying
their guts and bladders wherever they lay what a war.
Then God love me Charlie when all over give you a
stinkin' medal what for. Christ knows he knew all about
it that fellow. Mad Garrity. Pitched his in the fire what use
was that no use at all bastards starving everywhere why

the hell don't they tell the truth about the Salvation Army and bloody troops inoculated three times in a week lads only eighteen can't lift their rifles up for swellings in their arms and legs and other places – ssh! don't say anything, watch the poor bastards trying to carry a pack down that cargo shoot or plank or damned gangway bloody Turks did it on them rightaway three cheers for that fellow Churchill – swine –"

"What's he gassing about?" asked Duffy.

And suddenly the youth Maugham screamed rather than shouted: "How in Jesus's name do I know?"

"Cheer up, they said, war will soon be over you are good men brave and full of courage as good as the Navy. I should bloody well think so. Navy all my eye manned by whining lot of bastards kiss officer's backside. God love me Charlie I saw that soft mucker O'Dowd on a destroyer. Such a bleedin' nut came from our street thought he was a hell of a lad. If they only wrote a right true history of the war – *that* on Conrad and his tribe bloody masterpieces about Empire written in cabins with carpets and nice fires and more wine there tiger they're all right. What about bloody war in ship's bunkers ship's stokehold bleedin' authors shipping on tramps as passengers damn-all to do and down to Borneo and Gulf and other places and masterpiece written in London true story of the sea. Know nothing about bloody war they don't neither did daft O'Dowd. I know. Oh I know. Lying over the bloody rail in sunshine off duty an all sweat-rag round his neck and end of it in his mouth – laughing – the soft bastard whined later when Lieutenant came along deck and said HERE YOU. Like fellow calling his dog and he went – walked up to him no need to run as was off duty why should he – but Christ!

"Listen you, said he, when I call you next time you will come on the bloody double. That's Navy for you. Oh boy. O'Dowd runs back like a dog with his tail between his legs officer shouts HERE You! Soft bastard runs like a lamb. What a life! What a bloody war. Three cheers for the Starvation army. Three cheers for brave lads who died in Gallipoli – half of them s— themselves to death not their fault. Janet, why don't you let me bring you a nice pair of garters next trip you needn't say anything to Andy anyhow he doesn't matter – he mucks about with that Johnstone judy. Why – nothing wrong everybody who goes away brings judy a pair of garters must put them on for you why not – aw give us a bloody rest kiddo – "

"That poor fellow's mad!" shouted Morgan.

"Don't go near him," said the officer quietly.

IX

The tall building of the shipping company was situated on the Pier Head. It was the highest of all the buildings lining that part of the city that afforded the most magnificent view of the river. Through the massive swing-doors of the building men, women and children were now pouring, for it had been reported that the AO.2 had been torpedoed off the Irish coast. The staff in the office were almost driven frantic by breathless and anxious relatives of the crew enquiring after their husbands, sons and brothers. But the big gentleman standing at the door, with his nice new uniform and shiny peaked cap, was feeling a little ruffled by the continuous questions put to him, by excited women and children. And one of these happened to be Mrs Morgan. The children clutched desperately at her skirts as she swept down one corridor and up another, searching for the Superintendent, whom she said she knew personally. From time to time she dabbed a handkerchief to her eyes, and the children too were sobbing. It seemed as though the whole of the huge building had been suddenly turned into the Wall of Weeping. And when Mrs Morgan, choking back her sobs, asked a passing boy where the Super's office was, he directed her to the lift. She was carried quickly up to the top floor. When she stepped out of the lift the first person she met was Mrs Brady. That woman too was beside herself with grief. The harried clerks were in their various offices cursing this stroke of

fate – the ship or the men were not immediate matters
to them. They were only anxious for a little peace.
Each office, each room, was visited in turn by the frantic
tear-stricken women.

"Oh, Mrs Brady," began Mrs Morgan, when she
suddenly stopped, for Mrs Brady had collapsed into a heap
before her very eyes. Two lift girls came to her assistance
and sat her down on a near-by chair. And Mrs Morgan
kept saying aloud: "I knew it. Something told me this
would happen. O dear Christ! Nearly nine months out of
work and lands in that. O good God!" She burst into a fresh
fit of weeping.

Below, an excited crowd had gathered about the notice-
board which the company had had posted at the entrance
to the office. It gave the names of the crew of the unfortu-
nate boat, but no other information. There was none to
give. All kinds of rumours were flying about. The Ship had
been mined, she had been set on fire, she had sunk of her
own accord. But the long list of names staring them in the
face was enough. The AO.2 had been torpedoed. The
ceaseless Babel of sound, the continuous sobbing of
women and children, began to have its effect in those
hidden sanctuaries where relations of members of the
crew were never allowed to go. The offices were everywhere besieged, the clerks driven off their heads
answering questions. Mrs Morgan took her children down
to the ground floor. The corridor was jammed with people
wailing and shouting, and one amongst them, a slip of a

girl dressed in black, standing by the wall, or rather being crushed against it by the many bodies. The whole place was full of the warm smell of animal flesh, scores of handkerchiefs were being pulled from pockets, and above all this the ceaseless din of typewriters, the incessant ringing of telephone bells, the whir of the lift dynamos, the calls and cries of office-boys, porters, door-men, and baggagemen. There was one woman who for an hour had done nothing but run up and down stairs, never seeking any particular office, just running up and down and holding her hands to her face, as if this were the only kind of thing she was capable of. Upstairs, downstairs, along corridors, and asking and looking into everybody's face, and beating her hands against the walls of the corridors. Her name was Mrs Maugham. Her son was a trimmer in the boat. She screamed from time to time: "O my lovely lad. Dead through those Germans. O mother of God!" Shouting and beating the wall and the man with a face like a wolf in his office near by saying to his clerk: "Get that frantic woman out of here. It's getting on my nerves. Sounds like a confounded dog whining there all the time." His nerves were on edge. He had just answered the questions, some of them almost incoherent, of nearly one hundred women. He was getting tired of it. After all, what was one hundred? The war had to be won, and he was doing his best to beat those Germans. The clerk did as he was told and other women pestering him with questions, and he said to himself: "Holy Hell! Such whiners I never saw in all my life"; and aloud to Mrs Maugham: "How'd you do if you had to go away yourself?" Poor woman crazy with grief listening to him.

"How'd you like to go?" she replied. "Blast you. What about my poor lad? Dead! *Dead*!"

So it went on; huge crowds hanging around the shipping offices. Men selling newspapers about the Liverpool ship torpedoed by a German submarine, and other placards hitting one in the face and telling you all quiet on the Western Front and rations must be curtailed again. There was a poor woman with a shawl on her head and she was trying to get through the crowd, as she was intent on seeing the director of the engine-room department. The director in his office was sitting by a big fire and reading about "great lads fighting for us and that's the stuff to give 'em," and suddenly this woman outside his door, this woman whose name was Duffy, banging with hands of terror and pain on his door, and the director saying impatiently to his clerk: "Who's that? Good Lord! Am I never to have a single minute's peace? Damn it!" The clerk, who was very devoted to his boss, rushed to open the door to dispel this nuisance, and as soon as he did so there was the woman panting and sobbing, who nearly knocked him down as she pushed her way in.

"Oh, sir! Is Mr Duffy saved from this boat? Oh, sir, please tell me if he's all right. Poor darling. Oh, Jesus, please tell me he's safe, sir"; and as she said this, half of which was unintelligible to the harassed director, his face grew redder and redder with excitement and anger.

"Please go outside, my good woman. We can't tell you anything at present. We will advise everybody concerned as soon as we get the news through. Please go outside. Can't you see I'm busy?"

Mrs Duffy was terrible to see and all the blood drained from her face. Then she raised her two hands high above her head and, joining them, brought them down with a terrific thump upon the desk. Thump. Thump. All her heart and soul were in those hands now, and the continual thumping on the desk was only the poor hands themselves crying. She shouted continually: "Well, why don't you do something? My poor man, and never a one gives a curse. Darling! Darling!" she called out, and it seemed as though her very heart's blood were clouding the eyes, for all thoughts and all feelings were in those hands as she thumped.

"Take her out!" said the director. "The poor woman's gone light in the head," and she heard it and shouted again and again as the clerk dragged her out of the office. "Why don't you do something, you lot of devils? Why don't you do something, and my poor man dead? Damn and blast you, you pack of b—s," and only great grief was speaking in those words now. She was helped down the stairs. And she, along with others, crawled back to where she lived, and it was all dark there, and none saw these people suffering, poor people's blood, and none understood, for there was no time to think now, as Germans were winning, and what time was there to think of poor people? War had to be won.

All day and all night the offices were besieged and bombarded by the wives and sisters and brothers of the crew of the AO.2, and always their eyes were upon that board outside, devouring each name, trying to read into the plain black and white of a name a miracle, and no more than a miracle. Rain fell; it pelted down on this gathering, most of them poorly dressed and shivering with the east wind coming in over the Mersey. But they did not mind that; they could stand there for ever. They were thinking of their heart's blood staining earth and sky and ocean, and no kind words for them. They were calmer now, hardly uttering a sound, just standing in silence, like dumb animals, waiting, waiting. Were only poor people, must give their sons and brothers and husbands. War had to be won. Their eyes ransacked and sought and hungered, but no answer. No answer. The AO.2 was lost and all members of her crew had been reported missing.

X

When morning broke great rolling mists descended, blotting out the horizon, the surrounding stretches of water, whilst above the clouds seemed to move across the sky with almost funereal gestures. The thick mists almost blotted out one man from another. All heads were bowed. The mists touched these men, who sat with bowed heads waiting and wondering. In the night three oars had been lost, and now the boat itself had sprung a leak. Brady had been carried into the peak and laid down on a piece of boat canvas. The boat moved slowly, with an almost unearthly stillness, through the water. One heard the faint music of rolling water but could not see it. Everything appeared blotted out by the impenetrable mists.

"Give out – " said the officer in a husky tone of voice – "give out one biscuit and one teaspoonful of water."

The words were swallowed up in the fog. No answering voices. Five minutes passed. Again he spoke and again no answering voices. He made his way slowly along the boat, instinct telling him he had reached the stern. He put out his hand and felt around. Nothing there. The lamp-trimmer had disappeared. A lump came into the man's throat. Gone! And strangely no splash, no single sound had been heard. Perhaps he had fallen asleep himself. His mind was befogged. "Perhaps he just rolled over in his sleep," he muttered. He felt for the tank. Then he sat down. The man was lost. Now appeared to him the dim outline of the biscuit tin. But where was the water barrel? Suddenly he shuddered, his whole body shuddered violently. The water barrel was gone. He could not even think now, for the infernal fog swamped the mind as well as the heart. He clasped his hands. Looked up. And there was nothing to see. He tried to open his mouth, but his tongue appeared to have swelled – swelled only in that terrible moment of discovery. That the lamp-trimmer had gone. Rolled over in the night, and perhaps his arms clasped about that vessel containing the precious water. Perhaps. Perhaps despair too could roll a man over into the fathomless depths, the depths that harboured the memories of remembered voices, faces, looks and gestures. The man clasped and unclasped his hands. He shook from time to time. All oars were stilled. They hung helplessly in the rowlocks, for time had stolen certain power and courage from the hands. And the impenetrable fog seemed to hold each piece of fragmentary life in bond, had guarded and sheltered each life. Beyond the fog everything was huge, vast, the massive power and strength of the elements. The mist descended like a protecting cloak; it hid in those hours the external sights and sounds. It was like a great door shut against Rage, so that thought itself might not be imperilled. "Christ help us now!" he said, half aloud.

Maugham was crying, though he might well have been alone in that boat, for his sobs stirred nobody. The sounds wafted away into the eternity of space. He wrung his hands, he shivered. Suddenly he leaned sideways, put his hand in the water, let it be dragged and washed by the force whose very touch was the spirit of infinity. He withdrew it as suddenly, licked it, and with his mouth he sucked; and not alone that, but the eyes too seemed to devour the clinging drops of water, of salted water, that soon would send him mad.

"Duffy," whispered Morgan. There was no reply. He placed his hand in Duffy's, a cold, clammy, apparently lifeless hand, and held it with a powerful grip.

"We are lost. No bastard cares about us," and the thoughts that could not be expressed were: "No God either. Nobody. No miracle could bring a light into existence, no boat, no one of us could pray and hear a voice that could help us. My poor mother. My poor mother. What a war!" He stood up, and the head alone, of all his body, appeared to vanish, as though sudden despair had caused it to pierce this fog and shake and roll itself in a kind of frenzy. The arms hung limply. Words came, disjointed phrases, mutterings, murmurings:

"Where's the water? Where's the bloody water? O Jesus Christ, is everybody mad? Is everybody dead?"

He started to jump, to stamp his feet, first one and then the other upon the boat's bottom, to scream, and the wildly waving arms swept and hammered the air.

The officer sitting in the peak said quietly: "There is no water. It's gone and the lamp-trimmer with it. Be calm. We will have help soon. Go and sit down quietly like the others. Keep away from the salt water. Yes, the water went in the night. And in the night he went too."

Silence. Maugham suddenly ceased. They could hear the wash, the ceaseless wash of the water that licked her, the very bone of the boat, and minutely threatened her destruction. It was inevitable surrender, without protest, to a force that overwhelms and drags down all life. The floors of ocean were patterned by the life that surrendered and passed for ever below its surface. Four days and three of them given to courage and strength and blind faith. Now the fourth found them indifferent, unwilling, indolent, silent and sullen, unconscious of the passage of time, with each throb of thought and each physical movement atrophied by the indifference of the elements.

Morgan, who all this time had remained calm, now surrendered to the very forces which in his lifetime he had fought against valiantly.

"Why, why won't something come? Where are we? My poor wife and children."

Duffy too, whose mouth was closed like a steel trap, feeding on those words and so unharnessing the captive thoughts in his own brain.

"Blasted Germans! Who gives a damn about us? Nobody. No water. And that fellow in the bow half asleep when he should be doing something. Wake up, you bastard."

A warning voice sounded in the officer's ears. "Be careful."

Yes, one had to be careful when there was no water in the boat and men had been wilfully dipping their hands in the salt water, and sucking it from cupped hands. Treacherous salt water. One had to be careful.

"I hope," he said – it was merely a whispering – "I hope none of you fellows have been drinking sea water. There are a dozen biscuits in the boat. Let us shake off this apathy. It is our last chance."

These men, he had seen them and did not protest, had seen them do it in their caps, and put it to their parched lips. And whilst he meditated thus a body suddenly sprang, appeared to sail in the air, over the heads of Duffy and Morgan. It landed in the bottom of the boat near Brady. Upon Brady's mouth a white froth was forming and accumulating. The body that had hurled itself from some part of that boat was that of Maugham. He began shouting into Brady's ear.

"Now you b—, now you bastard. I can tell you. You loved my sister. Did it on her, too. I can tell you – "

"O mother," came from Brady's lips, and the officer said sharply: "Keep away from that man."

But Maugham picked up a rowlock and raised it above his head. In a second it would have split Brady's skull, but another arm shot out, gripped the upraised one and with the other brought the handle of a hatchet down upon Maugham's head. Duffy rushed forward.

"You, too. You lying swine. Officer. B— on you. Where are we now? Tell us before I fling you over the side."

"I warned you," stammered the officer, "against drinking salt water." He spoke no more, but in that instant hurled himself bodily upon Duffy. The two bodies locked themselves in an embrace. The boat rocked, a sea swept her from stem to stern, whilst the two men struggled, and one of them who towered above the other in height and strength knew not what he was doing. The officer's brain was as clear as a bell. He knew what *he* was doing. It was merely this action of Duffy's, the monstrous manifestation of that inner yearning for action, to do something. Sitting there hour on hour, and no stir or sound or motion, Morgan knew what he was doing and did not care. "Let them go! Let them go!" he muttered savagely. "Let the bastards fight it out. I'm thinking of my poor bloody wife and kids. I have to keep cool. Keep cool. Damn and to hell with them all. Who cares a curse anyhow?"

Then the boat listed violently and two bodies seemed to fling themselves over; there was a momentary thrusting out of hands, locked hands, high in the air. Then they vanished.

"Damn the bastards shouted Morgan. "I'm left here with two cringing lads," and he watched Maugham lying near to Brady, and the slobber running down the latter's chin.

"Mother! If you could – what's the use – bloody swine at home don't care if you only saw – Poor Janet!"

"Christ!" said Morgan, "he's off again."

"Janet, you remember what I said getting those garters for you next trip let's put them on who cares a damn what's the use of the bloody war anyhow. Janet. Janet! Stuck now. Your lousy brother saying what he did. Three cheers for all the judies in the world having a good time. Christ — " Suddenly Brady sat up, stared about him with a peculiarly vacant expression on his face. Then he waved his arms in the air, joined them as though preparing for a dive, and said: "Who are we! B— all. God save the king – B— on 'em all," and leaped over the side.

Morgan had sat watching this without a flicker of the eyelids. Now he walked along the bottom of the boat, knelt down, clutched frantically at Maugham's knees and burst into tears.

"Poor bastard. Where are you? Can't stop this bloody leak now with that soft kite Brady moving off the hole. Can't stop the leak. Maugham! Maugham! Wake up! Wake up! Wake up, you shivering, frightened bastard. Move your carcass and the water'll come in freely. Nobody gives a damn. Oh, my poor bloody wife and kids."

The tears streamed down his face. Nothing but the white face of Maugham staring up at him.

"Move your carcass, for Jesus's sake, and let's end this bloody game anyhow." With a lunge and a pull he dragged Maugham from the bottom. The water poured in. It filled the boat. It sank. The two bodies bobbed up and down in the water like well-manipulated marionettes. Morgan gripped Maugham tightly round the waist. The bodies sank. The waters murmured and the fog was clearing. Wilderness of water.